MW01253985

Aerthen

By Cathleen Ryan

To
amy,

the future is
what we make it!
Cathleen
Ryan

Sunflower Publishing

DEDICATION

Dedicated to Pluto, the ninth planet in our solar system!

In July 2015, New Horizons sent the first clear images of Pluto back to Earth showing the planet along with its moons.

Aerthen

COPYRIGHT

Copyright © 2015 by Cathleen Ryan

ISBN-13: 978-1515146445

ISBN-10: 1515146448

Sunflower Publishing

Mohawk, NY 13407

Other Books by Cathleen Ryan

Ardent Rising

Ardent Lost

Ardent Salvation

Ardent Alternate Universe

ABOUT THE COVER IMAGE:

A delicate sphere of gas, photographed by NASA's Hubble Space Telescope, floats serenely in the depths of space. The pristine shell, or bubble, is the result of gas that is being shocked by the expanding blast wave from a supernova. The bubble is the visible remnant of a powerful stellar explosion in the Large Magellanic Cloud (LMC), a small galaxy about 160,000 light-years from Earth.

The bubble-shaped shroud of gas is 23 light-years across and is expanding at more than 11 million miles per hour (5,000 kilometers per second).

Astronomers have concluded that the explosion was one of an especially energetic and bright variety of supernovae. Known as Type Ia, such supernova events are thought to result from a white dwarf star in a binary system that robs its partner of material, takes on much more mass than it is able to handle, and eventually explodes. Hubble's Advanced Camera for Surveys observed the supernova remnant on Oct. 28, 2006. With an age of about 400 years as seen from Earth, the supernova might have been visible to southern hemisphere observers around the year 1600. However, there are no known records of a "new star" in the direction of the LMC near that time.

Object Name: SNR 0509

Credit: NASA, ESA, and the Hubble Heritage Team (STScI/AURA)

Acknowledgment: J. Hughes (Rutgers University)

Retrieved from:
http://hubblesite.org/newscenter/archive/releases/2010/27/image/a/

Aerthen

1

"Youngsters, youngsters, we have to pack. Get what is important to you both and put it in your satchels. We are leaving in three days." Kaunda called to his two young ones who were in their rooms down the stone hallway of their home.

He headed into the cooking area where his wife was preparing their meal. "We received notice today. We leave in three days."

Turning, and looking at her husband, Milka started to shiver. "Is it coming that fast?"

"No, but the Provost does not want to take any chances."

"Are all the Dominions leaving now?"

"I do not think so, but at least ten have prepared to leave this week, the other twenty will be leaving not long after. No one wants to be here to see what is going to happen."

"How will we know what happens then?"

"Technology Command is placing an orbiter 932,000 miles from Aerthen in the star's direction so that we can monitor from the homeship once we leave. It will send data daily until we can return."

Continuing to prepare their meal Milka thought about Kaunda's brother, Domern, and how his family spoke about remaining behind and facing whatever was going to happen. She started to become concerned, "Kaunda, has Domern changed his mind?"

"No, I spoke with him today."

"Why is he staying? Are his wife and young ones still remaining with him?"

"I tried to convince him and all the members of the Aerthen Party to come with us, but they believe that no one should leave. They trust that once the cleansing is over that there will be many left to continue on and rebuild."

"He is your brother, why is he not listening to you?"

"I wish he would. I have shown him all the data and he just cannot believe that the resources would turn on us. Well, not totally anyway."

Milka continued to cook in silence. She was close to Domern's wife and truly feared for them. She turned to Kaunda, "Dinner is done, would you mind summoning the young ones please?" She asked not wanting to continue their conversation at that moment.

Milka set the table and then placed the stew made from roots and vegetables on the table while Kaunda informed their young ones that dinner was prepared.

Torem and Nishka each came to the meal and sat down in their usual spots around the table.

"Is that root stew?" Torem, the older of the two siblings, asked.

"It certainly is! There were fresh roots at the market today." Milka explained knowing the meal was a family favorite.

2

The family woke early the morning of the third day following Kaunda's announcement that they would be leaving. They gathered their belongings and packed them into their rambler.

"Is everyone ready?" Kaunda asked as they prepared to leave their home for the final time.

Once Milka, Torem, and Nishka acknowledged that they were ready to leave, Kaunda backed up, pointed the vehicle down the stone lain path away from their home, and headed toward the stone road leading into the metropolis.

Torem watched out the back window as they pulled away from the only home he had ever known. He felt a slight sadness as he watched the familiar surroundings disappear as they drove around a bend. He tried permanently imprinting into his mind the last image he saw of the large tan blocks of stone that made up their home as they shimmered in the light of the morning star. He wanted to remember how the moisture that had risen from the ground during the darkness was waiting to greet the bright yellow star that was starting to inch above the wooded tree line.

Torem continued to think about how striking his home had looked with the star rising in the background as they arrived at their departure site near the Technology Command. They drove through the gate of the Command's stonewall and onto the airstrip. Torem looked out the window at the huge number of home ships that were lit up with people standing around them. The feeling of loss started to be replaced with an excitement that grew the closer they came to the ships and Torem's thoughts changed to what their future would hold.

They parked, unpacked their satchels, and walked until they were near the steps leading to the circular opening in the side of a home ship with the words "Southern Dominion-A1" inscribed on the side.

"Wait here one minute." Kaunda requested. He then walked over to a group of scientists standing near the front of the home ship.

"Where are we going?" Nishka asked holding her mother's hand, afraid now that it was time to depart.

"I do not know exactly, your father will tell us." Milka answered.

Torem noticed his friend Larm heading toward them with his parents. "Larm! Over here!" He called.

Larm ran over to his friend. "I am glad you are on the same ship as us."

"Me too. I was worried I would not know anyone." Torem said as he and Larm sat on the bottom step of the home ship and continued their conversation.

"Is everything going as planned?" Kaunda asked as he approached the group of scientists.

"Everything is progressing as planned Captain; we are only waiting for twenty-five more families to arrive." Professor Bier answered.

"Good, once they have arrived and everyone is on the ships let me know."

"I will."

Kaunda returned to his family, "We better get aboard; I will show you where your cylinders are located."

"Nishka was wondering exactly where we are headed." Milka mentioned as the family started to walk up the steps of the home ship.

"I will explain when we are inside. Torem keep up, we need to stay together." Kaunda called back down the steps to his son who was continuing to talk to his friend. "They will be boarding soon."

"Okay, father." Torem replied, and then ran up the steps to catch up to his family knowing his friend would be coming up shortly.

When they walked onto the ship, Torem looked around. It was much larger than it appeared from the outside. Standing between the crowds of passengers already aboard, he stared at the silver cylinders that were in rows from one side of the ship to the other as far as he could see. Behind where he was standing there was a door that he noticed was ajar. He peered in and saw the instruments lit up on the control panels with a few flashing yellow, green, and white. He also noticed his father's superior Major Tarbuk talking with a few men he had never seen before.

"Torem stay close, it is too crowded for you to wander off." Milka called, noticing that her son was lagging behind.

As the family made their way to the far side of the ship the certainty of what was about to take place started to become reality. Torem and Nishka stayed close to their parents and Milka held onto her husband's hand.

"These are our cylinders, numbers 865 through 868. Your mother and I will be at the ends and you two will take the two in the middle. Place your satchels under your cylinders. There are compartments that slide open."

"Mom can I be near you?" Nishka asked, becoming afraid.

"Of course sweetheart." Milka answered her daughter and then looked at her husband to bring his thoughts back to their earlier conversation.

"Nishka, your mother said you wanted to know where we are going."

Looking up at her father from behind Milka, she answered. "Yes father, you have not told us."

"Let us put our belongings under our cylinders and then we will talk, okay."

"Okay father." Nishka answered smiling.

Torem looked at the bottom of the cylinder that was closest to him, number 866 and noticed his name engraved on a small plaque attached at the base. "This one is mine, you have 867 Nishka."

"Where is mother's?"

"It must be at the other end because this one has father's name on it." Torem said pointing to number 865.

"Oh goody. I am next to you mother!" Nishka said as she hugged her mother around the waist, relieved to know that she would be near her.

Kaunda smiled as he watched his daughter and wife. "Come over here, next to the wall where it is quiet." He said motioning to the left of their cylinders, which were in the second row from the wall. "I will explain the best I can what will happen in the next few hours, as well as where we are going."

The family stood in an area that was relatively quiet and away from the other families that were boarding and finding their cylinders.

"This trip has been planned for the last five years. I know that it has only been talked about for the last two years publicly. The reason for that was that we had to be sure of what we were doing and where we were going. Our scientists discovered proof that the resources were beginning to change."

"How are they changing father? I have not noticed anything different." Torem stated.

"That is a really good question son. The changes have been very slow, and have occurred mainly around the midline of Aerthen. I do not understand all of what is going on myself, since I am a protector and not a scientist, so I am going to try and explain the best I can."

"Alright, I will listen and not ask anything else until the end." Torem said seeing the disapproving look from his mother when he interrupted his father.

"According to the scientists the way the vapor works is changing. You all understand how the plants, rivers, and lakes all get their water. You were taught in early learning classes at the Academy how Aerthen's temperature decreases when the sun goes down and the vapors come out of the aerth and fill the lakes, rivers, and give life to the plants and trees and then go back when the temperature increases as the star climbs into the sky, right?"

"Yes father." Torem and Nishka answered in unison.

"Well that is what is changing. The vapors are not returning to Aerthen when the star rises in the sky. Instead, they are starting to gather in the troposphere at the midline. The more vapor that goes into the troposphere and not back into Aerthen has started to change the way the sky looks. There have developed puffs of condensed vapors that are white and have been growing more quickly the last six months. I saw a picture sent back from one of the flying eye rovers last week and some of the larger puffs are turning gray. That was the sign the scientists were looking for that would indicate that we have to leave our homes."

"I do not understand father, how is it possible for vapor to go up into the sky rather than to aerth?" Torem asked. He had been at the top of his studies in science at the Academy and hoped to be a scientist one day.

"I do not know. All I understand is that once there is too much vapor in the sky it will come back to Aerthen and cause great devastation. The darkening of the puffs is the first sign that it is going to happen in the near future. That is why we have to take everyone who wants to leave Aerthen and move to a new home."

"Father how far away is it?" Nishka asked.

"That I know about and can answer much better." Kaunda laughed and rubbed the top of his daughter's head. "We are going to another world that is far away from here. It is so far that we need to sleep in our cylinders until we get there. It is going to take almost twelve years going at high speed, but to you it will seem like you went to bed one night and woke up the next morning."

"Will I be seventeen when I wake up and be in higher learning? Will I be skipping middle learning? How will I know the class work I will have to do?" Nishka asked unable to comprehend what her father was saying.

"No sweetheart." Milka corrected her. "When we go at high speed we do not age, you will still be ten. It will truly be like you went to sleep and woke up the next morning."

"Oh, okay." Nishka sighed with relief.

"The world that we are moving to has a star almost exactly like ours, but instead of nine planets there are five, ours is the fourth in line from the star instead of the third like Aerthen. It has plants and animals on it and we hope our plants and animals will be able to survive there too."

"I am glad we are taking animals." Nishka remarked.

"Me too honey." Kaunda confessed.

3

"Can I have your attention please? Attention, Attention! We need to start taking our positions in the cylinders, we will be taking off in thirty minutes." A voice came across the intercom instructing the one thousand passengers aboard Southern Dominion-A1.

"Mother." Nishka called as she attempted to reach up and climb into her cylinder.

"It is alright Nishka; I will lift you up into the cylinder." Milka placed her daughter into the silver tube then both she and Kaunda gave her a kiss and a hug.

Kaunda pushed a button on the cylinder that began closing the see through glass lid while at the same time dispensing a mist that put Nishka to sleep within three seconds.

"Torem, it is your turn." Kaunda said as he turned toward his son.

Torem climbed into his cylinder and laid face up with his head on a pillow. "Father?"

"Yes."

"How many ships are there?"

"Twenty-three. Twenty with a thousand people on each and the other three with animals, seeds, preserved foods, and other items we will need until we are established on the new world."

"What about the other Dominions?"

"They have about the same. Almost everyone is leaving."

"How many are remaining behind?"

"Only about twenty to twenty-five thousand people from all the Dominions. Some are staying in caves, some have built water ships, and some are going into the mountains."

"Do you think Domern and his family will be okay?"

"I do son. I really do." Kaunda said as he pushed the button on Torem's cylinder to close the lid and put him to sleep.

"You are next." Kaunda smiled at his wife.

Milka took her place in the cylinder next to Nishka. Kaunda leaned over and kissed her. "I will see you in the morning."

Milka smiled, "Sweet dreams my love." She then pushed the button on the inside of her cylinder and closed her eyes.

Kaunda checked on his family one last time before heading to the front of the ship. As he walked past the inhabitants of the ship, he glanced at many of their sleeping faces. They seemed so peaceful in their cylinders. He hoped that the voyage and subsequent landing on the new world would be uneventful.

Major Tarbuk was standing with Professor Bier when Kaunda approached. "How is everything going?"

"The last family just arrived and will be embarking on Southern Dominion-A18 shortly." Professor Bier replied.

Kaunda glanced over at his superior, "Is there a problem, you seem worried?"

Smiling Major Tarbuk turned toward Kaunda, "You always were observant. Actually nothing is wrong; I am just going to miss this piece of dirt that is all."

"I am too."

"It is not going to be easy once we land. The information that we have from the starscopes is sketchy. All we know for sure is that there is air, water, and temperatures that do not fluctuate much." Professor Bier remarked.

"I really hope it is as beautiful as Aerthen, once we land we have no choice but to stay and settle on the planet." Major Tarbuk replied staring out the window of the home ship. After a few seconds of reflection, he turned to the other crewmembers. "When we take off we will orbit Aerthen and then deploy the stationary orbiter that will relay information to us on the way to the new world. Are you two ready?"

"Yes." Professor Bier and Kaunda answered in unison.

"Are you three ready?" Major Tarbuk asked the pilots who were seated in front of them.

"We are." Samgi the lead pilot answered.

"Okay let us get buckled in." Major Tarbuk ordered Professor Bier and Kaunda to sit, pointing at the seats against the back wall. He then turned to the pilots and in a commanding voice ordered, "Take off when you are ready." He then sat in his seat between Professor Bier and Kaunda's seats.

Seated behind the pilots, the three men listened as the ship's engines began to rumble, and the lead pilot communicated with the other ships. They would be taking off in order from number one to twenty-three, and would meet on the far side of Little Aerthen. Once all were accounted for they would go to high speed and begin their journey.

Southern Dominion-A1 would take off first, orbit around Aerthen and deploy the orbiter between Aerthen and its star before heading to the far side of Little Aerthen where the other ships would be waiting.

Kaunda leaned his head against the back of his chair as the home ship started to make its way onto the runway. He felt the centrifugal force push him into the chair as the ship picked up speed and took off. The sky changed from blue to black as they headed out of Aerthen's atmosphere and began to orbit around their home world.

"Professor we are at the coordinates for the deployment of the orbiter." Samgi informed Professor Bier.

"Thank you Samgi." Professor Bier said as he unbuckled himself and stood. He was a little wobbly on his feet since the artificial gravity had not yet completely filled the ship. After a few seconds the professor made his way to the control panel, opened a small pull out door revealing three buttons. He pushed the first one on the right, which opened a smaller door at the rear of the home ship. Once it lit, he pushed the second that ejected the orbiter. When that light lit, he then pushed the third that closed the home ship door. When it lit, he then closed the small door and went back to his seat next to Kaunda.

"Take us to the rendezvous point." Major Tarbuk ordered.

When the ship approached the rest of the fleet, Professor Bier was looking at a hand held screen that he had pulled out of his satchel. "The orbiter is starting to send information." He looked up at the other two men. "It is working exactly as intended."

"Samgi, contact the fleet and make sure we are all present." Major Tarbuk ordered.

Kaunda listened as the ships reported in one after another. When all the ships were accounted for Major Tarbuk took a deep breath, "Set the spontaneous controls to go to high speed in twenty minutes. That should give us enough time to get to our cylinders. Have the rest of the fleet follow suit one by one."

Kaunda knew it was time to take his place in his cylinder. He nodded knowingly toward the Major and Professor Bier who would be following suit shortly along with the three pilots. He walked out of the ship's control hub to check on his family. Assured that Milka, Torem, and Nishka were asleep and safe he climbed into his cylinder and pushed the button on the inner right side. He closed his eyes feeling himself starting to lose consciousness as the white mist sprayed out from the small circular openings around his head.

4

"Welcome freshman, my name is Professor Walters and this is Introduction to Archeology. We will be meeting on Thursdays in this lecture hall, and will have a number of field trips that we will embark on. At the end of your freshman year, there will be an optional trip over the summer to Bolivia if you have any interest in taking this trip let me know by the end of next week. Today's lecture encompasses chapter one and two in your text . . . ."

"Hey how ya doin? My name's Thomas Torem." He whispered so as not to disturb the professor who continued to speak.

"Oh . . . hi. I don't remember seeing you around." Dominick remarked looking at the student who sat next to him even though there were plenty of other seats available in the auditorium. He was older, maybe a junior with sandy blonde hair and blue eyes.

"I just transferred from the west coast. I got tired of the quakes." He said with a slight laugh.

"I thought you looked a little old to be a freshman."

"Yeah, I'm a third year student I started late instead of right out of high school I waited until I knew what I wanted to do with my life."

"Shh, we better listen; the professor just glanced our way." Dominick whispered covering his mouth as he spoke hoping his professor would not realize he was still talking.

Thomas nodded in agreement. The two sat silent listening to the lecture for the next forty minutes.

"Read up to and including chapter four and there will be a quiz when you return next week on chapters one and two." The professor said ending his lecture.

When the professor concluded his instructions, Dominick gathered his note pad and books. Once the professor left the lectern and began to walk toward the door at the side of the hall, Dominick left his seat without acknowledging the student next to him. It was close to lunch and he wanted to grab something to eat before heading to his next class.

"Dominick, hey Dominick."

Dominick turned around and saw the student who had sat next to him calling his name. He waited until he caught up. "Did you need something?" He asked.

"I was wondering if you wanted to meet for lunch or dinner today. I don't know anyone on campus yet and thought maybe you could introduce me around."

"I'm heading to the cafeteria now if you want to come, but I don't know who'll be there."

"That's fine. I'm pretty hungry I got up too late for breakfast."

"It's not that far but we have to hurry to beat the crowd." Dominick said as he turned to walk.

The two young men walked to the campus buffet and were one of the first in line. After paying for their meal, they sat near the window in the back of the room.

"So you said you just transferred from the west coast, what school did you go to?"

"Caltech."

"That's a pretty big jump from the technical institute to a community college."

"Yeah, well I had my reasons. So is archeology your major?"

"I'm taking my prerequisites here and then transferring to finish my degree. I really like archeology but my major is marine biology."

"That's interesting, I'm into archeology myself. My major in California was electrical engineering but I'm not sure what direction to go into now. What do you do for fun here? Are you dating anyone who might have a friend?"

"I'm not dating anyone at the moment. If you like gaming they have overnighters here once in awhile where we go online and play other students around the world, and that can get interesting. Other than that, I just study and hang out at the rec center. They have a gym here with equipment that I enjoy using to do my workouts; I like to keep in shape."

"I find it hard to believe you don't have a girlfriend!" Thomas exclaimed.

 Dominick felt the question was intrusive since they had just met, but he continued the conversation. "I haven't dated since high school. I went out with a girl named Mandy for a few years, we went to the proms and the movies, but we knew she was moving to Georgia for college so we didn't get too attached."

"The overnight gaming sounds interesting; maybe I'll check it out the next time they have one."

Dominick wondered where Thomas was coming from; he seemed a little too old to want to hang out with freshmen. "They usually post flyers around campus when it gets close to one, you won't miss them their everywhere!" Dominick laughed.

Thomas looked at his watch. "Well, I need to get to my next class I'll catch you later." He said as he stood and left the cafeteria.

"See you later." Dominick responded. As he finished his lunch, Dominick pondered the last hour, and wondered why Thomas made such a point to get to know him. He also thought that his story about moving here seemed off somehow.

Patrick took the seat across from Dominick. "What's you doing buddy?"

"Not much. I have to be at geometry in fifteen."

"Me too! I didn't know we were in the same class, that's great!"

"Did you eat?"

"Oh yeah I just finished. I saw you sitting with that other guy and didn't want to butt in so I waited until he left. Who is he?"

"It's kind of weird. He sat next to me in lecture this morning and then came to lunch hoping I could introduce him around. He like . . . really wants to be my friend or something."

"It's the 'something' I would worry about." Patrick added. "Oh yeah, after dinner there's a couple of us getting together at Mark's dorm room, do you want to come over?"

"Sure, I don't want to be an outcast my first semester at college." Dominick remarked with a laugh as they stood and started walking to their geometry class.

5

"I've been asking around and no one seems to know that Thomas guy who has been hanging around with you."

Patrick told Dominick while they waited for the professor to start geometry class a few weeks later.

"What do you mean?" Dominic asked a little unnerved by Patrick's statement.

"I mean that no one has heard of him and I asked at the office where his room was and there's no record of him attending the school."

"Come on Patrick, that doesn't make sense, he's in my archeology class. He's been there every week since class started."

"He isn't enrolled Dominick, I'm telling you. Ask the professor if he's registered for the class."

Dominick turned pale, "You know it's been bothering me that he knew my name."

"What do you mean he knew your name?"

"The first day we met and I was leaving class he called me by name. I tried to remember if I introduced myself after he told me what his name was and I don't think I did."

"Let's find him after class and see what he's really up to." Patrick said with a stern tone in his voice feeling protective of his longtime friend. They had been friends since junior high and did almost everything together. In high school, they were in many of the same classes, on the same soccer team, studied together, and worked out at the YMCA whenever they could.

"I don't know maybe we should just report him and let security take care of it." Dominick wondered, not wanting trouble.

"He'll deny it to them. We can get a couple of the other guys together. Max and Donald will go with us to question him, I'm sure of it."

"Alright, I would really like to know what's going on."

After class, Patrick called Max and Donald. Neither went to the community college but still lived in the area taking jobs after graduating high school. Both agreed to meet at the college on the following Thursday before Dominick's archeology class was scheduled in order to talk with this Thomas person whom they were told was bothering their friend. Both Max and Donald were on the football and wrestling teams in high school and together gave the appearance of a formidable force to be reckoned with. Patrick new that just the site of them would be intimidating, and couldn't wait to see Thomas squirm.

"It's all set. Max and Donald will be here next Thursday morning at eight. We'll find Thomas and figure out what he's up to." Patrick stated with a smile, always in the mood for a confrontation.

"I can't even imagine what he would want to stalk me for? I'm nobody." Dominick stated starting to feel a little nervous about the situation.

"Who knows why people do the things they do. But we'll do our best to get him to tell us what he's up to." Patrick stated putting his arm around Dominick's shoulders. "What do you say we go to the gym and work out just in case things get physical?"

"I don't want any trouble, Patrick."

"Let's just get rid of our frustration then, working out will get your mind off him."

24

"That sounds like a better idea. I wish I had never met him right now. What the heck, why does he have to want to be my friend? There are plenty of other students here he could hang with."

"That's what I hope to find out." Patrick stated as they walked up the steps leading to the gymnasium door.

+++++++++++++++++++++

Dominick and Patrick waited for Max and Donald to arrive by the statue of the school mascot, an eagle flying with a fish in its claws. At seven forty-five, they could see their friends heading across the parking lot. The sheer size of them along with how they carried themselves was unmistakable as they came into sight.

"Over here, hey over here!" Patrick called and waved his arms as he and Dominick headed across the lawn to meet their friends.

After exchanging high fives Max asked, "What's this Patrick tells us that some older guy is bothering you?" He said looking at Dominick.

"It's crazy but there's this guy named Thomas Torem who seemed to know my name and has been trying to be friends. Patrick found out that he doesn't even go to school here! But he's been sitting in on my archeology class since the first day, we think just to get close to me!"

"That's crazy. Has he done anything other than that?" Donald asked.

"No, that's what's weird it just doesn't make any sense." Dominick remarked.

"Let's head over to your class and wait for him to show up, then we'll see what's up." Max said clenching his right fist and hitting his left palm.

They laughed and walked to the building where Dominick's class was going to be held in a little over an hour.

The boys sat under an oak tree on a brick wall filled with dirt that surrounded the base of the tree. While they waited, they caught up on the goings on back in their hometown. It was less than an hour away but living on campus seemed to keep Dominick and Patrick out of the loop.

"Here he comes." Dominick whispered seeing Thomas turn the corner of the building at the far end of the walkway.

As Thomas drew near, he noticed Dominick and the three other boys. He waved and said, "Good morning." Sensing something was up, he wasn't sure if he should stop or keep walking.

Max answered his unspoken question by stepping forward and blocking his path. He held out his hand, "Hi, I'm Max a friend of Dominick's. I hear there might be a problem here?"

Thomas eyed the two hundred pound six foot brick wall in front of him. "Problem? I don't understand what you mean?" Thomas stated as he held Max's gaze unflinching.

The two young men stood looking at one another without moving.

"The problem is that you don't go to school here and you seem to be paying a lot of attention to our friend!" Patrick said breaking the silence.

Donald stepped forward and stood next to Max seeing the standoff between the two as they continued their staring contest. "Do you have an explanation? Well!" Donald said raising his voice to get Thomas's attention.

"I think you should answer the question." Max said in a monotone voice waiting for a reason to pounce on Thomas.

Suddenly Thomas changed his posture to a more relaxed one, took a step back, and started to laugh.

Max and Donald glanced back and forth at each other confused by Thomas's reaction.

"It's all good guys, I've been trying to figure out how to introduce myself to my cousin, and you have given me the perfect opportunity."

"Hold on! I know all my cousins on both sides of my family, and you are not one of them!" Dominick said moving closer to Thomas, Max, and Donald getting angry now that he felt Thomas was taking him for a fool.

"What are you trying to pull?" Patrick said backing Dominick up.

"Nothing. It's true. Our ancestors go back many generations, we're not first, or second cousins but we are cousins. We're descended from two brothers."

"That seems like a stretch. Do you have any proof to back up your statement?" Max asked.

"I actually have a lineage tree that my family has kept since the brothers separated and went in different directions thousands of years ago. I can show it to you, it's the reason that I knew who you were." Thomas explained looking over at Dominick.

"For real?" Dominick asked.

"Yes, for real." Thomas answered.

"Why all the secrecy then? I was getting nervous and was starting to believe you were some kind of a crazed stalker or something, and that you were up to no good!"

"I didn't know how to approach you and thought that if we were friends it would make it easier to explain all of this at some point. That's all."

Max, Donald, and Patrick relaxed feeling that Dominick was no longer in any danger. Even though Dominick was still a little upset over the revelation of who Thomas said he was, they realized that Thomas wasn't a threat to their friend.

Dominick looked at his watch; he felt awkward and wanted to get away from the situation for the time being. "I'm going to be late for lecture I have to go, but we can talk later." He said looking at Thomas. "Thanks guys, I appreciate you coming here. Sorry it was a false alarm! Are you going to go to the gym with Patrick?"

"Yeah, the gym and then the cafeteria at Patrick's expense!" They said laughing and pushing Patrick back and forth between them.

Dominick laughed, "See you later."

"I'll be around and we can talk after lecture." Thomas said, in answer to Dominick's earlier statement.

Dominick turned and briskly walked toward the door that led into the building nearest them.

"So you're related to Dominick then?" Patrick asked knowing the answer.

"Yep. I came here to get to know him and his family better. So tell me, how is it that Dominick has friends that seem so different than him?" He said looking at Max and Donald.

"Oh, we've been friends for years; we met at the YMCA when we would go after school in junior high." Donald explained.

"Yeah, Dominick and Patrick were shrimps but they could sure play basketball, we had a great time back then." Max added.

"That's nice I'm glad he has such good friends, that's important." Thomas leaned back against a tree and smiled at the three of them as they started to walk in the direction of the gym.

"Can you mention to Dominick that I'll meet him in the cafeteria for dinner . . . say around six?"

"Do you mind if I come with him?" Patrick asked walking backward alongside Max and Donald.

"Not really. The more the merrier!" Thomas answered, shaking his head at the three young men as they walked away. They were so carefree and youthful, if they only knew what was coming down the road in the not so distant future. For a second he found himself hoping things could be different, that his reason for being here was truly only to meet Dominik and his family.

6

Thomas drove to his apartment twenty minutes from the college campus. He went into his bedroom, opened the top drawer of the bureau, and removed a device that looked similar to a cell phone. He pushed a button on the side and waited the couple of seconds it took for the front to open to the correct page and link to the receiver. He then used the touch screen and touched one of the icons to connect him to the appropriate recipient.

"Hello, this is Trent Tarbuk."

"Hi Trent it's Thomas."

"Oh, hi what's going on down there?"

"I met Dominick Domern and told him I was his cousin."

"Did he believe you?"

"I think he's a little skeptical, but yes, for the most part I think he does."

"Good a little skepticism is healthy." Trent stated. "Have you heard from Bethany Bier or any of the other team members?"

"Only Diane Dineen and Vince Visor and so far all is going as planned. They have both been successful in infiltrating their objectives and are waiting for further orders."

"Good, contact me as soon as you have your quarterly meeting. Your father is getting antsy."

Knowing his father as he did, he was not surprised in the least. "I'm meeting Dominick for dinner I'll see how receptive he is and if we can bring him on board."

"Keep me informed. Oh before you go I wanted to let you know that I spoke to your father yesterday, he wanted you to know your mother is doing much better."

"Thank you Trent I needed to hear that."

"No problem my friend, take care."

"You too, Trent."

Trent put his communicator down. When he looked up, he saw Timothy Torem come into the room. "I just spoke to your brother."

"How's it going over there?" Timothy asked.

"He met your cousin and is going to start talking to him in more detail tonight. Hopefully he will be successful."

"He will, when Thomas puts his mind to something he doesn't stop until he reaches his goal."

"That must be why your father sent him."

"I have no doubt. He's cut from the same piece of material as my father, neither one will stop until they reach whatever goal they have set."

"You must take after your mother then?" Trent said with a smile knowing that Timothy was quieter and less of a risk taker than his father or brother.

"If you mean that I think before jumping into a situation, yes I suppose I am. That's why I oversee the program and my little brother does the footwork." Timothy snickered, and then asked a more serious question, "What has the latest data shown?"

"Look for yourself." Trent pushed a few buttons on the console in front of him bringing up pictures, facts, and figures. "We received this information two days ago from the orbiter at the hover position near the star. As you can see, the overall atmosphere is starting to become unstable. It won't escalate for a few decades but it's noticeable to anyone who is willing to open their eyes and take look."

"From what I understand there's a great deal of misleading information and unwillingness to acknowledge the truth." Timothy stated with a tone of displeasure.

"Unfortunately there is, and it has caused mistrust and fractionalization among the inhabitants." Trent remarked shaking his head in frustration.

"That's what is going to be our impasse I'm afraid." Timothy acknowledged placing his hand on Trent's shoulder.

7

Patrick met up with Dominick after his lecture, "Your so called cousin wants to meet you for dinner. I told him I would be there too, and he didn't seem to care."

"Do you doubt his story?" Dominick wondered.

"I don't know if I do or not. But it really seems odd to me that he just showed up out of the blue like that."

"Yeah I know it does. I called my dad before my lecture, and he said that he didn't know of anybody in our family that had the last name Torem. But Thomas did say the split went way back so we'll just have to see what he has to say and what he is going to show us tonight."

"It should be interesting. I have to go to class now so I'll meet you at our dorm room around five."

"Okay." Dominick said. He watched as Patrick walked out of sight as he headed to his class. He felt lucky to have such a loyal friend.

+++++++++++++++++++++

While he waited for Patrick's class to finish, Dominick spent the time lying on his bed looking out the window of his dorm room thinking about what he was going to say to Thomas. He was curious to see how far back the lineage, Thomas supposedly had proof of, actually went.

Patrick went straight to his dorm room right after his class ended. He was excited about what the evening might bring when they met up with Thomas. Opening the door he called to Dominick, "I'm here! Are you ready to go to dinner?"

"Oh hey, yeah. I didn't hear you come in. I was thinking about what to say when we get to the cafeteria."

"Have you decided?"

"No, what do you say to a long lost stalker cousin!" He said laughing.

"I don't know but I guess we'll find out soon won't we." Patrick replied also laughing.

Excited the two friends walked to the cafeteria. They went to the buffet, filled their plates with food, and then waited in the booth near the window where Dominick usually sat and where he had eaten with Thomas previously.

"There he is." Dominick said covering his mouth that was full of potatoes.

Patrick turned around and saw Thomas standing at the cash register paying for his dinner.

Thomas nodded toward them to let them know he saw where they were sitting. After paying for his meal, he headed toward the familiar window booth.

Thomas took a seat across from Dominick and next to Patrick. "I really don't mind the food here, they offer a nice selection. Although it's not quite like home, but what are you going to do, right."

"Right. So tell us why you think you and Dominick are related." Patrick said getting right to the point.

"You don't waist much time do you?" Thomas said glancing at Patrick. "And I don't think we're related I know we are. My side of the family has kept very careful records since our ancestors split over 20,000 years ago."

"Hold on one minute!" Dominick said offended by what Thomas was insinuating. "Do you really think I don't know that that's ridiculous? There was no civilization that far back in time, I study archeology! Did you forget about that?"

Smiling Thomas looked directly into Dominick's eyes. "Answer me a hypothetical question. If you became an archeologist in the future say 20,000 years from now and went to the Amazon or the Pacific Islands and studied the life of the inhabitants there believing that the entire world was inhabited by men who lived that life style what would you think the world in the 20th century was like?"

"I suppose I would think that everyone lived in grass huts and wore very little clothing." Dominick answered.

"That's my point! Your books are full of a history with that exact scenario. How does your education system explain the stone cities that are submerged off the coast of Okinawa, Japan? Or the stone cities that are in Peru and Bolivia in South America?"

"Well, they really don't." Dominick relented.

"I thought they used stone tools and tree logs to make those places, you know like the pyramids in Egypt." Patrick remarked.

"That's what they say because they have no other explanation for them. Or I should say they have no explanation that fits into the history they originally developed, and nobody wants to rewrite all those history books." Thomas added in a slight sarcastic tone.

"How could you possibly even know all this?" Dominick questioned.

"How did they build them then? They didn't have machinery like we do today?" Patrick continued to question, not knowing much about archeology since he was a computer science major.

"I know because when our families split my side watched carefully. We have come back, visited at certain points in time, and tried to help, but we haven't always been successful. Your half of the family, I mean all of you here that are descendants of those who remained, not your family in particular, have become greedy and somewhat selfish."

"You're beginning to sound like a nut." Patrick said. "What do you mean anyway by our half of the family and your half of the family?"

"I mean your half of the family are the people who stayed behind and now populate the earth."

"Whoa! What the hell are you trying to say?" Dominick interrupted, realizing exactly what Thomas was eluding to, and he was astounded.

Thomas laughed, "I see you're starting to think a little bit cous."

"What you're insinuating is a bit crazy. You have to admit that." Dominick said.

"How do we know that you haven't escaped from an insane asylum or something?" Patrick added as he lowered his voice now that a couple of students sat down in the booth across from them.

Thomas continued to laugh and sat back in his seat. "Listen, why don't we go back to your dorm room where we can talk in private, and I can show you the documentation I brought."

"That would probably be for the best. I really don't want anyone hearing this conversation." Dominick stated as he leaned toward the center of the table and spoke in a low voice so that no one would be able to hear him. The cafeteria was starting to get crowded, and loud, as more students were coming in for their supper. He was skeptical of Thomas, but if anyone overheard what they were talking about they might ask questions or repeat what they heard. Being known as the freshman with the crazy ideas about history was the last thing Dominick wanted right now.

The three young men finished eating and walked back to Dominick and Patrick's dorm room.

"Where do you live?" Patrick asked as they headed into their dorm building.

"I live in town and have an apartment over one of the stores."

"Alone?" Dominick asked.

"Yes, but I have associates that I work with who live nearby and in the Virginia area."

"Are they from your home town?" Patrick asked not really sure how to put it since he eluded he was from somewhere other than earth.

"They are. They have their own reasons for coming, actually there are over five hundred of us here scattered over the globe for different assignments."

Dominick stopped just before the elevator, "What do you mean assignments?"

Turning around Thomas winked at him, "I'll tell you soon, one thing at a time. Okay?"

"You're going to have to be pretty convincing, because right now we think you're crazy." Dominick said looking at Patrick who shook his head in agreement.

"All I can do is tell you the facts, it's up to you to believe or not." Thomas said with a serious look on his face.

The elevator dinged and the door opened, after a number of other students exited the three young men entered and Patrick pushed the number three button to take them to the third floor. They rode the elevator in silence, when the door opened they exited and walked to room 318 where Patrick unlocked the door and they stepped inside.

"Have a seat." Dominick said pointing to the chair at his desk.

Thomas sat, as did Patrick who pulled up his desk chair. Dominick sat in front of them on his bed. "Well?" Dominick asked.

Thomas reached into his backpack and pulled out a black and brown covered journal. He opened it to the first page and turned it around for Dominick to see, then pointed to the first sentence.

Dominick looked at the spot that Thomas was pointing. "I don't understand? It's not English how do you expect me to read that?"

"I don't. It's the original language of all humankind. I just wanted you to see it."

"There is no original language. What are you talking about?" Patrick asked.

"I'll give you a history lesson, the actual history of this planet not one shrouded in myth and supposition." Thomas answered.

"I have to hear this!" Dominick replied sarcastically.

Thomas observed Dominick for a few seconds before beginning his account. "The first civilization began close to 78,000 years ago on a large continent called Luremia that was in the middle of what you call the Pacific Ocean. Everyone spoke the same language and they eventually spread throughout the entire globe. Everything that they built was done by using stone so that it would last throughout the ages. All of their major metropolitan areas were evenly spaced at 36 degrees longitude in order to be able to send power easily to everyone. There were ten major metropolitans that were surrounded by smaller districts, and these were located within Dominions and each had a separate body of governance. We are all descended from those original humans."

"That's quite a story, Thomas. But where is your proof to back that up? If they really did build everything to last, then where are all the buildings?" Dominick found the whole tale a little absurd.

Patrick was more interested in the journal, "So if what you're saying is true, are you going to read the journal to us and expect us to believe what you're reading is what it says?" Patrick asked sarcastically.

"No, I have a translation of the book. We had each family line translated into whatever language the descendants have developed over the centuries. That way, each family could read for themselves."

"Do you have copies of each of these journals?" Dominick asked not truly buying into his story.

"No, I only have one written in English that shows your line, which was all I needed."

"Let's see it then!" Patrick demanded getting a little frustrated.

Thomas pulled a second journal from his backpack and handed it to Dominick. "There you go!"

Dominick opened to the first page and started to read it to himself. "This begins 24,000 years ago." He exclaimed.

"That's when my ancestors left for our new world and yours stayed behind to take their chances."

"Take their chances? What were they taking their chances against?" Dominick asked.

"The atmosphere of the world we called Aerthen, was changing. We knew that many of us would die so we left for a stable planet."

"You called Earth, Aerthen?" Patrick questioned. "Don't you think they sound an awful lot alike?"

"Language changes over time. Think about the first settlers in America who spoke English, it wasn't spoken the same way you speak it today!"

"Alright I'll give you that." Patrick relented. "But that still isn't convincing."

"How was the atmosphere changing?" Dominick wondered not really understanding how it could have been so extreme to cause them to leave the planet.

"It all started at the equator and spread from there. There was no rainfall like there is now; there was a condensation cycle rather than a rain cycle. The plants and aerth were watered at sunset and sunrise when moisture in the form of fog and mist would rise up from the ground when the temperature cooled."

"By aerth, you mean earth, right?" Dominick wondered thinking that if nothing else this was a good story.

Thomas shook his head showing that he agreed with Dominick's question.

Before Thomas could resume his account Patrick asked, "What started at the equator?"

Thomas was glad to see an interest in what he was saying start to peak in the two, he continued where he ended. "Clouds started to appear around the equator because moisture started to go into the atmosphere rather than back to the ground. The scientists said that the white puffs where actually the moisture gathering in the sky and eventually it would fall back to Aerthen."

"That's rain! So what's the big deal?" Patrick wondered.

"Today its rain back then it was a pending disaster. We left before the planet was covered by the clouds but eventually they engulfed the entire sky, they started to turn from white to grey and then almost black. That's when the water fell from the sky and the destruction began."

Dominick and Patrick looked at one another.

"We know that there was a flood, the Bible tells about it and so do some of the writings from other early civilizations. There is no mention of technology like you're talking about or people flying off to another planet!" Dominick stated with a scowl on his face.

"There is if you look for it." Thomas said.

"Where?" Dominick and Patrick asked in unison.

Aerthen

"The writings from India speak about many of the ships and types of technology that there used to be." Thomas said matter of frankly, as if this was common knowledge.

"Oh. Well we're not familiar with that." Patrick said as he and Dominick continued to look back and forth at one another.

"Tell me more about the disaster, how did the rain become so bad?" Dominick asked curious to hear the rest of the story.

"The world was quite different then than it is today. The oceans were smaller and many landmasses that were above sea level are now submerged. The planet revolved around the sun in 360 days not the 365 it does today and the days were longer than 24 hours. There wasn't as much turbulence in the sky, or wind as you call it, and it was warmer."

"How did the rain change that?" Patrick asked engrossed in Thomas's tale.

"It wasn't just the changing climate that was responsible for the differences; there was also a pole shift."

"A what?" Patrick asked.

"The north and south poles reversed." Dominick added.

"That can happen?" Patrick exclaimed with a surprised tone in his voice.

"Yeah, and they say there's another one coming." Dominick added.

43

"How do you know that?" Patrick asked Dominick.

"From science class, but the scientists don't know what will happen or when exactly it will take place." Dominick answered.

"Why doesn't everyone know about this?" Patrick wondered getting a little loud, and excited by the idea that something was happening this huge and it wasn't making headlines.

"I don't know, I suppose nobody really believes it." Dominick answered.

"That's right. It's part of the reason we're here." Thomas divulged.

"Part of the reason?" Dominick was getting anxious. "What do you mean, and what other reasons are you here for?" Dominick asked.

"To reunite our family of course." Thomas stated with a smile from ear to ear.

"Why are you so concerned with Earth, doesn't your new world have these problems?" Patrick asked noticing that Dominick was starting to believe what Thomas was saying.

"No it doesn't. Aerthen II, as we call it, is larger and older than this planet and that makes it more stable."

"So you are saying that Earth is unstable!" Patrick practically yelled at Thomas, his nerves were on edge and the continued conversation wasn't getting any better.

"It's been unstable since we left. What do you think that earthquakes, volcanic eruptions, and storms like hurricanes and tornadoes are? It wasn't like that before the flood and polar shift. When the oceans grew and volcanic activity increased after the flood, the ecosystem changed. Nuclei produced raindrops and the change increased the atmospheric turbulence causing the weather you have today!"

"That's mind blowing if it's really true!" Patrick said feeling a little shaky as he started to look at the weather and think about natural disasters in a different light.

"Our scientists knew the rain and flooding was coming, but the polar shift was more than they expected. They were so focused on what they found and what we needed to do to survive that they didn't see the whole picture. Those who stayed behind lost all of their technology in the aftermath and that's why it didn't pass down to the generations of today. Your history doesn't pick up until after our ancestors were able to gather at a central location. They grouped together hoping to salvage what was left before they lost everything."

"Where was that?" Patrick asked.

"In the area around what is known as the Middle East, they called it Aden. Before their communication devices and ships stopped working they relayed the coordinates to each other and eventually they all gathered in one place to survive."

"What did they do to survive such a devastating catastrophe?" Dominick wondered.

"People from every Dominion on Aerthen stayed behind, and they each chose different methods to try and make it past the flooding. The metropolis where the Mediterranean Sea is today built boats to float on the waters so they could withstand the floods. The Dominion that existed where India and Asia are decided to go into the extensive cave systems that were high in the mountains. Your ancestors lived in what today is South America and they felt that they could go to the higher elevations around the metropolis that was in the Andes Mountains. The only reason they survived was that the polar shift caused the continent to be thrust upward more than 13,000 feet above sea level to the elevation it is today. Even though they had gone to higher elevations they would have been submerged and all killed if not for the upheaval."

Patrick looked at Dominick who was enthralled with the tale Thomas was telling and looked a little pale. "So what you're saying is that your part of the human race left this planet and now are coming back?" Patrick asked.

"No . . . not exactly." Thomas stood up and walked over to the window looking out at the scenery. "It is beautiful here; we don't have seasons like this at home." He remarked taking in the changing fall colors of the trees.

"So why are you here then?" Patrick asked in an uneasy tone sensing something in the way Thomas was acting but not sure what that something was.

Thomas turned and looked at the two friends "We have been coming back for centuries. After we left, it was almost fifteen years before we realized how devastated our home world had become and we feared that no one would have survived. My ancestors had to assure our own survival on a foreign world before we could even think about returning. Once they established themselves on Aerthen II, they sent a ship and crew back to see the damage first hand and bring survivors back with them to Aerthen II. By then it had been almost thirty years, because we were only able to travel as fast as the speed of light, making the distance between the planets a problem."

"So why don't we know about all this? I mean if you came back that long ago." Dominick wondered.

"We sent scientists and medical personnel back so we could understand what had happened and help those who survived. We knew it had been bad because of the information we had received from the orbiter we placed in space nearby Aerthen before we left. The readings it relayed to us about the atmosphere and planet were shocking, it still sends us data to this day, well an updated version does, but it couldn't tell my ancestors what happened to the inhabitants on the planet. Once they were able to return they attempted to make contact with the survivors, but by then most of the leaders had passed away and the younger generation was bitter, they felt that they had been abandoned by my ancestors and didn't want their help. The descendants of the people who stayed behind became violent and told us to leave them alone."

"But you still kept coming back you said." Patrick interjected. "Why?"

"Yes we did. We improved our technology and were able to come here and return much more quickly. We have also had some of our members join your society to try and help you by leading you in the right direction so to speak, but have not been as successful as we hoped."

"What do you mean?" Dominick asked.

"I think that I have said enough for now. There is a lot more I want to tell you and I will. What I have told you so far is alot to take in and digest." Thomas smiled, turned, and continued to look out the window.

"What is your world like?" Dominick asked.

Without turning around to look at them, Thomas answered. "It's not all that different. It isn't tilted on its axis as it is here so we don't have seasons. The temperatures stay relatively the same wherever you happen to live. The planet is four times larger and most of us live in the warmer climate zone. Our star is yellow like yours but it's older and only emits forty-five percent as much light. We only have five planets in the system, we live on the fourth planet, but the fifth is also inhabitable and is even larger than ours."

"Do people live on the other planet?" Patrick asked.

"Not really it's more of a vacation spot. We keep it natural without the use of any technology."

"Couldn't you let us know that you exist now? Our society wouldn't be bitter anymore we don't even know about you?" Dominick wondered, and then realized that he was starting to believe his story.

"You're society has become too corrupt." Thomas answered.

Patrick and Dominick looked at one another hearing the tone in Thomas's voice. He sounded disgusted.

8

After Thomas left for the night, Patrick and Dominick began to discuss what he had revealed to them.

"Do you believe him?" Dominick asked Patrick.

"I don't know. It sounds more like a science fiction movie than real life."

"I know that there are ancient cities that we can't explain their origins from studying archeology. I also know that there are mysteries surrounding them like how the large blocks of stone were moved and shaped considering we believe they had no technology."

"Maybe there is some truth to what he's saying then." Patrick relented.

"You would think that if they had space ships and other forms of transportation that we would have found one of them buried somewhere! We've found the bones of dinosaurs that were alive long before he claims they were here." Dominick stated.

"Who knows? Maybe we did and it's a big government secret or something."

"What do you think he meant that we are too corrupt anyway?" Dominick questioned.

"Maybe they're perfect . . . who knows. But we better get to sleep, I have a test tomorrow." Patrick concluded and turned off the light next to his bed.

Dominick laid awake for some time thinking about what Thomas had said. Some of it made sense, which gave him a sick feeling in the pit of his stomach. He still didn't really understand why Thomas would be contacting him though he wondered if it could really be just because he wanted to meet a relative.

+ +

At seven the next morning, Patrick's alarm sounded waking the two from their sleep. Patrick rolled out of bed and walked to the bathroom to take a shower. Dominick laid awake listening, waiting for his turn. Once they were both dressed and ready for the day they headed to the small coffee shop on campus to eat a quick breakfast of coffee and bagels before separating and attending their first classes for the day. Neither one spoke about the conversation of the previous evening, it had made them frustrated since they could not prove nor disprove most of what Thomas had told them.

The day passed without incident, Patrick took his test in computer language, and Dominick attended his biology and chemistry classes. Neither of them ran into Thomas and neither of them spoke about him. Each on his own had decided that whatever Thomas was up to, or was talking about, wasn't going to be the focus of their life.

On Thursday, Dominick went his lecture for archeology and really hoped that Thomas wouldn't show up and sit next to him. His hope soon turned to reality as time clicked by and there was no Thomas. He found however, that Thomas's absence was turning out to be a distraction. He couldn't seem to stop his thoughts from wandering, wondering where Thomas was and why he hadn't been around for the last few days. He had been at lecture every Thursday and showed up for meals at least three times a week, now there wasn't any sign of him.

After lecture, Dominick decided to talk to his professor, Dr. Walters, and see if he knew anything about the things Thomas had eluded to him and Patrick about the past. "Dr. Walters do you have a minute?"

"Sure son what is on your mind?" The sixty-two year old man with graying hair asked.

"I was wondering about the trip next summer and thought that I might want to go with you."

"That would be wonderful, Dominick." Professor Walters exclaimed as he continued to pack up his books and lecture notes.

Surprised that he knew his name considering there were almost a hundred students in the lecture hall. "Um...yeah. I was a little curious about the site that we are going to. Where is it . . . in Bolivia?"

"The trip is to an ancient city called Puma Punku in the Andes Mountains. I wanted to study the stones used to build the city and thought that it would also be a good learning experience for any students who wanted to tag along."

"I only know a little bit about those places, when do you think they were built?" Dominick was really hoping for an answer to the questions he had concerning Thomas's assertions.

Professor Walters looked at Dominick and smiled. "That's hard to say son, since you can't carbon date rock and there are many theories and conflicting opinions on the subject."

"Oh I see. I was wondering because I've heard some of those same theories. The one I was interested in said that it was over 20,000 years old and that there used to be a technologically advanced culture on Earth at the time it was built." Dominick wanted to see the professor's reaction to what Thomas had told him.

"That's interesting you should bring that up. Mainstream science won't consider those theories, but they have no other answer either. I'm glad you have such an open mind for a young man."

"Thank you. I . . . have to go now." Dominick was getting uncomfortable as he started to feel exposed and didn't want to reveal the source of his information to anybody.

"I'll put your name on the list of students interested in going to Bolivia." Professor Walters called after him as he started to walk up the stairs leading out of the lecture hall.

Aerthen

"Okay." Dominick called back, turning quickly to respond to the professor, before running up the remaining stairs and out of the hall.

Dominick felt even more frustrated, he was hoping that Dr. Walters would have had a decisive answer for him about the ancient cities so that he would know if Thomas were telling the truth, or if he was psychotic.

Dominick started to head back to his dorm room when he heard Patrick calling his name. "Dominick, Dominick, wait up."

Out of breath from running, Patrick caught up to Dominick and leaned over with his hands on his knees. After catching his breath, he began to explain his excitement. "We were let out early today. My professor has an appointment that he has to go to, so I have the rest of the day off."

"That's great! Since tomorrow's Friday that gives you a longer weekend." Dominick said smiling, knowing that neither he nor Patrick had classes on Fridays.

"Yeah, I was wondering if you wanted to go back home or stay here. I was thinking of visiting some of the guys over the weekend to get my mind back to reality." He said nudging Dominick with his shoulder.

In a serious tone, he answered, "I was thinking of going home too, I want to talk to my dad."

"Are you still thinking about what Thomas said?" Patrick asked.

53

"I can't stop thinking about it. It's like I'm haunted by it." Dominick answered putting his hand to his eyebrows and rubbing.

"Going home is probably the best thing for you then, maybe you can get your mind off of all those things that he was saying."

"I hope so. I need to concentrate on my schooling instead of his craziness!"

"Yeah, me too!" Patrick said laughing. "You know, if you think about it, it really does sound crazy doesn't it!"

"It sure does, he really had me going though let me tell you. I'm glad he hasn't been around the last few days. I've had time to clear my mind and rethink some of the things he told us."

"Maybe he got bored with us and moved on to someone else, some other cousin someplace!"

"Maybe." Dominick answered, but he couldn't help feeling a little sad at the thought of Thomas really being gone. He did enjoy his company, despite their conversations.

When they returned to their dorm, they each packed clothes for the weekend. Patrick had a car so they would ride home and then back to their dorm on Sunday night.

Dominick packed his books planning to do some homework over the weekend and noticed the journal Thomas had given him right where he had left it on his desk. He picked it up and put it in his backpack with his other books so he could show his father. "Are you ready Patrick?"

"Yeah, I just have to get my tooth brush." My mom will have my head if I forget it.

"You know what's strange?" Dominick asked Patrick as they walked down the stairs from their dorm room instead of taking the elevator.

"What's that?"

"Ever since Thomas told us all that stuff he hasn't been back around."

"He wasn't at your lecture earlier today?" Patrick asked a little surprised.

"Nope. I was glad he didn't show up too. I just don't know how I feel about all of this, or him."

"Maybe he's just a story teller and really did move on to bother someone else?"

"That would probably be for the best, but somehow I doubt it."

Patrick unlocked his car doors with the button on his keychain as they approached the car. Dominick watched as the lights flashed and a beep could be heard coming from the car signaling that the doors were unlocked.

They drove the forty minutes it took to get home in relative quiet, both concentrating on the upcoming weekend. Patrick was thinking of what he would do when he hooked up with his buddies from high school. He hoped that they could get a game of basketball together on Saturday afternoon if enough of them were available on such short notice.

Dominick wondered what his dad would think of the journal when he showed it to him.

Patrick pulled up into Dominick's driveway, "I'll call you and let you know what's going on."

"Okay." Dominick answered. He shut the passenger side door and opened the back door of the car to take out his suitcase. He walked up the walkway and into his house where he smelled food cooking. "Mom, I'm home."

His mother was in the kitchen making fried chicken; she stopped peeling the potatoes, washed her hands, and came into the living room. "Give me a hug." She said reaching for her youngest child. "How were your first few weeks of school? I didn't get much of a chance to ask when you called."

"I like my courses and I might take a trip to South America with my archeology professor next summer, if it's okay, oh . . . and the food is pretty good." He answered smiling.

"We'll talk about that trip later." She said with a concerned tone in her voice. "I'm making fried chicken for dinner and your sister is coming home too."

"How is Donna doing this year so far?" Dominick asked, knowing that she had changed majors.

"She says that she likes early education better than she did nursing. She doesn't have to take anatomy and physiology if she is going to be an elementary school teacher."

Dominick laughed, knowing how squeamish his sister was when it came to blood and guts. "I'm going to take my things upstairs. When will dad get home, I have something to show him."

"Around six." His mother answered as she headed back into the kitchen.

Dominick went to his room and put his suitcase in the corner. He emptied his backpack and took out the journal. He knew his mother would have dinner ready by six when his father came home so he had an hour and a half until that time. He decided he would start to read the journal, it was the first chance he had since Thomas gave it to him. He examined the material the journal was made from, the cover seemed to be some type of a cardboard that was stained brown and held together with metal rings like a three subject notebook, but smaller. The paper was off white, and was thicker than normal writing paper. He could tell by the paper the journal was written on, along with the ink that was used, that it seemed unusual. It was not the way paper and ink usually looks or feels. Of course, he knew that didn't mean it came from some planet light years away either. He opened the cover and turned to the first page:

In the year of our creator 54,000, the Torem Clan left for Aerthen II leaving behind the Domern

Clan who chose to face their fate and remain on our home world.

The purpose of this chronicle is to trace the Domern descendants throughout history for the sole purpose of reuniting with said descendants when the timing is deemed appropriate.

Domern, father of Drake Domern, father of Dougal Domern, . . .

Dominick read the first page and turned to the second, then the third. He realized that the entire journal only consisted of names, one after another with the words father of, father of, before each name. He decided to turn to the last page and see how it ended, he took a double take not sure if he could really believe what he was reading.

Douglas Domern, father of Drew Domern, father of Dominick Domern. The legacy of Domern, the brother of Torem in the year on Aerthen 2015 and the year on Aerthen II 78,000.

His grandfather and father's names followed by his own name! The whole issue mentally exhausted him. He couldn't help falling asleep in bed while holding onto the journal.

"Dominick, Dominick! Are you awake . . . it's time for dinner?"

Hearing his mother's voice Dominick opened his eyes and stretched. "Coming."

Dominick placed the journal on his night table and then went to meet his family for dinner.

When he entered the dining room, his father stood and walked toward him. "Give me a hug." Drew wrapped his arms around his son lifting him off the floor and then patting him on the back as he returned him to his feet. "Look at you." He said as they parted, "You look like you've grown since you left home a couple of months ago!"

Laughing Dominick answered his father, "I may have put on a few pounds eating in the cafeteria. The food there is pretty good and we can eat as much as we want from the buffets."

"You look the same to me." Donna said approaching her brother and giving him a quick hug.

"Mom said you like the courses you're taking for teaching."

"Oh yeah, there's none of that dissecting animals or cadavers for me!" She said, laughing as she returned to her seat at the table followed by Dominick.

"It's nice to have the family together again for the weekend." Rebekah Domern remarked watching her family fill their plates with mashed potatoes, lima beans, and fried chicken.

After taking a few bites, Dominick remembered the journal. "Oh dad, do you remember me telling you about that guy who said he was my cousin?"

"Yes. You told me he had some kind of proof or something."

"Yeah, he gave me this journal with pages and pages of names that end with you, me, and grandpa."

"Really? Do you have it with you?"

"It's upstairs, I'll show you after dinner."

"What is this? Some guy's been approaching you and saying he's your cousin? How old is he?" His mother asked a little concerned.

"I met him at college, I'm not sure how old he is, maybe twenty. He told me we were cousins. But dad said that he had never heard of his last name, its Torem. He gave me this journal to show me the records that his family has kept and the list ends with my name."

"That's creepy! My brother has a stalker!" Donna stated in a serious but sarcastic tone.

"How do you know what he's up to? I don't want you alone with him do you understand?" His mother demanded.

"It's okay mom, Patrick and the other guys won't let anything happen. They know about him and made sure he knows not to bother me."

"I'd like to meet this person, what did you say his name was?" Drew Domern asked.

"It's Thomas Torem. He said that our many times great grandfathers were brothers."

"What do you think about the journal he gave you?" His father asked.

"I don't know, anyone can write a journal that doesn't make it real!"

"Well I'm glad you're being mature about this." His mother added.

Dominick smiled realizing he had not mentioned to them that Thomas said he came from another planet. That would just make the whole thing sound ridiculous and they certainly would not believe anything he said after that. He laughed to himself realizing that he barely believed it.

+ + + + + + + + + +

Once the table was cleared and his mother was finishing putting the dishes in the dishwasher, Dominick went to his room to get the journal and bring it to his father.

When he came back downstairs, his father was sitting in his favorite chair in the living room watching the evening news.

"Here's that journal I told you about." Dominick said, as he walked over to his father and held the journal out for him to take.

"Oh, thank you. Let me see that." Drew Domern took the journal and opened it looking carefully at the first page. He looked up at Dominick with a confused look on his face, "Did you see this first paragraph?"

"Yeah. I did."

"What is Aerthen II, and the year written here doesn't make any sense either. This looks like some work of science fiction!" He shook his head and turned a few pages shortly realizing, as did Dominick that each page was made up of just name after name. He opened the journal about three quarters through, glanced at the page, and then went to the back of the book. He read the final paragraph and looked at Dominick with a perplexed look on his face.

Dominick had taken a seat on the sofa to the left of his father. He watched his expressions as he studied the journal in order to be able to tell what he was thinking. It wasn't very hard.

"Well, other than the last four names I can't say for sure if there is any truth to any of this. What is the name that is written here? Aerthen? What is that?"

Wanting to change the course of the conversation Dominick attempted to focus on the names in the journal, "I only recognized the last three, is the fourth one your grandfather?"

"Yes, that was my grandfather's name. Now what did that Thomas fellow say about this name written in here?" He asked with a stern tone while he pointed at the word Aerthen.

Realizing his effort had failed, he tried to answer his father's question. "He … he said that it is what they use to call Earth." Dominick could barely bring himself to tell his father knowing how it sounded.

"Who are they?"

"The people that use to live here and then left before a supposed catastrophe thousands of years ago."

Drew looked at his son and noticed he was uneasy with the way the discussion was going. "I would like to meet Thomas and talk to him. Do you think that would be possible?"

"I don't see why not, but . . . he wasn't at school today. I suppose that he will be back next week."

"Can I hold onto this?" Drew asked, as he held the journal out slightly as he referenced it.

"Sure, I really have no use for it. It's just full of names that I could never just sit and read, it would be just too boring. Besides, there's no way to validate them."

"I just want to have someone look at it, as long as you don't mind that is."

"I don't mind but who do you want to show it too?" Dominick didn't want his father to look crazy.

"Well . . . my father first of all, to see if he knows any of the other names listed. Then I want to get the paper and the ink checked out, they seem odd don't you think."

"I noticed that too. Alright, well . . . I have to do some homework so I can spend time with the guys tomorrow." Dominick looked at his father wondering why he was taking this thing so seriously. He really expected, and hoped, that he would say that it was some sort of a scam. Then he could just forget about it and tell Thomas to get lost. Now he felt like he was stuck in some sort of a practical joke that kept sucking everyone into it when he tried to get them to agree with him that the whole thing was crazy.

9

"Hey, what's up?" Dominick asked, answering the phone after seeing Patrick's name and hearing the ring tone he had programmed for him.

"We're meeting at eleven o'clock at the Y for a game of hoops, are you in?"

"Yeah, I'll be there."

"Good, see you then." Patrick said before hanging up.

Saturday mornings were still the same as they had always been at his house. Ever since he was a young child, his parents slept in until at least ten, leaving him and Donna to fend for themselves when it came to breakfast. He made himself toast with butter and jelly, showered, and then went to his room to surf the internet. He wanted to do some research on the stories that Thomas had told him. He started to do a search on ancient civilizations and was surprised to find multiple web pages devoted to all kinds of theories. He clicked on the one that sounded the most legitimate. A professor of archeology had created the site and had traveled around the world to visit many ancient civilizations, including the ones that Dominick had mentioned in his search. He was glad that there were plenty of photographs on the pages; it made it easier to relate to what the man was explaining.

The first ancient city on the site was the one Professor Walters had talked about, Puma Punku in the Andes Mountains in Bolivia. According to what was written on the web page, it was made of carved stones that were twenty-six feet long and weighed one hundred tons each! The H shape allowed the blocks to fit together almost perfectly. It said that a piece of paper couldn't even fit between the stones. The web site went on to state that the stone blocks had to have been hewn by some sort of mechanized tools or lasers due to the intricate work and perfect right angles that were as smooth as glass.

Dominick thought about what he had just read for a minute, he couldn't even imagine how big the stones must be. He scrolled down until he saw a photo of the professor standing next to one of the huge H blocks; it looked gigantic having the professor next to it for scale.

Dominick clicked the 'next' button at the bottom of the page to go to the second city, a place called Tiahuanaco, that wasn't far from Puma Punku. The city had megalithic stones that were situated in a way that made the structure able to withstand earthquakes. The explanation for this was that the stones would shift and move during a quake, but that they would not move out of place. It stated that they used polygonal construction techniques, which made this possible.

The idea that early people, that were uneducated, were able to build these places with stone tools like chisels seemed quite irrational to Dominick. He continued to read the web site intrigued by what he was discovering.

The next section was about cities that were submerged under the ocean off the southern coast of India, under the Mediterranean Sea, and off the Japanese coast near Okinawa. He thought he remembered Thomas mentioning something about this. It seemed that the cities in each of these places were also made using huge pieces of stone.

This was getting too much to deal with at one sitting, so Dominick exited the web page, powered down his computer, and closed the lid to his laptop. He sat in his desk chair staring into space wondering if maybe there was some truth to all of this, that the possibility of an ancient civilization existing thousands of years ago could be a reality. Of course, that didn't mean that what Thomas said about their ancestors was true. He could have went to a similar web page, researched similar information, and made the whole thing up. He also could have created the journal. After all, how hard would it be to make up generation after generation of names? But why would he do something that was so extreme? It really didn't make any sense to him, what would he have to gain by doing it?

Dominick glanced at the clock on his bedside table, it was ten-thirty, he would have to leave shortly if he was going to get to the YMCA on time for basketball. He went downstairs to find his parents sitting at the kitchen table. His father was reading the morning paper and his mother was washing the few dishes that were in the sink.

"Is it alright if I borrow one of the cars? I want to go and meet the guys at the Y."

"You can use mine." His mother said. "But you'll have to put gas in it; I have less than a quarter tank."

"Okay. Do you want me to use your card?"

"It's in my wallet. My purse is in the living room."

Dominick went to the living room and took the gas card from his mother's wallet. "I'm leaving. I should be back around three."

"Okay." His mother called.

"Dominick!" He heard his father's voice.

Dominick went to the kitchen knowing that was what his father wanted from him. "Yeah dad?"

"I'm going to take the journal over to George's house and get him to look at it. I hope that he will have some answers for us. When I called your grandfather he verified a couple of the other names in the journal, my great-grand father, and third great-grand father."

"That's crazy, how could someone know that?" His mother's reaction was exactly what he was thinking.

"I don't know, but if these are correct it might be safe to say the rest are also." Drew added.

Dominick was starting to become a little freaked out, so he thought he would get his mind off the subject by getting out of the house quickly. "Alright, I hope he can tell us something. I'll be back later."

Dominick knew George was a co-worker of his father's at the lab where he worked. They both were in the same department, his father worked on analyzing blood and other crime scene evidence while George was a document expert.

After stopping to fill his mother's car with gas, he drove the last few streets to the YMCA to meet his friends.

They played basketball for over two hours in teams of two, Max and Dominick against Donald and Patrick. When they finished, they decided to head downstairs to the basement to work out in the gym.

"Hey let's hit the showers, I smell like a wet dog!" Max said putting back the weights that he had been lifting.

"That sounds great! I haven't worked up this much sweat in quite awhile." Patrick added.

"Hey Dominick, I saw Mandy last week. She came back for the weekend to visit her parents and said to say hi." Donald just remembered as they headed to the showers. He and Mandy were neighbors they lived two houses away from one another on Bleaker Street.

"Oh, well if you see her again tell her I said hi."

"What happened with you two anyway? You seemed like the perfect match our senior year! Shit, you were practically inseparable!" Donald added.

"I don't know. I think we got a little bored with each other, she wanted to go down south for college to get away from the winters, and I didn't want to go with her. After that things changed and we started to drift apart."

"That sucks, but you could have stayed together anyway, plenty of our classmates went to different schools and still kept dating." Max interjected.

"Yeah, I know. Mandy just wanted us to go to college together and was pissed when I didn't do what she wanted."

"I never liked her, she was just too pushy." Patrick interrupted. "She was used to getting her own way, and she usually did. I remember when she wanted to be the head cheerleader in junior high. When they picked Cheryl instead, she turned half the squad against her and made her life miserable until she quit. Then Mandy got what she wanted."

"I didn't know that." Dominick said a little surprised. "You never mentioned that before."

"I know, I didn't want to do anything that would hurt our friendship, coming between you two would have been a mistake. She would have tried to turn you against me."

"I don't think she would have succeeded." Dominick replied. "I've known you a long time, we've done alot together, our friendship means more to me than anything she could have said."

"I didn't want to take any chances, I was glad when she left." Patrick confessed.

"Let's go play some pool; we have about an hour before they close down to get ready for the middle school basketball game tonight." Max said wanting to move on, he never cared for Mandy either.

The other three agreed, so they headed back up to the main floor across from the gymnasium where the poolroom was located. Dominick was glad to move on from the discussion about Mandy, he didn't want to admit it but he truly did not miss her, and Patrick was right she was pushy.

They played in teams, this time Patrick and Dominick against Max and Donald. When the staff announced it was time to leave for the day, the four went their separate ways. As he drove back to his house Dominick realized how much he missed living in his hometown. He also knew that once he finished college he would return, get a job and life would settle down and be somewhat close to what it was when he lived here. He would have a weekly routine that included going to work and then a weekend full of excitement with the guys. He started to hope that the next four years would go by fast.

10

"Come on in, do you want a beer?" George asked Drew Domern when he answered the knock at his door.

"Absolutely! What are you drinking these days? Is it still that light stuff?" Drew asked in a tone that reflected his dislike of the beverage.

"No I gave that up the day after I started them. Not quite the same, you know."

Drew laughed; thankful he wouldn't be forced to tolerate a light beer.

After taking two beers from the refrigerator, George turned to Drew, "Let's go out on the deck, I don't want to miss one of the last nice days before winter sets in." George opened the sliding glass door that led out onto his deck.

Drew followed taking a seat at the picnic table. He placed the journal down and slid it toward George. "This is what I was telling you about. I need you to see if there is anything out of the ordinary about the paper, ink, or lettering, whatever you can analyze."

George picked up the journal and leafed through the pages. He stopped after a few of them and looked closely, lifting the page toward the light and running the tip of his finger over it. "This is very interesting . . . I'm going to have to take this into the lab and look at it under the microscope."

"Is it peculiar?"

"It may be very peculiar. Do you want to take a ride?" George asked eager to analyze the document.

"Sure, there's something I wanted to get from the lab anyway. It's best if I do it when no one is around to ask questions."

George took his eyes from the journal and looked toward Drew. "Like what?"

"I want to get a blood sample from someone and test their DNA against my own. The boy who gave Dominick the journal said he was a cousin, a distant cousin, of ours. I thought I would check out his story."

George shook his head smiling, "You really want to get to the bottom of this don't you. It's the forensic scientist in you, I think!" He said with a short laugh after.

"It maybe, but I'm beginning to think that there is something to what Dominick has been telling me about this character, he calls himself Thomas Torem."

"What, that he's a distant cousin?" George felt that Drew was getting a little extreme for someone just claiming to be a relative. "Are you rich and never told anyone?" He asked sarcastically. "Is he coming after your millions?" George laughed knowing that Drew lived paycheck to paycheck just as he did.

"There's more to it than that. Just read the first paragraph."

George flipped back to the first page and started to read. He looked up at Drew, "What is it talking about?"

"The journal supposedly starts when people from centuries ago left Earth to avoid some type of disaster. Or so Dominick was told by Thomas."

"Does Dominick believe him?" George wondered.

"He's skeptical but curious . . . as am I."

"Well, let's get going and see what we can figure out from this." He said lifting the journal now that his curiosity was peaked.

+ + + + + + + + + +

The drive to the lab took twenty minutes. When they arrived, everything was locked up for the weekend. The offices and labs were empty with the exception of security and the cleaning staff.

"Hi Wayne." George said as he and Drew walked down the hall to one of their labs.

"How is everything?" Drew asked as they approached the security guard.

"Good. What are you two doing here?" Wayne wondered.

"We needed to run a few tests on this book." George stated raising the journal toward Wayne.

"Oh, too bad you had to come in on a Saturday! It's too nice out to be at work." Wayne said as they passed each other in the hall.

"You can say that again." Drew said with a smirk on his face agreeing with Wayne.

George took his keys from his pocket and unlocked the door to the lab where they both worked during the week.

While George turned on the equipment around his work area, Drew gathered the articles he needed to draw a vial of blood from Thomas if he would allowed him.

Drew stood next to George as he looked at the journal paper under the microscope.

"Can I cut a small corner off one of the pages?" George asked.

"Yeah, whatever you need to do." Drew said as he walked over and stood behind George.

He watched as George put on a pair of gloves, took a small scalpel, and sliced a piece of the paper off at the top corner of one of the pages. He then placed the small slice into a glass vial and placed a few drops of liquid on it. Next, he cut another small portion of paper with ink on it from one of the other corners that had a page number on it. He did the same thing with that slice except he used a different liquid.

Once the ink dissolved, George took the vial that contained the piece of journal paper with ink and used the chromatographic method to identify the ink. "This will compare the pattern of the dyes used with the ink database to give us the formulation that was used."

After a few clicks and pings, the printer printed out a sheet of paper. "That will be your result." George nodded toward the printer with a smile revealing the pride he had in his work.

Drew picked up the sheet of paper and read the result. "You better look at this George." He said with a puzzled look on his face.

He handed George the paper, he stared at what was written, he had never come across a result like this. INCONCLUSIVE. NO KNOWN MATCH IN DATA BASE.

George went to his computer and entered a few codes then reran the sample. "I expanded the search to include other chemicals that could possibly be used." He stood by the printer waiting until it spit out a piece of paper. He read the findings then looked at Drew. "Whatever was used to write the words in that journal is made up of an unknown ink. Not one of the dyes in the ink is made up of anything we use today."

He then went to the sample of paper that had finally dissolved in the other solution and placed it into the molecular spectroscopy. "This will tell us what organic compounds are in the paper that was used in the journal." George said.

"You don't sound confident." Drew stated observing George.

"I didn't expect the ink result. I have never placed a sample through the system without at least some of its chemical components popping up. And I have put thousands, hell, tens of thousands through over the years."

Drew felt a little nervous twinge in the pit of his stomach. What if what Thomas has been saying is true? Then what? He thought.

The printer started to print out sheets of results. Drew peered over George's shoulder as he picked up the papers and noticed the peaks and valleys of the wavy line.

"What is it made of?"

George looked a little pale as he leaned against the counter. "It's organic, most likely a plant. But it's not a tree or plant that we have in the database. Drew . . . I don't know what this is made out of!"

Drew ran his fingers across his jaw and paced back and forth while George collected the samples and placed them into the freezer to store them. "I don't know what to do with the samples. If I take them anywhere for further analysis it will open us up to a good deal of questioning. Do you want that?"

"NO!" Realizing he sounded panicked Drew regrouped, "I mean that I don't want to go that route, not yet anyway. I wouldn't be able to answer whatever would be asked and who knows how far reaching it would go."

"I think we, or you, need to talk to your son's friend and find out what is really going on here before we do anything else."

"I agree. Do you want to be involved?" Drew asked not wanting intentionally to drive his friend away from the situation, since he helped him analyze the journal.

"Just let me know what you find out, I don't want to scare the boy by both of us questioning him." George stated, then he stared at the floor as if he was in deep thought.

"Yeah, you're probably right." Drew answered. They sat for a few seconds contemplating what had just taken place before Drew spoke again. "Maybe we should get going; Rebekah's going to wonder where I am."

"I have to lock the freezer first." George said, as he reached down and turned his key in the keyhole, he then pulled the handle to make sure the freezer was indeed locked. "Okay, let's go."

The two men drove back to George's home with little said between them. Drew walked to his car and turned back to George, "Thank you for helping me with this."

"No problem. I wish I could have found more of an answer for you."

"In its own way it is an answer." Drew acknowledged knowing that it answered one question, the fact that what Thomas was saying may very well be true.

+ + + + + + + + + +

Dominick returned to his home a little later than he had said, it was close to four, he knew his mother would have dinner ready before six and didn't want to miss her home cooking. He had forgotten about Thomas, the journal, and all that it entailed he was having such a good time with his friends playing basketball and running into other people he knew from town at the Y.

When he came into the house, his father was talking to his mother and telling her about something that seemed to cause quite a bit of tension. He felt it as soon as he entered the room. At first, he thought it was because he was almost an hour later than he had said he would be, but dismissed the idea as fast as he thought of it. His parents stopped their conversation when they saw him.

"I was just telling your mother about the journal and what I found out when I took it over to George." His father said in a serious tone.

"Oh?" Dominick answered. He could tell that he had found something, or he wouldn't have been so serious.

"Listen Dominick, I really need to speak to Thomas. Call me when he is at school so I can come over there to meet him."

"Okay . . . but what about the journal? What did you find out?"

"I really didn't find anything out, that's the problem. George put it through a couple tests to check the ink and the paper it is written on, the substances are not in our database."

Dominick thought about what his father just said. He knew a little about the testing that the lab handled where his father worked. They conducted testing for many criminal cases for the State and even the Federal Authorities. The databases they had access too were extensive. "How can that be?"

"We don't know. The paper the journal was written on is made from a plant of some sort but nothing that grows around here. The chemical makeup of the paper and the ink are foreign."

"Foreign . . . like from Europe or the rain forest?" Dominick said with a hopeful tone.

"No. Foreign like from another planet!" His father answered. "It is important that you don't tell anyone about the findings. George and I aren't sure what the best way to handle this is, so I want to talk with Thomas first."

"Who would believe me anyway?" Dominick remarked.

"You're right about that." His mother said, "It does really sound too farfetched."

Dominick noticed that there wasn't anything cooking on the stove, "When is dinner going to be ready?" He asked.

"We wanted to surprise you and your sister with pizza tonight, the delivery boy should be here any minute." His mother said with a smile.

"That's great! I haven't had pizza from Marco's since last summer." Dominick answered excited, pizza was the only food he liked better than his mother's fried chicken.

"Take this to your room." Drew handed Dominick the journal. "Put it away someplace safe, okay."

Dominick nodded his head and walked to his room passing his sister on her way down stairs. "Is dinner here yet?" She asked.

"Not yet." He answered as he continued to walk to his room.

11

On Monday, when he wasn't in a class or lecture, Dominick walked around campus hoping he would run into Thomas. He never asked him for a phone number or exactly where he lived which left him with no way to get in touch with him. He was beginning to get worried that

Thomas might have moved on and left him hanging with no answers to all the questions he had.

He ate by himself and then went back to his dorm room where he studied and then took a nap. He woke to the sound of Patrick coming in the door and throwing his backpack onto his bed.

"What's up, I missed you at dinner."

"Oh, I ate earlier. I didn't feel like socializing." Dominick stated.

"Have you run into Thomas?"

"No, I'm beginning to wonder if he really did leave the area."

"I suppose it's possible, but I really don't think he would just leave if what he has been telling you is true. He seemed to have a purpose in mind, if you ask me."

"I hope you're right, Patrick, because this whole thing is starting to interfere with my life."

"What do you mean?" Patrick asked concerned for his friend.

"Well . . . I don't know . . . I just can't focus on anything. The stuff Thomas said is always in the back of my mind distracting me."

"That's not good, if he doesn't show back up you'll have to move on and forget about it. It all seemed ridiculous anyway, I don't see how what he said could be real that's why he probably left. He left before you could prove he was a liar."

Dominick looked at Patrick, he wanted so badly to tell him what his father had found out over the weekend but had promised not to talk about it. "Yeah, I suppose." Was all he could think to say. He felt like he was betraying his best friend.

+ + + + + + + + + +

When Dominick woke on Thursday morning, the first thing he thought about was what to get for breakfast. Then realized it was the first time he hadn't thought about Thomas first since last Friday. Patrick was in the shower already so Dominick rolled over and waited until he came out.

On their way to the campus coffee shop Patrick noticed Jenny walking down the sidewalk. "Hey." He called and jogged over to her. "Why don't you join me, I'll buy you a cup of coffee."

"That sounds nice, I would like that." Jenny said as they headed back to where Dominick was standing.

"Hi." Dominick said when they were close enough to hear him.

"Hi Dominick. I didn't see you guys last weekend."

"We went home for a couple days." Patrick explained.

Dominick walked beside Patrick who was between him and Jenny. He listened as Patrick spent the rest of the way to the coffee shop talking to her.

Jenny was from Connecticut and came to this particular community college in New York so she could transfer her credits to the Technical Institute that was on the other side of town. This way she could save money by not spending her first two years paying the higher cost of the tuition at the Institute. She didn't want to move a second time so chose the closest community college she could find.

Dominick thought she was pretty; she had blonde hair, blue eyes, and was very petite and feminine. She was Patrick's type but not his, he preferred girls that were more athletic.

Dominick ordered a breakfast sandwich and coffee. The three talked and laughed for the next half hour until they had to leave for class. Dominick walked ahead of Patrick and Jenny as they left, and overheard Patrick ask her to the movies on Saturday. Dominick smiled hearing her response; she seemed genuinely excited that Patrick asked her out.

Patrick jogged along the walkway to catch up to Dominick after saying bye to Jenny.

"I think she really likes you." Dominick said as Patrick stopped beside him.

"I hope so, she's really something. She's smart and pretty." Patrick said with a smile.

Dominick laughed realizing Patrick had a crush on her. He dated frequently but had never really been serious about any of the girls from high school. He would usually became friends with them more than developing a romantic relationship.

"I'll catch you later." Patrick said. He then headed down the pathway that led to the building where his class was held.

Dominick headed to the lecture hall and sat in his usual spot. Professor Walters was a few minutes late but didn't waste any time getting the lecture underway once he arrived.

"Good morning class, today I thought we would discuss some of the better known archeological sites starting with the pyramids of Egypt. One of the more interesting aspects of the Great Pyramid is the tunnel system that . . ."

"Hey, did you miss me?"

Dominick turned, startled by the voice behind him. It was Thomas. Who then slid around the last couple of seats in the aisle to the seat next to Dominick.

"I thought you left or something, where have you been?" Dominick whispered.

"I went to DC to visit my girl. She came back with me; and I'd like you to meet her."

"What does she do in DC?"

"She's a political advisor to one of the senators."

"Oh." Dominick felt he needed to stop talking before his professor noticed. "We can talk after; I have something to tell you."

Thomas smiled as if he knew already what Dominick had to say.

After the lecture, Dominick waited until most of the students left the area where he and Thomas had been sitting.

"My father had the journal analyzed at his lab." He looked at Thomas to see his reaction; he seemed to be listening with interest but was expressionless. "There are no matches to the ink or the material the pages are made from on this planet."

Thomas smiled, "Is that what your father said?"

"Yes, and he wants to meet you to talk about it."

"I'm glad. How about we go this Saturday, I'll bring Bethany with me."

"Is that your girlfriend? Is she . . ."

"Yes, she's from my world. This is great Dom I've wanted to meet your dad." Thomas said sitting back in his chair and facing forward with a triumphant air about him.

Dom? Dominick thought. "No one calls me that!" He answered agitated at Thomas.

"Sorry, I thought it fit you."

"It doesn't!" Dominick answered again in an agitated tone, already annoyed at the fact that Thomas was even in his life let alone making assumptions about what his name should be.

"I'll come to your dorm on Saturday, late morning, say elevenish. Then we can go to your house, okay?" Thomas placed his hand on Dominick's shoulder as he started to stand.

Dominick glanced at Thomas, "Yeah, I'll see you then." Dominick only agreed because he knew his father wanted to meet him. Right now, he had had about enough of Thomas. He didn't like the feelings he felt when he thought Thomas was gone, he was starting to think that Thomas had some sort of hold on his life, manipulating him and controlling his emotions even more that some girl he might be yearning for.

When he returned to his dorm, Patrick was sitting at his desk doing homework. "Thomas is back." He said in an emotionless tone.

"You don't seemed enthused!"

"I'm not. He was acting like a jerk and called me Dom. What right does he have to think that would be alright?" Dominick shouted.

"Wow, why would he call you that? I've never even thought to shorten your name." Patrick answered seeing how disturbed Dominick was by it.

"I don't know, but I let him know I didn't appreciate it."

"Good, maybe he'll leave you alone now."

"I doubt it." Dominick sat down on his bed, "That's enough about him. I heard Jenny accept your invitation to the movies Saturday. What are you going to take her to see?"

"I don't know, I thought I would let her pick." Patrick said in an almost shy voice.

"You really like her don't you?"

"Yeah, I think I do!" Patrick answered with a huge smile.

12

Saturday seemed to inch along as Dominick paced back and forth in his dorm. Patrick had left to take Jenny to lunch before the movies leaving him without a distraction as he waited for Thomas.

He had called his father Thursday evening to tell him he would be bringing Thomas and his girlfriend home for the day. He was surprised at his father's response, he seemed almost nervous during their conversation. The thought of his father being nervous made him even more agitated at Thomas.

He looked up at the clock; it was now ten forty-five so he headed to the dormitory lobby to wait for Thomas.

While he waited, he talked to John, the student whose job it was to monitor who came into and left the dorms.

Dominick signed the book at the desk that kept track of the students who lived in the dormitory. This way the school would know that he would be off campus for the weekend. While he signed, he and John discussed the upcoming football game on the following Sunday that was going to be broadcast on the television in the student lounge. The student government was going to provide pizza and soda and they were hoping for a large turnout, as this was the first official student get together of the fall term. John was part of the student government and hoped Dominick and Patrick would come.

"I'll try to make it, as long as I don't go to my parent's house." Dominick answered when John asked if he was planning to attend.

Dominick turned to look out the window and saw Thomas coming up the walkway with a dark haired woman whose hand he was holding.

"I'll see you later, John. My friend is here."

"Take care."

Dominick exited the dorm and walked over to Thomas. "Is this your girlfriend?" He asked.

"It is, Bethany Bier this is Dominick Domern."

"Hi, it's nice to meet you." Bethany stretched out her hand to shake Dominick's hand.

Dominick hesitated a second, then reached out to shake her hand. "Nice to meet you too."

"Let's talk in the car where no one can hear us." Thomas practically ordered them making Dominick even more agitated.

Dominick followed as they headed to the parking lot and stopped at an older maroon Ford Tauris. "Is this your car?"

"Yeah, it gets me where I want to go." Thomas unlocked the driver side door and pushed the button on the inside of the door to unlock the rest of the doors. Bethany sat in the passenger seat and Dominick opened the back door and took a seat directly behind Thomas.

"Do you need directions to my house?" Dominick asked.

"Of course, do you think I'm that much of a stalker?" Thomas asked glancing in the rear view mirror and smiling at Bethany.

"Just take Route 9 East and get off on Route 206 North. It will take about forty minutes. When we get into town I'll tell you which street to turn at." Dominick was in no mood to joke around.

Thomas started the car and followed the direction Dominick gave him. "So, I can tell you're upset with me about something." Thomas stated glancing in the rear view mirror at Dominick.

"I felt like you were jerking me around. I didn't know you went out of town and thought you might have taken off or something, leaving me hanging."

"Sorry, it's just hard. I'm not sure exactly what I should or shouldn't say, this whole thing is somewhat new to me too.

I have never been this honest with anyone who is a native born before."

"A what?"

"Someone who was born here and not on my world."

"Oh."

The silence seemed awkward so Dominick decided to change the subject. He looked toward Bethany, "Thomas says that you're a political advisor in Washington."

"Yes I am. I work for the senator from your state, New York."

"How long have you been doing that?"

"Almost three years now. He's up for re-election next November, so I may be out of a job." Bethany answered.

"When did you get here?"

"A little over three years ago, right after Thomas."

Dominick was startled by her answer, "You've been here for three years Thomas! What do you do? And how old were you?" He asked looking at Thomas thinking he was only a year or two older than he was.

"I was eighteen when I left my home and came here, the same age you are now. I use to monitor the weather conditions but now I connect with others from my world in order to send information back home. My father, Tegan, is in charge of the Aerthen Project and my older brother Timothy is one of the directors. He's the person that I report to."

"So you're like a middle man then?" Dominick wondered.

"Yes, you can say that I suppose. It's easier to send all the collected information through one person rather than have everyone sending it at different times."

"I don't understand why do you need to send information about Earth back to your planet anyway?"

"That's hard to explain, so we should probably have that conversation a little later. I think we're close to the turn up ahead."

Dominick looked out the car window and saw that Thomas was right. They turned onto Route 206 a minute later.

When they came near the bridge over the small river that ran parallel to his town, Dominick gave Thomas further directions. "Take the first turn on your right after you go over the bridge, then the first left."

Thomas followed Dominick's direction.

"Okay, turn right at the next street. That's where I live, Spruce Lane. My house is the third one on the right, number 76."

Dominick noticed his living room curtains were being drawn back as Thomas pulled the car up to the curb in front of his house. His mother was peering out the window trying to see if Dominick was in the car.

After Dominick got out of the car and turned toward his home, both his parents were already standing on the front porch waiting for him.

13

Dominick waited on the sidewalk for Thomas and Bethany to exit the car. They walked up to the front porch together where Dominick introduced them to his parents. "Mom, Dad, this is Thomas and his girlfriend Bethany."

Drew held out his hand to Thomas. "Hello, nice to meet you." He said as they shook.

"Same here." Thomas answered.

He then shook hands with Bethany, "It's nice to meet you too."

"Nice to meet you." She said.

"Welcome to our home." Rebekah said smiling as she opened the screen door to allow Drew, Bethany, Thomas, and Dominick to enter the house.

Everyone stood in the living room, Dominick was waiting for his father to speak, Drew wasn't sure where to start so Rebekah began the conversation. "Can I get you something to drink? We have cola, water, and iced tea."

"Water would be nice." Thomas said smiling.

"I'll also have water. Do you need any help getting it?" Bethany asked.

"That would be nice, thank you. Ice tea Drew, Dominick?"

"Yes." They answered in unison.

Rebekah walked into the kitchen followed by Bethany.

"You have a lovely home Mrs. Domern."

"Thank you. Do you live around here?"

"No. I live in Virginia and work in Washington, D.C. for one of your state senators."

"Dominick said that you and Thomas are dating. Is that correct?" Rebekah asked, feeling safe in doing so since they seemed to walk very close together up the walkway.

"Yes, we have been together for almost four years now. We met back home and Thomas's father recruited me to work on the Project that we are both involved with. It was very intriguing since my major at the Academy was Environmental Science."

"So you're a scientist then?"

"I have an education in science, but my job is a political advisor for environmental change."

"That sounds interesting. There is a great deal of discussion on that these days. Do you believe what they say about climate change? I'm not sure if it's true or not, there are scientists who say it is and others who say they are just pawns of the government." Rebekah asked Bethany as she took out five glasses from the cabinet. Put ice cubes from the icemaker on the front of the freezer door in all of them, then poured water from two bottles into two of the cups and into the other three she poured iced tea.

"I do believe that there is something changing in the planets climate." Bethany relayed curious to see Rebekah's reaction.

"Do you think it's because of car fumes and factories?" Rebekah asked as she handed Bethany two of the glasses.

"Not so much, it's more of a natural reaction to the unstableness of the planets rotation, axis, and the solar system being as young as it is. As your solar system ages all these things will become more stable and the climate will become very stable without any further change."

Rebekah found her answer not to be exactly what she expected to hear. She smiled awkwardly and motioned for them to return to the living room.

As they reentered the living room, Drew and Thomas were standing in front of the sofa talking about the journal as Dominick came down the stairs with it in his hand.

"Thank you," Thomas said, as Bethany handed him a glass, "We were just discussing our family lineage."

"Did you find a common ancestor?" Rebekah asked as she handed her husband a glass of ice tea and sat Dominick's on a coaster on the table next to the sofa.

"We haven't progressed very far." Drew answered taking a sip of tea.

Rebekah then turned and went into the kitchen to get the glass of tea she had poured for herself.

"Here's the journal." Dominick said handing it to his father.

Drew flipped open the cover and pointed to the first paragraph. "What is meant by Aerthen and Aerthen II?"

"Well you certainly get right to the point don't you!" Thomas said smiling as if he was proud of Drew. "Aerthen is what we call this planet, you call it Earth, and Aerthen II is the planet we live on now."

Everyone was silent, a little stunned at the openness and frankness Thomas displayed while answering Drew's question with his unbelievable reply.

"I took a sample of the ink and paper the journal is made out of and analyzed them at the lab I work at." Drew confessed.

"And?" Thomas asked.

"Why don't we all sit down?" Rebekah said, she had just returned from the kitchen and overhearing her husband's statement she felt everyone needed to be more comfortable for the conversation they were about to have. She pointed toward the sofa and chair to encourage her family and guests to take a seat. She also realized this could end up being a very long afternoon.

Thomas and Bethany sat on the sofa next to one another; Dominick sat at the other end of the sofa next to where his mother had placed his glass of iced tea. Rebekah sat in the chair nearest to Dominick and Drew took the recliner that was closer to Thomas.

Once they were settled, Drew began where he had left off. "As I was saying, the analysis came back without a match, it was inconclusive. The paper is definitely organic, so I know it came from a plant, but it didn't come from one that grows here . . . on this planet. Unless it is extremely rare and not one that is normally used for paper production."

"Your right, it was written and published on Aerthen II, my home planet. I brought the journal with me to share with your family so you could see your lineage all the way back to the Riven."

"The Riven? What exactly is that?" Drew asked.

"That's how we refer to the separation that occurred between our ancestors. It took us close to thirty years to return once we left for Aerthen II, and when we did the next generation of people that we contacted rejected us."

"Is that why we don't know about you?" Rebekah asked.

"Yes, that's right. We decided that it was best to remain inconspicuous when we came here so that there would be no further problems." Thomas explained.

"So who was our common ancestor?" Dominick asked.

"The journal starts at the most distant common ancestors that we have together. They were brothers named Torem and Domern. Torem left with the majority of the population to find a new home on Aerthen II while Domern remained here on Aerthen. Nearly eighty percent of the population escaped in ships before the catastrophe occurred. That meant that only about twenty percent of the population remained here to face whatever the resources where going to throw at them."

"Resources?" Rebekah asked. She was shocked by what she was hearing and had no idea what Thomas meant by resources.

"He means the elements or the forces of nature." Bethany explained.

Rebekah nodded her heard showing she understood, finding it hard to talk any further. The whole concept of Thomas being from another planet was making her a little uneasy and she didn't want it to show.

"So your records only go back to this split or Riven that you referred to, and not any farther?" Drew asked still trying to remain skeptical about what he was hearing.

"No, our records go back almost 78,000 years. Our ancestors are the same before the Riven. Each family has kept a record of their relatives who stayed here so we wouldn't lose track of any of you."

"That doesn't make sense." Dominick chimed in. "There have to be more relatives of yours here than just us. Domern had more than one child I'm sure, and even if he didn't his grandchildren or great-grandchildren did. What do you have . . . separate journals for each of them?"

"You're absolutely correct about that Dominick, and we know who all of them are. However, it isn't prudent to tell everyone the truth. My father, brother, and I chose your family line to divulge the truth. We were hoping that you will assist us in what we need to do to help your half of the population."

"What do you mean? Help with what?" Drew asked with a hint of fear in his voice. "What kind of plan are you talking about?"

"Don't worry it's not anything illegal or immoral. We can discuss it more when the time is right. There is so much more for you to see and learn about before then."

"Let's get back to this story that you're telling us . . . that we're related." Drew stated wanting to get back on track for his plan to take a DNA sample from Thomas.

"Alright." Thomas answered leaning forward with his forearms on his knees.

"If we are related then it would be possible for me to run both of our blood samples and there should be a genome match showing a distant relation." Drew said searching for a reaction in Thomas's expression.

"Sure, there should be enough DNA that will match. I need to warn you though that because we split so long ago that there will also be different strands within my DNA that may not be in your database. Have you ever heard of the bottle neck that appeared in the genetics of your people?" Thomas asked.

"Of course I have." Drew stated feeling almost insulted by the insinuation that he wouldn't have heard of it.

"Well, we don't have that within our population since the vast majority of the people moved on with my ancestors."

Drew thought about what Thomas was saying. Either he was a real crackpot or he was the real thing. He certainly knew what he was talking about and if he made it all up, well it would be just nuts to make all this up in such detail. "Do you mind then if I take a sample of your blood? I have what I need to do it right here."

Thomas held out his right arm, "Be my guest."

Drew went to the kitchen and brought back the small black leather zipped bag that he brought home from the lab. As he walked over to sit next to Thomas, Bethany scooted down closer to Dominick.

"This will pinch for a second." Drew said as he pushed the needle into Thomas's ante-cube after wrapping a rubber tourniquet above his elbow and wiping the spot he intended to stick with an alcohol wipe. He then filled two tubes with Thomas's blood, pulled out the needle and held pressure at the site with a cotton ball. When it stopped bleeding, he placed a Band-Aid over the cotton ball.

Drew turned the tubes of blood back and forth a couple times and then slid them behind a strap in the leather pouch, zipped it, and placed it back in the kitchen.

When he left the living room for the kitchen, Bethany returned to her spot next to Thomas and picked up his hand. Thomas looked at her, winked, and smiled.

Dominick had watched the conversation between his father and Thomas as well as their expressions. He was becoming convinced that Thomas was telling the truth even though it was really more like a science fiction story than reality.

"Do you ever go back to your planet, or are you stuck here?"

As Thomas started to answer, Drew returned from the kitchen. "We take trips back rather often, we've gone back twice in the last three years."

"I thought you said it took twelve years to get there? That's why the mistrust developed between the people who left, and the ones who stayed behind. Didn't you say they didn't return for more than twenty-four years?" Dominick questioned remembering word for word what Thomas had told him when they were on campus.

Smiling, Thomas explained as Drew stood listening. "I did say that, you have an excellent memory! But if you remember, I also said that we have developed advanced technologies since then!"

"So what does that mean?" Drew asked.

"We can bend space-time now. When we lived here we were only able to go as fast as the speed of light and the planet we left for was twelve light years away." Thomas explained.

"So how long does it take for you to travel back and forth now?" Rebekah asked. She was sitting on the arm of the recliner since the rest of the seats were taken.

Drew returned to his seat and placed his arm behind her resting his elbow on the armrest and hand on the small of her back. He wanted to listen to every word Thomas was saying.

"We need to leave the solar system first, which we can do at light speed. That takes a little over five hours. Then once we are in open space we can open up a bridge between here and wherever we want to go. For our planet it opens just outside the solar system there, as it does here."

"You mean an Einstein-Rosen Bridge!!!" Drew exclaimed standing back up raising his arms, apparently shocked at the thought of it.

"What's that?" Rebekah questioned seeing her husband's reaction.

"You might know it better by the nickname it has here . . . a worm hole." Bethany explained being familiar with the word.

"Like in the movies?" Dominick asked.

"Yes." Bethany said.

"How long will it take to travel through that?" Dominick asked not wanting to get off track from his original question.

"Once we enter the tunnel on this end it takes only a few minutes to exit at the other end." Thomas answered.

"How is that possible? I learned in school that you can't go faster than light!" Dominick added being suspicious of Thomas once again.

"You actually go slower than light speed once you enter the tunnel." Thomas answered. "The bridge folds space, for example it takes about three days to drive to California from here, right."

"Pretty much." Dominick said.

"But it only takes an hour to drive to Albany from here."

"What's the point?" Dominick asked.

"Well if you were able to take Los Angeles and bring it to where Albany is you could reach it in an hour instead of three days."

"Oh, I see. So you bend space and only travel a short distance rather than the actual distance." Dominick added.

"Exactly, we have been going back and forth like that for thousands of years now."

"Then why haven't we heard anything about you coming here?" Rebekah asked.

"That's complicated, after our experience the first time we returned, and our cultures began growing farther and farther apart, we decided to be more elusive in our dealings with you."

"What kind of dealings?" Drew asked.

"We've influenced many men and women throughout your history for one thing." Bethany began, "Sometimes we were able to achieve our goal and at other times we weren't."

"Name me one instance." Drew demanded.

Thomas and Bethany looked at one another, "Well . . . electricity is the best example I can think of at the moment." Bethany said.

101

"What about electricity?" Dominick asked.

"We manipulated your society to move in the direction of alternating current rather than direct current." Thomas added.

"We learned in school that alternating is better! That's why it was used!" Dominick blurted out thinking Thomas didn't know what he was saying.

"If you read about the battle over the two currents you'll see that Thomas Edison was pushing for direct current and had already built up the eastern seaboard with electrical powerhouses. He was extremely influential and wasn't going down without a battle." Bethany added.

"Is that true Dad?" Dominick questioned looking at his father.

"It's true son." Drew related.

"What did you have to do with it?" Dominick asked.

"Our people worked behind the scenes encouraging Nikola Tesla and motivating Mr. George Westinghouse to support him." Bethany continued.

Dominick and Drew looked back and forth at one another knowing that this statement could neither be proven nor disproven.

"Who was Nikola Tesla?" Rebekah asked. She wasn't familiar with scientists or inventors.

"He was a genius from the country that you know as Croatia. He became an American citizen and was an inventor, electrical engineer, mechanical engineer, physicist, and futurist who held many patents around the world. The only other scientist that was truly his rival was Albert Einstein." Bethany explained.

"Oh. I'm surprised I never heard of him."

"More emphasis was placed on Albert Einstein at the time and he faded to the background I'm afraid." Thomas answered. He then turned to Drew, "I suppose that we'll just have to wait for the bloodwork to come back to verify that we're related. Then we can continue with our conversations, I'm sure you will have more questions once you think over what we talked about today." Thomas said. He realized that the conversation was becoming tiresome, and felt they all needed a break.

"I think you're right. Would you or Bethany like some snacks? I have chips and dip that I can bring out." Rebekah added.

"That would be nice; I'll help you get them." Bethany said.

After they left for the kitchen the conversation between Drew, Thomas, and Dominick lightened up. Over the next hour, they discussed many other subjects, none of which had to do with space travel or ancestry.

14

Dominick had decided to stay home for the weekend, rather than drive back with Thomas. His parents drove him back to his dorm Sunday evening after dinner. They hadn't talked much about the afternoon spent with Thomas and Bethany on Saturday. The day left them mentally exhausted, and with many questions and doubts. As Dominick prepared to exit his parent's car he asked, "How long will it be until you get the results from the DNA sample you took from Thomas?"

"It's going to take a few weeks I'm afraid." Drew answered.

"What if it comes back that we are related?"

"We'll worry about that when it happens. Until then concentrate on your school work, okay." His mother said in a supportive tone. She didn't want to worry him or let him see that she and his father were very concerned over the situation.

"Okay, but will you let me know as soon as you get any results?"

"You'll be the second to know!" His father said with a laugh to lighten the mood.

Dominick smiled as he opened the car door and proceeded to go to his dorm room.

Patrick wasn't home when Dominick entered the room. He noticed a note taped to Patrick's computer screen, he pulled it off to read it.

Decided to hang out with Jenny and a few friends.

I will be back later tonight.

Patrick

Dominick thought that he would take advantage of the quiet and opened his computer to do some homework and keep his mind off Thomas. After a couple hours, he started to have trouble concentrating so he decided to call it a night and went to bed. Dominick's dreams that night were disturbing, he dreamt of floods, disasters befalling unfamiliar cities, and planets far off in another galaxy with strange creatures that were roaming in every direction he looked. He woke with a start. Glancing over at Patrick's bed he could see the shape of his body under the covers, he must have crept in silently so as not to wake him.

Dominick had a hard time getting back to sleep, he tossed and turned for over two hours and finally fell back to sleep close to dawn. His alarm went off at seven-thirty; he pushed the snooze button twice before finally sitting up and stretching. Patrick was still asleep, today was his late day, and he didn't have any classes until the afternoon. Dominick however had a class in an hour; he washed and headed to the café for a quick cup of coffee.

"Dominick, hey Dominick!"

Dominick turned quickly recognizing Thomas's voice and saw him and Bethany walking across the café.

"I couldn't leave without letting you know."

"You're leaving?" Dominick blurted out in a surprised voice.

"Not leaving, leaving. I'm taking Bethany back to Virginia she has to be back at work tomorrow morning."

"Oh, I was afr . . . I mean wondering if you meant you were leaving for good." Dominick remarked catching his words, not wanting Thomas to know how much his friendship was starting to mean to him.

"I'll be back on Thursday for lecture." He said with a sneaky grin.

Dominick laughed, "How do you get away with attending a lecture when you don't even go to school here?"

"We all have our secrets my friend." Thomas said patting Dominick on the back. "I didn't want to take off without telling you know where I was going, and when I'd be back. If you're going to trust me I need to give you a reason, right."

Bethany laughed, "He just doesn't want to upset you like he did last time he disappeared for a couple days." Turning to Thomas she smiled, "You can be so dramatic, my love."

They kissed gently on the lips and Dominick turned away feeling like he shouldn't be watching such an intimate moment.

"So anyway, I'll be back and we can continue our talks, okay?"

"I'll see you at lecture on Thursday then." Dominick said as he stood, "I need to get to class before I'm late." Dominick smiled after his back was to Thomas, he felt he had won a small victory of sorts with Thomas letting him know his whereabouts.

15

Thomas and Bethany arrived at her apartment close to five o'clock Monday evening. They relaxed after the long drive from New York and turned in close to ten. The next morning they drove from Bethany's apartment in Virginia to a hotel located in Richmond. Thomas parked the car and they walked to the elevator, pushed the button for the second floor, and walked to room 209 where Bethany knocked three times.

The door opened revealing an older gentleman who was dressed in a suit with black hair and a closely trimmed beard and mustache. "Come in my friends." Vince Visor announced with a smile and look of relief on his face.

"Why the look?" Thomas asked.

"We're just about to get started, the only one not here now is Tony Tarbuk. His plane was late taking off from the west coast." Vince explained.

"Should we wait for him?" Bethany asked.

"No, we can get his report later; Trent is waiting for my call." Thomas said.

Thomas and Bethany walked into the hotel room and greeted their fellow Aerthen II citizens. "How are things going?" Thomas asked Diane Dineen who was an oceanographer.

"Not good, the monitoring equipment in the Sargasso Sea has been sending back some odd readings and the Gulf Stream current has slowed 1.5 mili-seconds over the last six months."

"Has anyone noticed?" Thomas asked.

"No, our instruments are more sensitive. Even I don't understand what's happening with the Sargasso Sea, the biology of the seaweed is changing with each new generation. Some of the specimens I've collected and studied have started to develop a thick exterior and it is spreading on the surface. It doesn't bother the sea life and is having no ill effects with the food chain that I can tell. The odd thing was when we went to collect it, we had to find the edge and get a specimen from there where the new growth had not developed the harder casing. We couldn't penetrate the center of any of the flows of the weed."

"That is odd. Why do you think that is?" Bethany asked.

"Not sure, a mutation maybe. I sent Lawrence Larose to keep a close eye on it."

"Good." Thomas acknowledged then turned to Vince. "What's up with your end?"

"The poles are still losing ice extremely fast, but not having any large effect on ocean levels which is surprising. Though it is effecting the Gulf Stream, as Diane said, and a few other currents slightly. But I don't think there will be any significant effects for about three to four more decades." Vince explained.

"Bethany how's the political end?" Thomas asked. They never really discuss work unless it was of great importance when they were together; they had so little time to spend as significant others recently as it was.

"The corruption is just as bad, if not worse. Instead of banding together for the welfare of the people and the environment, they use the information, or disinformation in some cases, for political leverage with voters. However, nothing they do ever seems to make any real strides on the issue. If that doesn't change they are going to be caught completely off guard and be too unprepared to save themselves."

Thomas thought that Bethany sounded frustrated. "Do you think the political arena is a waste of our effort?" Thomas asked.

"I'm beginning to think so. The scientific community might be easiest to reach. Hopefully someone will listen to them." Bethany stated.

"What about the UN or another of the influential countries?" Vince asked.

"We'd have to get the okay from Program Directors for an undertaking like that." Thomas said. "And to be honest I don't think they want to keep beating a dead horse, so to speak."

"What do you think will happen then if we can't influence them enough to recognize the danger they're headed toward?" Diane asked.

"I don't know." Thomas stated with a look of despair. "What I do know is that it's been discussed at the highest levels. My brother, Timothy, confided that to me the last time I was home. He didn't know what exactly was discussed however."

"Then I suppose a change in plan and assignments might be coming at some point!" Bethany said reaching for Thomas's hand, fearful they might be separated by an even greater distance.

Thomas squeezed Bethany's hand to reassure her, "If anything we might be called home." He said. He could feel the relief in Bethany's grip as he held her hand. He turned and smiled, she smiled back, squeezed his hand, and then let go. He knew she was reassured.

"The only other order of business that I need to relate is that Wilton and I might be escorting a few Aerthen citizens to Aerthen II in a few months." Thomas heard the gasps from his colleagues. Not revealing their true identities had always been one of their highest priorities, not to mention the fact that there had never been a citizen from Earth taken to Aerthen II.

"What?" Vince, the oldest member of the team, asked in disbelief.

"Provost Golan asked my father to have me make contact with a family from our bloodline, only as test subjects. In order to see if individuals could be made to accept the truth without fear, even if their society as a whole or some of their governments couldn't." Thomas explained.

Diane and Vince glanced back and forth at one another. "Sounds like the Program Directors may already be losing hope in reaching the politicians and are looking into plan B." Diane proclaimed.

"It's very possible." Thomas agreed. "But in the meantime we still have our assignments. Have Tony get in touch with me when he gets in. I have to contact Trent on Wednesday with our reports. I'll be with Bethany until late afternoon and intend to call home before I head back up north."

Before dispersing to continue their official business, the group relaxed and talked about many things including speculations about what the plan might be with the new information they all just learned.

16

Thomas heard from Tony late Tuesday night. On Wednesday, he called Trent and relayed to him all the information he received from his associates. Tony Tarbuk had no new information, the molten interior and volcanic activity was as unstable as ever, but normal for the age of the planet.

Timothy wasn't at the control room when Thomas called, he had hoped to ask his brother a question or two, but it would have to wait.

After eating dinner, he started the drive back to New York. His separation from Bethany felt as agonizing as ever, they hated being apart, but it was necessary for the moment. He arrived back at his apartment late Wednesday evening, and went straight to bed.

+ + + + + + + + + +

Dominick arrived at his lecture early anticipating Thomas to show up as promised. He sat in his usual chair and looked toward the door leading into the lecture hall. A few minutes before Professor Walters was due to begin he noticed Thomas walk through the door. A sigh of relief left his lips before he realized it, again he felt the odd effect Thomas had over him.

"Hey buddy. Everything alright?" Thomas asked seeing Dominick's expression.

"Yeah, I was a little worried you might not show."

Thomas laughed, "Believe me you are not going to get rid of me that easily. Are you going to go with the professor over the summer break to Peru?"

"I mentioned it to him, and was thinking about it. Why? Do you think I should go?" Dominick asked, thinking it was strange Thomas would be interested in Peru. "Don't you have bigger things to worry about?"

Thomas eyed Dominick with suspicion. "Why would you ask that?"

Realizing he said something wrong Dominick answered, "No reason. Just with all you have said I would think a trip by an archeology class wouldn't interest you."

"I'm interested in everything you do. I don't want to lose my relatives after just finding them! Ya know." He said rubbing the top of Dominick's head and laughing.

Dominick felt like Thomas was becoming more like an older brother than a distant, long lost cousin of some sort. He liked the feeling.

"Good morning class . . ." Professor Walters started his lecture the same way every time.

Dominick and Thomas sat side by side listening to the hour-long lecture. When he was finished his lecture, Dominick thought he noticed the professor nod in his direction. He couldn't imagine why.

"Here, take this." Thomas said handing Dominick a piece of paper.

Dominick took it from Thomas and opened the paper that was folded in half. There was a phone number on it. "Is this yours?"

"In case you ever want to call."

Dominick stood up, took out his wallet, and placed the piece of paper inside. "I will."

"Let's go backstage." Thomas said to Dominick.

"What?"

"I want to show you something."

Dominick followed Thomas down the stairs of the lecture hall, then up the four steps that led to the stage. They walked behind the curtain to an area where the drama club had props and costumes hanging on hooks.

When Dominick's eyes adjusted to the lower light level, he noticed Professor Walters standing across the room. He felt that he shouldn't be there and started to excuse himself, "I'm sorry Pro. . ."

Thomas interrupted, "It's okay Dominick, this is what I wanted to show you."

Dominick was confused; he looked at Thomas and then Professor Walters.

"This is Wilton Walters! He's part of our team in the U.S." Thomas said reaching out to shake the Professor's hand.

"Yes, well . . . I'm, we're sorry that it took so long to let you know who I really am, Dominick." The Professor said as he shook Thomas's hand and then reached toward Dominick.

"Who are you?" Dominick asked as he shook the professor's hand. "I'm a little confused? Aren't you a professor here at the community college?"

"Yes I am, but I'm also from Aerthen II like Thomas here. My mission was to educate the nest generation in your area about history and climate change."

"Oh, I see. I think." Dominick felt like nothing was the way he had been led to believe. "Is there really a trip to Peru?" Was the only thing he could think to say.

Thomas and Professor Walters looked at each other and smiled, "There is a trip, yes. But not to Peru, and not this summer." Thomas stated losing the smile and looking more serious.

Dominick's shock learning his professor was not, well, who he thought he was, started to turn to anger. "I'm beginning to think that no one is who they say they are! Who else is with you Thomas?" Dominick demanded as he started to raise his voice in frustration.

"No one else that you know, I promise." Thomas answered crossing his heart with his right index finger.

"Why did you deceive me about the trip? I don't get it, why was it announced to the entire class?" Dominick added.

"That wasn't a deception; I am taking a group to Peru this summer to explore the ruins that our ancestors used to live in. The trip that Thomas is referring to is another one that we really hope you will be interested in going on. We are planning to go home to visit Aerthen II as well!"

"To another planet! Are you crazy?" The thought scared Dominick; he had butterflies in the pit of his stomach when he thought about going to South America let alone another world.

"Don't worry little cousin, I intend to invite your father too!" Thomas added with a smile.

Dominick had nothing more to say. This whole thing was getting to be too much for him. "I need to get going." He said as he started to walk back to the stage. He overheard Thomas telling Professor Walters that he would be in touch with him later.

"Wait up Dominick, are you sure that you're alright?"

Dominick stopped right before the stairs that led off the stage and turned around to face Thomas. "Why are you here? Why do you want to get to know my family and me, and why tell us all this stuff? What is really going on here Thomas?"

Thomas sensed that Dominick had been pushed to his limit, revealing that Professor Walters was not just his professor must have been the last straw. "Listen Dominick, I realize this is alot, okay. But I promise you will understand soon, I just can't tell you everything right now."

"Why the hell not? You think this is a game. You like jerking me around, does that make you feel superior to us Aerthen left behinds!"

Thomas looked at Dominick a little dumbfounded. "Aerthen left behinds?" If Dominick wasn't so upset he would have thought the remark was funny. "Do you really believe what you just said?"

"I don't know . . . why can't you just be honest with me?"

"Do you see how you've reacted by finding out that Wilton was one of us? If I told you everything that I know you would really freak out. Believe me when I say that I will tell you when the time is right. Please."

Having let his anger and frustration out, Dominick was feeling more agreeable and rational. "Okay, I'll tell my dad you want us to go to your planet. I can't believe those words just left my lips!" He looked at Thomas who seemed relieved. "We okay?"

"Yeah, we're okay."

Dominick turned and walked down the stage stairs and out the door. He went straight to his dorm hoping Patrick would be there.

When Dominick opened the door to his room, he realized Patrick was in the bathroom, "You decent?" He called.

Patrick poked his head out the door with his toothbrush in his mouth, "Yeah, what's up?" He asked as toothpaste dripped from his mouth and fell into his hand cupped under his chin.

"I just left lecture and Thomas was there."

Patrick finished brushing his teeth and came out to talk to Dominick realizing he was unnerved about something. "What else?"

"I don't think I'm supposed to tell anyone this, but . . ."

Patrick looked at Dominick realizing this was going to be big, "What?"

"On Saturday when he met with my dad Thomas told him that he was from another planet."

Patrick laughed it sounded so outlandish. "He really is crazy isn't he?" Then Patrick realized Dominick wasn't laughing and had an odd expression on his face. "You're not kidding are you?"

He shook his head no. "My dad had that journal tested and it's made of materials that are not from our planet. It's made from some sort of plant that doesn't grow here!"

Patrick sat on his bed thinking, and then looked up at Dominick. "Another planet? He's an alien like the big eyed little grey things in the movies?"

"Well I don't think he's an alien exactly. His ancestors supposedly left here a long time ago and they come back here now and again."

Patrick stood up, "You can't be serious. Do you really believe that?"

"I'm starting to . . . I think." The two boys just looked at each other for a few seconds. "My dad took a blood sample from him and he's checking it." He said in a flat tone.

Patrick ran his hand through his hair, and walked across the room. "Wow, this is crazy. I don't know what to say or think."

"Me either, but like I said, I don't think I'm supposed to really say anything. Oh and my archeology professor is one of them." Dominick said as he looked down at the floor still not over the shock of that revelation.

Patrick looked at Dominick, speechless. After a few minutes he said, "I don't understand?"

"There are more of them here besides Thomas, he has a girlfriend, my archeology professor, and who knows who else. He said there were around 500 of them worldwide."

"What for?"

"I don't know, he says he can't tell me yet!"

"You know I won't say anything. If your dad is involved then this must be legit." Patrick conceded.

"Yeah, he started to think it was after the results from the journal."

"Wow that's all I have to say, just wow!"

17

Drew Domern sat at his desk with the results of Thomas's blood sample in front of him. He opened the sealed envelope and felt a cold chill run through his abdomen as he looked at the report. The comparison was unmistakable; they were related, and very distant, as Thomas had said.

Drew looked at the second report he had asked for. A summary of Thomas's heritage, his family origins compared to other populations that had been tested worldwide from the genealogy bank.

Drew put the paper down, then picked it up again, trying to digest what he was looking at. Thomas only had 45% of his DNA that could be matched to regions of distant human origins around the globe. Moreover, these were the same as his ancestral line, extreme Northern European, what are Scandinavia and Finland today, as well as the British Isles. The rest were unknown. No other human populations had the same allele segments that Thomas demonstrated. The only thought that came into Drew's mind was 'the bottleneck' that the human race had gone through, which there was no real explanation for, only theory and conjecture.

Drew felt a tingle, which turned into a shiver; envelop him as he remembered the conversation he had with Thomas almost a month ago. There was no way this could be a con or made up, the evidence was the evidence, and it was reality! Now he had to inform his wife and son, and he wondered where it would lead.

+ + + + + + + + + +

Dominick and Patrick were heading for the overnight get together of the gaming club that was named 'The Knight Players'. A play on words since the games were held overnight in the gymnasium on campus. They were excited about the overnight activity that would be held against many other college students all over the world.

"It's amazing how we can play this game with so many other students and we don't even speak the same language." Patrick was contemplating aloud as they walked up the stairs to the gym entrance.

"Yeah, I know. I suppose moving characters around and smashing in the brains of other guy's avatars doesn't need alot of talking." Dominick said with a laugh hitting Patrick in the upper arm at the same time.

"The first attack I make is going to be your man!" Patrick said pointing at Dominick as he regained his balance from the force of Dominick's impact on his arm.

"I don't think so. You need me if we are going to beat those Irish kids who won last time!" Dominick said as he opened the gym door.

"It seems a lot different coming here as actual college students and not high school geeks anymore, doesn't it!"

"It does, I'm not quite so intimidated by the college guys anymore since I'm one of them now."

From the door to the gym floor was about twenty feet, the two young men ran to it in seconds, excited about the evening ahead of them. They wanted to be sure to sit at computers next to one another so that they could share with each other as they played.

As they sat and waited for everyone to arrive and take their seats Dominick's phone buzzed in his pocket. He pulled it out and looked to see who was calling, "It's my dad." He said to Patrick as he answered.

"Hi dad."

"I told you that I would let you know when I got the results from the blood test."

Dominick felt instant anxiety hearing his father's words. He had managed to push the whole thing out of his mind the last couple of days focusing on the gaming night and not running into Thomas at all. He looked over at Patrick, who was already looking at him.

"Hold on dad, I need to get to someplace quiet." He motioned to Patrick that he was going out into the hall. Once he closed the door and it was quieter, he resumed his conversation. "Okay, I'm back. Tonight's game night and everyone was being really loud, I couldn't hear you very clear."

"I have the blood test results. It's true, we are related. It's very distant like Thomas said but we are family."

"Wow." Was all Dominick could say. "Now what?"

"I don't know, but I told you I would call. I just received the results late today. We can talk more about it when I see you. Go back with your friends and have a good time with your gaming."

"Alright, I love you guys."

"We love you too, bye."

Dominick heard the silence on the phone then placed it back into his pocket. He stood in the hall for a few seconds thinking about what his father had told him. He had prepared himself to hear the results and felt he would have been more surprised if his father had told him that there was no blood relation between them and Thomas. A loud yell came from the gym bringing him back from his thoughts of Thomas to the present. He opened the gym door and went back to his seat knowing that it was getting close to the start of the games.

"Are you alright?" Patrick asked when he sat down.

"Yeah, the blood test is back . . . we are related."

Patrick and Dominick looked at each other without saying a word.

"You already kinda knew that didn't you?" Patrick finally replied.

"Yeah, I think I did."

+ + + + + + + + + +

At four o'clock in the morning, Dominick and Patrick returned to their dorm room.

"What a night!" Patrick exclaimed.

"I can't believe those guys from California this year. Last year they were out early on, I didn't even consider them a challenge!"

"They must have been practicing 24-7." Patrick said as he pulled back his bedding and climbed under the sheets.

Dominick did the same, "Next year, we'll get them . . . next year!" He said with a laugh. "I'll see ya in the morning."

"Goodnight." Patrick said with a laugh showing his agreement to Dominick's remark about getting them next year, he then reached over and shut the light off on the table next to his bed.

Dominick laid in bed thinking about the conversation he had with his father. He thought that he should call Thomas in the morning and tell him the results. He wondered what he would say as he dosed off.

18

Thomas was watching the morning news and drinking a glass of juice when he heard his phone ring from the bedroom. He sprinted to the phone and saw that it was a number he didn't recognize.

"Hello."

"Thomas?"

"Yes."

"It's . . . it's Dominick."

"Oh, hey buddy. What's up?" He was surprised, but glad that Dominick called. He had given him his cell number almost a month ago and had not received any calls from him. They still only had contact when he went to the college campus.

"I just wanted to let you know that my father called me last night and said he had the blood test results.

"Okay . . ." Thomas answered waiting for Dominick to continue.

"He said that it showed we really are related."

"How do you feel about that?" Thomas asked.

His response caught Dominick off guard; he expected a response that was more ecstatic and emotional.

"I think I expected it."

Thomas was relieved at his answer; he had feared he might panic at the realization. "I'd like to set up another meeting with your father, can you take care of that."

"How about next weekend? I'm sure he won't mind."

"That sounds good. I haven't met your sister yet. Do you think she will be there?"

"I don't know, I can call and ask her to come. Her college is only about two hours away."

"That sounds good. How was your game night?" Thomas wanted to continue to bond with Dominick.

"We lost. But we did better than last year and it was fun, we didn't get to bed until after four o'clock in the morning!"

"I remember hanging out with my friends when I was a teenager back home, we had video type games too."

"Really!" Dominick was a little surprised; he then realized immediately that he saw Thomas, and his people, as being more serious and not very carefree and fun loving.

"Yeah, they took up a whole room and we interacted with them instead of having avatars."

"I've seen articles about that kind of thing. Supposedly, we'll have that soon too! It'll be a blast actually being the character."

"It's a different experience that's for sure; I believe that you'll like it. Listen, I won't be around till Thursday I have a few things to do." Thomas explained.

"Okay, I'll call home today and make sure it's alright with my dad for next weekend."

"Good, see you later."

"Yep." Dominick said as he pushed the end call button on his phone.

"That sounds like it went well." Patrick stated from his bed. He hadn't gotten up yet and was planning to stay in bed for most of the day.

"I suppose I'm over the shock. How much more could there possibly be?"

"I don't want to know." Patrick said. "At least not today. I'm too tired." He rolled over to face the wall and pulled the covers over his head.

Dominick was also tired but was motivated by hunger more, so he showered and went to find something to eat. It was now eleven o'clock and lunch was being served so he decided on a couple slices of pizza and a soda. After he ate, he sat down on a bench near the dorm and called his dad.

"Hi son, you okay?" His dad asked answering his phone.

"Yeah, I'm fine. I talked to Thomas; he wants to come over the house next Saturday. Is that okay with you and mom? He also wants to meet Dianne."

Dominick sensed hesitation from his father, "What does he want?"

"I don't know, maybe he just wants to talk about things."

"That should be alright, I'll let your mother know. I'm not sure about Dianne coming home though. We haven't told her anything about this. I don't know how to even begin to explain it to her."

"She's going to freak!" Dominick said almost laughing at the image of his sister spazzing out.

"Be nice son."

"I know dad; but it would be funny to see."

He heard his father exhale, probably annoyed with him. He used to tease his sister mercilessly when they were younger.

"I'll be in touch later in the week, let me know if anything comes up with Thomas."

"Okay dad, bye." Dominick sat on the bench enjoying the sun that was bringing warmth to his face. After a few minutes it began to be a little too warm so he decided to head back to the dorm and maybe take a nap.

19

Patrick planned to spend the weekend with Jenny since they hadn't spent much time together the weekend before when he and Dominick attended the gaming weekend together. Dominick felt that it worked out well for them both then, since he planned to go home this weekend and take Thomas for a second visit with his parents.

It was raining when he woke up so he decided to wait at the bus stop for Thomas instead of the campus park where they had planned on meeting. A glass box surrounded the bench where students who rode the bus sat as they waited; it did a good job of keeping him dry while he waited. It was only a short distance from the bus stop to the parking lot, so he would be able to see Thomas's car when he arrived and run over to it, hopefully not getting too wet.

Thomas was five minutes early, Dominick watched his maroon Taurus pull in from the main road and slowly make its way to the parking lot. He jogged over to where Thomas parked, and was able to get to the car without getting soaked.

Thomas saw Dominick as he came across the parking lot and pushed the button to unlock the passenger side door.

Once Dominick was inside the car it started to pour. "Good timing." Thomas said as lightning struck and thunder clapped.

"That was loud." Dominick said with a slight laugh.

"We have to wait for someone else. I hope you don't mind."

"Who?" Dominick asked feeling a little nervous knowing his family only expected Thomas.

"Professor Walters wants to meet your dad. He felt that if someone older was there it would help your dad feel more comfortable."

"Oh, okay, I suppose." Dominick said, he didn't say anything but felt that he would be a little uncomfortable with his professor there. While they waited for Professor Walters, they watched the lighting strikes and listened to the thunder that followed, Dominick began to wonder if Thomas's planet had storms like this. "Do you have thunder storms on your planet?"

"No, the weather is more like this planet was when we lived here."

"That's interesting, I never really thought about how the weather was that long ago."

"It's changed quite a number of times over history actually, you've learned about the ice age, right."

"Yeah, you're right, I also saw a TV show on how once, before the dinosaurs lived that the Earth was completely covered in ice, and then when the dinosaurs existed how it was tropical everywhere."

"There have certainly been some extremes! Look, here he comes now!" Thomas said pointing toward the entrance to the parking lot.

Dominick looked in the direction Thomas was pointing. A tan colored SUV was heading toward them.

"He's going to drive on his own." Thomas explained. "He'll follow us."

Dominick was relieved. "I'm going to text my parents and let them know so they are prepared to meet someone else from . . . you know . . . another planet."

Thomas laughed heartily as he started his car and began the drive to Dominick's home.

"You know what's weird?" Dominick remarked.

"What's that?"

"It's beginning to seem so normal that you're from so far away."

"Good."

"How is Bethany doing?" Dominick asked keeping the conversation going.

"She's fine. We're planning to go home over Christmas recess so I'll get to spend more time with her then. It's hard being apart like we have been lately."

Dominick realized that this was the first time Thomas had shared anything quite so personal with him. "Are you planning on getting married?"

Thomas looked over at Dominick surprised by his question.

"I'm sorry. I didn't mean to pry. It's just that you seem to really like her, that's all."

"That's alright. I was just surprised by your question. We are planning to be a couple, yes. We don't have any kind of a formal declaration of our union like you have here. We just choose a partner and go from there."

"Really, people here think that you need something to keep you together, if you're not married then you can just split up or leave at any time." Dominick thought about what Thomas said for a few seconds. "So there's nothing binding you together, legally on your planet."

"No there isn't. That's one of the differences between our cultures."

"What do you mean?"

"I really don't know how to say it without you getting insulted."

"I won't get insulted. There are plenty of people here who just live together without a legal marriage. They feel they don't need a piece of paper."

"That's true but like you insinuated, it's not your society's norm and I find that it is frowned upon in general."

"Yeah, I suppose so. Why is it so different with your culture?"

"Because we're different. Our society is a peaceful one, we don't have war, we don't scam one another, and have no lawsuits against each other. Your part of the family lines changed after the flood and apocalypse. We aren't quite sure why it happened but it did, that's one of the reasons we have never revealed ourselves to you. Well, until now."

Dominick thought about what Thomas had just said. "You have never been in a war with each other?" He found that very hard to believe. "What do you do when one group wants another's land or animals or whatever?"

"That just doesn't happen; we work together and respect each other. You'll find that there are many ways that we are different from your people."

"Like what else?" Dominick asked.

"We don't eat meat. That's another thing your part of the family started after the flood."

"What do you do with your animals then? You said you took some with you."

"We use their fur for clothes much the same as you do with sheep. They are companions to us like your dogs and cats, and at one time, they helped us plow fields. Much of our relationship with our animals is similar. We just don't eat them."

"I never noticed that you didn't eat any meat at lunch or dinner. Umm . . . that's interesting. Does it gross you out that we do?"

"I'm used to it now, but at first it did. I just couldn't understand it. Especially when I would hear someone talk about it. Like on TV commercials for barbecues when it would show pictures of bloody meat. It made me feel sick."

"Do you drink milk, eat cheese, or eggs?"

"Oh my gosh! NO! I don't understand that either, cow milk that is meant for baby cows, what is with that?"

"It has calcium and other vitamins." Dominick said defending his culture.

"So do vegetables, seeds, and roots." Thomas remarked.

"Well I suppose they do, we have people here who are vegetarians and seem to do okay. I don't think I could only eat just fruit and vegetables all the time though." Dominick conceded. "Oh, don't forget to turn up ahead."

"I won't. Thanks for the reminder though."

Dominick smiled, happy that they were getting to know one another better.

+ + + + + + + + +

When they pulled up to Dominick's house, Professor Walters was right behind them. Dominick led the way to the front door. The weather had cleared and it was no longer raining, and his parents hadn't come out to greet them this time.

Dominick held the front door open allowing Thomas and his professor to enter. Once he was in he called out to his parents, "Mom, dad. I'm here with our company!"

His mother came around the corner of the living room, having been in the kitchen. "I didn't hear you pull up. I'm sorry." She held her hand out, "Welcome once again, Thomas."

Thomas shook her hand, "It's nice to see you again, too. This is Wilton Walters, an associate of mine and Dominick's professor at college."

Rebekah was taken back hearing that Thomas's associate was Dominick's professor. "Oh, what class do you teach?" She asked as she shook Wilton's hand.

"Archeology. It's nice to meet one of Dominick's parents; he's a fine young man." He stated glancing over at Thomas who was slightly blushing.

"Well, it's nice to meet one his professors. My husband had to run out to the store but he'll be back shortly. Would you like to come into the kitchen until he returns? I'm in the middle of cooking."

Thomas nodded and followed Rebekah Domern into the kitchen. They sat down at the table and Dominick offered their guests a drink. Looking into the refrigerator, he saw that there was cans of soda, water, or apple juice. He asked Thomas and Professor Walters what they wanted.

"I'll take some water." Thomas stated.

"Apple juice for me, please." Professor Walters replied.

Dominick handed each man what he had requested and took a cola out for himself.

"What are you preparing?" Thomas asked to start a conversation.

"Since my daughter will also be home, I thought I'd make fried chicken. Everyone here likes that, I hope you do too?"

"Mom . . . Thomas and Professor Walters don't eat meat."

Rebekah Domern turned from the counter where she was breading the chicken and looked at the two men. "Oh, do you eat salad, potatoes, and broccoli?"

"Yes." Thomas answered.

"Will that be enough for you then?" She asked.

"It will certainly be enough. We appreciate your generosity." Wilton answered.

"If I had known we would have had a more vegetarian type of meal, I'm sorry." She looked at Dominick questioning why she wasn't told about this with her eyes.

Sensing her meaning, Thomas added, "Dominick didn't know himself until today. The subject just never came up."

"I see, well, will it bother you if the rest of us have chicken?"

"No. Of course not." Thomas stated.

Drew Domern opened the door that led from the garage to the kitchen just as Thomas finished. "Hello everyone." He said smiling as he placed two grocery bags down on the counter.

He turned and held his hand out to Thomas, "Nice to see you again." Then he glanced over to Wilton Walters, "Hello, Drew Domern." He held his hand out.

"Wilton, Wilton Walters, nice to meet you."

"Wilton is one of Dominick's professors at the college." Thomas added.

Drew looked over at Dominick then back to Wilton.

"He's doing well. I teach archeology which is one of Dominick's electives."

"Well, I'm glad to hear that." Drew walked over to Rebekah, "Do you mind if we go into the living room and talk?"

"No, go ahead. I'll join you in a few minutes."

"Let's go into the living room and relax, I have some information I want to share with you." Drew said looking over at Thomas and Wilton.

After they walked into the living room and sat on the sofa and chairs, Drew began the conversation. "So, Wilton, I suppose you are from the same place as Thomas then?"

Thomas laughed enjoying the directness Drew continued to display, which only strengthened his resolve that he had chosen the right relations to reveal himself.

"Yes, that's right." Wilton answered, looking at Thomas surprised by his reaction.

Thomas redirected the conversation. "So, you said you have something you wanted to tell us?" He asked looking at Drew.

"I wanted to tell you more about the results of the blood test that I ran. Not only did it show that we are related, but it also showed that there are parts of your genetic material that do not match any of the known haplogroups."

"How do you feel about that?" Wilton asked.

"Actually, I'm surprised to say that I find it exciting." Drew laughed. "I'm beginning to believe the wild stories you've been telling us!" He exclaimed looking at Thomas.

"I'm glad because I have an even wilder question to ask you!" Thomas replied as he continued to laugh. "How would you like to take a trip to Aerthen II with us? Both you and Dominick?"

"Are you asking what I think you are asking? You want to take us to another planet?"

"You're right. That is exactly what I'm asking. Wilton, Bethany, and I are going over winter break at the end of December into January."

Dominick sat watching his father and Thomas as they spoke. He was speechless listening to them as they laughed in between serious conversations.

Drew burst out into laughter, "I can't believe we are having this conversation! It is insane, and I'm laughing because it's just unbelievable!"

"What conversation? What's unbelievable?" Rebekah asked as she came into the living room hearing the conversation getting louder.

Dominick spoke up seeing his father was still laughing, which seemed odd to him. "Thomas wants us to travel to his home planet during Christmas break!"

"Don't be silly Dominick, I'm serious what conversation is unbelievable?"

"Dominick isn't kidding." Wilton explained. "That is what we are discussing."

"Drew . . . Drew!"

"Yes dear. I'm sorry but this conversation is beyond belief and I find it really insane." Drew explained as he tried to stop laughing.

Rebekah sat next to her husband. "What exactly is going on?"

Clearing his throat with a cough Drew looked at Rebekah. "Thomas is going home for the winter break and invited Dominick and I to join him."

"Home . . . you mean . . . your real home?" Rebekah asked looking at Thomas.

"Yes, Mrs. Domern. That is what I mean."

"You can't be serious about doing this." Rebekah looked at Drew.

"This is the first I've heard of it, hun. We'll have to discuss it and then we'll decide together."

Rebekah didn't want to discuss the issue in front of their guests. However, she did not intend to let her husband and son go to another planet with almost total strangers.

"Dad, Thomas was telling me that they are all vegetarians and that they don't have any wars like we do."

"Is that right?" Drew asked, being drawn away from his previous mindset and feeling more serious. Drew turned from Dominick toward Thomas and Wilton. Before he could say anything else, Thomas continued.

"It's true. We don't eat meat or use any animal products for that matter, and our society hasn't changed very much for over 70,000 years, well . . . with the exception of our technology." Thomas explained. "I remember when I learned about what your world is like. I was horrified and shocked because everything was so different from how we live."

"How old were you when you found out about us?" Dominick asked.

"I always knew about you. Your existence isn't a secret on our world. You don't realize it, but you're all very much apart of our lives. We never forgot about our home world, most of us have relatives here. When we are in higher learning, which is equivalent to college here, we can learn more details about your world if we choose to. I was fifteen when I decided I wanted to join my father and work with the people who monitor Aerthen, so it was required to learn about your history. I had nightmares and couldn't sleep after seeing and hearing the details of your history."

"Fifteen? I thought you said college?" Dominick exclaimed.

"Our education system is different; we have three levels of learning, a lower, middle, and a higher level. The lower level is where we learn our basic skills of reading, writing, and math.

At the middle level we expand math, learn our history along with some of your history. Then when we're around fourteen we move on to higher learning where we learn the skills we'll need for our future careers."

"Oh, alright, so if you pick a career at fourteen or fifteen, what happens if you change your mind later and want to do something different? Can you choose something different?" Dominick wondered.

"Of course you can. No one is limited to what they can do or when they can do it, it's best that way." Thomas stated matter of fact.

"Oh, do you get paid for being here?" Dominick asked.

"We don't get paid and we don't have money!" Thomas stated bluntly as if insulted by the question.

"Sorry!" Dominick felt bad for asking but didn't get why Thomas would be so uncomfortable with the question.

"Don't be sorry, I just get frustrated because of how everything revolves so much around money here. I told you there where things here I didn't agree with. Well . . . money is one of them."

"You see, Drew, Dominick." Winston began. "We all work together to create a society that benefits everyone. We participate in the overall wellbeing of each other by doing what we enjoy. I enjoy teaching, others enjoy farming. Still others enjoy building or making clothing, we all contribute according to what our interests and talents are. Everyone benefits and no one does without."

"That sounds too good to be true." Rebekah remarked.

"I suppose that from your point of view it does, after all you only know what you live. At one time, your ancestors lived the same way we do now. We believe that the flooding and atmospheric changes that took place after we left may have been the reason they changed. The harsh conditions created a survival mechanism within your ancestors that we never experienced." Wilton tried to explain the best that he could.

"That makes sense." Dominick thought aloud.

"It's the only thing that makes sense to us, and would explain why there would be such a dramatic change in the nature of the people that stayed behind." Thomas added.

The front door opened drawing everyone's attention. Diane came in, just arriving home for the weekend at her mother's request. "Oh . . . hi everybody." Diane said looking around at the unfamiliar faces. "I didn't know we were going to have company!"

"Hi sweetheart, this is Thomas and this is Wilton." Rebekah said introducing Diane to the men.

The two men stood, "It's very nice to meet you. I'm one of Dominick's professors at the college."

"Oh, hi." Diane said as she shook Wilton's hand.

"I'm Thomas. Dominick's . . . friend." Thomas was going to say cousin but decided against it at the last minute.

"I've never heard Dominick mention you before. Did you meet at college?" Diane asked suspicious at the age difference between Thomas and her brother.

"Yes we did, as a matter of fact."

"Well, I'm glad he's making new friends. If you'll excuse me, I just want to put my things upstairs. I'll be back in a minute."

Once Diane was upstairs, Thomas lowered his voice, "I don't want to cause you any problems, why don't you explain things to Diane once we leave."

"That's probably a good idea." Rebekah stated. "When she comes down she can help me in the kitchen, that way you can continue your conversation."

Everyone nodded in agreement.

"As we were saying." Thomas continued. "It's true, we would like Dominick and Drew to accompany us when we head back home for a few weeks."

"I think that would be the best way for us to build our relationship and our trust in one another. Once you see how we live then you won't have any doubts about us. We also have some scientific research from our studies that we want to show you." Wilton added.

"Studies about what?" Drew asked a little concerned since he still didn't know the whole reason for all of this, there had to be more to it than just finding long lost relatives.

"We told you about why we left so long ago." Thomas added.

"Yeah, you said it was an environment change and a polar shift." Drew answered.

"Well . . . we believe that it's happening again. Not the exact same change as we experienced of course, but weather patterns are changing and there are signs that indicate that a pole shift is also starting."

Rebekah, Drew, and Dominick looked back and forth at one another. The fear created by Thomas's words was evident.

"The pole shift isn't going to take place for about thirty years, but the climate is another story. At least that's what our calculations say." Thomas said hoping to calm the family's fears.

"Then why are you here now?" Rebekah asked.

"To monitor the situation first hand, and try and make your leaders aware of the possible severity of its consequences. We would like to help, we just don't know if they will accept our help or not." Thomas added.

"I don't understand." Rebekah said. "We have nothing to do with the government. Why would you contact us? Or do you contact a lot of people?"

"You are the first of our relations to be contacted. I don't know if we will contact others or not!" Thomas stated.

"But why?" Rebekah pushed for an answer.

Wilton thought he should answer, "If your governments won't listen we want to save as many people as we can. If our contact with you, Domern's descendants, is successful then we will contact others."

"So we're like guinea pigs to you then!" Dominick remarked in a tone that showed how annoyed he was at the thought of that.

"In one sense . . . well . . . maybe. But this is something we have wanted for thousands of years and could not come to an agreement on how to go about approaching any of you, until recently." Wilton stated hoping to stop the feeling that he knew was rising in the family.

"What Wilton is saying is correct." Thomas continued. "When your ancestors didn't want anything to do with us it was very hard for our predecessors to accept. They struggled with the rejection along with the guilt over what caused it for a long time. We were hoping to avoid anything like that again, plus you have all forgotten about us! How to reintroduce ourselves is something we are still working on."

As Diane came back down the stairs from her bedroom, Rebekah stood and asked, "Honey, would you mind helping me in the kitchen. I have a few last minute preparations that need to be done."

"Okay mom." Diane answered looking around the room, sensing something was off.

When they were alone in the kitchen Diane asked her mother what was going on. "Mom, what are they talking about in there? And why would Dominick's professor be here, is everything going alright for him at school?"

Rebekah looked at her daughter. She wasn't use to misleading her, nor hiding anything significant from her. "Well honey, the truth is that the young man out there is a relative of your fathers. A distant cousin on his father's side."

"Oh." Diane thought about what her mother just said. "Why does there seem to be something weird going on then? I felt it as soon as I came into the house."

"It's just that he wants your father and brother to go with him to visit where he was born."

"What's the big deal about that?" Diane asked as she started to peel the potatoes. "How far away could it possibly be? I mean he doesn't seem like he has an accent so he must live in the country somewhere. Where would they be going?"

"I'm not sure exactly how far away it is." Rebekah replied.

"Oh, do you think I could go? I'd like to meet our relatives too!" She asked probing further not really understanding what was going on, but not wanting to be left out.

"We'll talk about this with your father, okay!" Rebekah said in a tense voice.

"Geez mom, I was only asking! Sorry!" Diane answered sarcastically.

"I'm sorry too honey. There's more to it than just that, but we need your father to tell you about it. Please wait till later, okay."

Diane could tell that whatever was going on was hard for her mother to talk about. "Alright, mom." She said continuing to peel potatoes, but not happy about it.

Rebekah and Diane continued to make dinner without much conversation, the tension becoming thicker as Diane mulled over their conversation.

"Wait here." Rebekah asked Diane after a few minutes. She then went to the living room and called to Drew. "Can you come in here for a minute?"

Drew excused himself and went to see what his wife wanted. "Is everything alright?"

"We need to tell Diane, now." She said without leaving room for Drew to refuse.

Drew shook his head and walked to the kitchen with Rebekah.

Diane saw her parents come in through the door and turned. They had a serious expression on their faces.

"Come sit down." Drew said to his daughter pulling out a chair at the kitchen table for her to sit on.

Diane was nervous, what could be so serious? She wondered.

Drew began to explain everything that had happened since Thomas and Dominick met. Diane listened in silence.

When her father finished she looked back and forth at her parents, "Is this some kind of April fool's joke or something?"

"No dear, your father has proof to back up Thomas's story."

Diane stood up and walked toward the living room; she looked through the door at the two men in the living room and then returned to her parents. "This is crazy!"

"We know. It took us some time to accept it but apparently, it's not a joke. I'm sorry we didn't tell you before this, but we wanted to talk to you in person. Do you understand that?" Drew asked, concerned for her.

Looking at her father and seeing the pain in his expression, she answered. "It's okay dad. I'm not mad. But, I'm not quite sure I believe all of this either. Isn't he the guy you were talking about last time I was home, the one stalking Dominick?"

"He is, but it turns out that he just wanted to find a way to approach us about this whole thing." Rebekah stated.

"Do you want to come and join us in the living room until dinner?" Drew asked. He didn't want her to feel like she was unwelcome around there quests.

"No, that's okay, I'll stay and help mom."

Drew smiled and glanced at his wife before returning to the living room.

"We told Diane, and she's seems okay with everything." Drew said matter of factly as he sat down.

"Good, she's welcome to join us in December as is your wife." Wilson added.

"We'll discuss it and see. So, tell me when would we leave and return." Drew asked.

Thomas was excited. He knew that if he was asking then he was considering on going. "We would leave December twentieth and return on January third."

"Where would we leave from?" Dominick asked, having wondered about where they could possibly keep a spaceship.

"Virginia. There's a level plain in the mountains that we leave and return from." Thomas answered.

"We would drive down together and then drive you back to New York when we return." Wilton added.

"Dinner's ready!" Diane called from the doorway.

"Okay, we'll be right there." Drew answered.

"Think about what we said, we can continue our conversation another time." Thomas said, "Let's just enjoy the company and the conversation for now."

"That sounds good." Drew answered. He was also a little relieved; this was becoming alot to digest.

After dinner, Dominick decided to ride back to college with Thomas instead of staying at his parents until Sunday. On the drive back, the two continued to joke and laugh becoming closer friends.

After dropping Dominick off, Thomas called Bethany. "Hey, how are you doing?" He asked when she answered.

"Good, how did your dinner go?"

"Excellent. I'm getting closer to Dominick, and his family is accepting everything I've told them. I think we're making progress. I'm pretty sure that at least Dominick and Drew will be coming home with us in December."

"That's great." After a sigh Bethany continued. "I miss you."

"I miss you too, especially at night." He laughed.

"I bet you do." She replied.

20

"What do you think they are up too?" Jim asked, looking over at his partner.

"They have certainly gone off their usual protocol, there's no doubt about that now." Wayne replied.

"This is the first time that it seems that they've revealed who they are to anyone, that has me worried."

"It means that they're going to make some sort of move, but what that is, is the question?" Wayne remarked.

"Yeah, I don't know what there up to. Thomas will head back to his apartment from here so let's get back to the base and see what else is going on." Jim said, as he began to drive out of the college parking lot and head toward the air base.

When they arrived at the base, Jim and Wayne went toward their offices. They occupied one of the two small rooms at the far end of one of the hangars. The second office was also used by their organization. Two other men, named Ron and Luke, were busy in the second office when they arrived.

"What did you find out?" Ron asked.

"Since Walters went along I think it's safe to say that this was not just a social visit." Jim said.

"I agree." Wayne continued. "We believe they may have revealed their identities to the Domern family. Whatever the reason for that is we haven't been informed, at least not at our level."

"They have no political or scientific connections that would make them valuable to their usual agenda." Jim added.

"We found one thing this morning that is of interest." Ron stated, turning to his computer and pulling up a report that he had minimized on his screen.

The other three men gathered behind him. "See this. It was sent to me from Central Headquarters this morning."

"What is it?" Wayne wondered.

"It's a DNA comparison. Drew Domern ran it a few weeks ago." Ron pointed to the top results, "I was told that this is Drew's DNA."

"Whose result is under it?" Jim asked.

"Not sure, but whoever it is, isn't from earth." Ron said, looking back at the other three. "See these last segments on the right of the screen? According to the results, whoever this is has enough genetic similarities to Drew to be related, how be it distantly. However, the person also has DNA that isn't a match to any databases of collected DNA samples here on Earth."

"What does that mean exactly?" Wayne asked.

"It means that no humans on earth have anything in common with that specific part of the DNA, it's alien!" Luke stated as he brought his hands up to his mouth creating a tunnel between them and his mouth causing the words 'it's alien' to sound ghostly.

"Alien! Come on Luke, don't be so dramatic." Jim said, laughing.

Luke also laughed as they all joined in.

"It only means that there are no descendants here that have that portion of the DNA within them. The people who stayed behind aren't represented by it, namely us, only the ones who left." Luke restated.

"So do you think that this is proof then, to show Drew Domern that they are being honest with him about their origins?" Wayne wondered.

"I would say so. I would also bet my last dollar that the sample belongs to Thomas!" Luke stated.

"He did go out of his way to befriend Drew's son, Dominick." Jim began yelling over the sound of helicopter engines starting up in the hangar beyond their offices. He then placed his hands over his ears.

The four men waited, and waited. Finally, the engines cut off.

"We have to talk to someone about a better office location!" Jim said, after taking his hands away from his ears.

"At least out of the mechanics hangar, that would really help." Luke added.

"Being part of a shadow government has its drawbacks." Ron remarked. "It's not like we can rent office space downtown and hang out a sign!"

"Why not?" Jim asked.

"Yeah, we could call ourselves the 'Shadow Chasers' or something cliché like that!" Wayne laughed at his joke along with Jim and Luke. Ron was more serious.

"How about, 'Alien Busters', you know like the movie about ghosts!" Wayne continued to laugh and patted Jim on the shoulder.

"Alright you guys." Ron finally said, attempting to get them back on track. "We need to find out what they are up to."

"Don't be a fuddy duddy Ron. We finally have some intrigue." Jim said.

"It gets boring just keeping tabs on these guys. Now that it's getting cloak and dagger it's exciting." Wayne said, in agreement.

"Alright, I'll give you that." Ron said, as he turned and picked up the phone.
"I'm calling Europe to see if anything similar is going on there, or the Far East."

Jim and Wayne went into their own office to file their reports while they waited to hear from Ron.

"How many years has the SG been following and watching them?" Wayne asked. "And nothing even remotely as exciting as this has ever occurred."

"Yeah, it's really pathetic if we're that excited over this! I mean, all they did was confide in a family with no real importance, that we can tell anyway."

"I know, pretty sad. You have to admit that this is significant though. They have been coming here and manipulating things, or at least trying to, for as long as civilization has been around. Not once in all that time have they divulged their true origins to anyone!"

"What do you think Central will tell us to do?" Wayne wondered.

"I have no idea? Maybe watch them!" Jim added, laughing and putting his hand on Wayne's shoulder.

"Well that's a novel idea." Wayne answered in a disappointing tone.

Jim's desk phone rang. "Hello, Jim speaking." . . . "We'll be right there." He looked over at Wayne, "That was Ron, he wants to see us." Jim said laughing.

"He's five feet away! He couldn't call from the door?" Wayne laughed.

"Makes him feel important I suppose. Let's go."

The two men walked out of their office door and into Ron and Luke's office a few feet away.

"What's up?" Wayne asked.

"According to our overseas associates, none of the others have done anything different. They are still following their normal routines of trying to convince politicians and scientists to take climate change more serious. So all we have different is Thomas and Walters contacting the Domern family." Ron reported.

"So we have to figure out why they did that!" Jim stated.

"That's right." Luke chimed in. "What are your suggestions on ways to do that?"

"Drew works for the State, he understands protocols. He might be open and cooperate; he did run that blood test using lab equipment after all." Wayne reminded them.

"The last thing we need is drawing attention to ourselves." Ron grumbled. "Remember we don't even exist!"

"They don't know that!" Jim added. "We don't have to threaten or coerce him. We can just have a friendly chat.

There's nothing wrong with that, at least last time I checked there wasn't." He added smiling.

"And how would you go about doing that?" Ron asked as he leaned back in his chair and put his pencil in his mouth.

"We could approach him scientist to scientist, using the blood sample and the DNA as a starting point. Hopefully he'll start talking without much effort on our part once we mention the strands that don't match our databases." Jim said.

"And if he doesn't?" Ron asked.

"Then I suppose it's a dead end!" Jim relented.

"We could always just ask Thomas. I mean he is at the center of this whole thing, we've never tried that!" Wayne said sarcastically.

"I'm sure he would just start spilling all he knows, the fear of us fallen humans, and all!" Ron exclaimed.

"You know the rules we've lived by since the start of all this. We don't have any direct contact with them." Luke stated in a loud voice feeling frustrated by the discussion.

"We won't be the ones who broke the rules. They aren't supposed to be revealing themselves to anyone either!" Jim stated almost yelling. "Besides, those rules are archaic. Our ancestors created them to protect everyone concerned a long time ago when we were barbaric. Do you really think anyone would be drawn and quartered, or burned at the stake today over this?"

"Jim, calm down." Wayne said walking in front of his partner. "You know full well how it all works and why our forefathers started this agency."

Jim turned around and ran his fingers through his hair, and then turned back, facing the other three men. "Of course I know why. Our families are the only ones who have always known who they are, the only ones who remember where we actually came from! No other families trusted them when they came back, so why do we keep so distant, especially in this day and age. I mean it's not like we haven't known who each other are generation after generation."

"We're here if they need us, and that's it! If Thomas contacts us then we'll open communication with them. It's always been their call, not ours." Luke reminded Jim.

"I realize that's how it has always been; I just think maybe it's time to change things. That's all!" Jim remarked in a calmer tone.

After a few seconds of quite Ron began, "Alright then, let's all relax and think about this. First, let's review the facts that we have so far."

"The one thing we know from the blood work is that they are related to someone, possibly Thomas." Wayne spoke up first.

"Thomas and Walters are the only two who have approached anyone on a nonprofessional level." Luke stated.

"Anything else we can say is a fact?" Ron Asked.

"Bethany visited them with Thomas a few weeks ago, right before the blood sample was run in the lab." Jim remembered.

"That's right, she did. I wonder if the sample came from her." Wayne blurted out, thinking there wasn't an answer either way.

"Sorry Wayne, but the sample showed that it came from a male not a female. Anything else?" Ron asked.

The three other men shook their heads relaying that they had nothing more.

"Alright then, from where I sit these are the facts." Ron took out a notepad from his desk drawer, "I keep a record of all their meetings, who they see, where they go, and so forth. Until recently, it has been the same basic routine. Then Thomas came up north and rented an apartment, we followed from DC since he is the center of this group. He then visited the college, we thought to work with Walters in some way, but now it seems it was to meet up with Dominick Domern. Everyone agree so far?" Ron asked.

When no one disagreed, Ron continued. "Then Thomas and Bethany Bier visited the Domern family, the blood sample surfaced, and then Thomas and Walters visited the Domern family." Ron looked up from his notebook, "I do believe, as you have assumed, that they are attempting to prove who they are to the Domern family, the question that remains, is why?"

"That's what we'll have to find out!" Wayne acknowledged looking at Jim and winking.

Taking a deep breath, Ron asked. "Now, give me a few logical explanations to what they are up to."

"They want to reveal their identity for a reason; the DNA was a way to convince the Domern's. If it works, then they could show others." Luke stated.

"That could be very possible. But what would they gain by that?" Ron questioned.

"They could be looking for support from the public in order to convince the politicians about climate change. After all they haven't been very successful in that area and if the politicians thought they would lose support they might see the issue in a different way." Wayne said.

Jim thought about it, looking from a different angle than he had been. "Okay, that could be, but I think it might be more than that. There could be a larger plan, something more than just revealing themselves. What if this is the beginning of a new tactic!"

"A new tactic? Like what?" Luke asked.

"You know as well as I do that they haven't made much headway. They've convinced individual politicians, presidents, and other leaders worldwide. But, that's as far as they get, once the men and women who control the money start their campaigns to convince whoever they can that the tree huggers are getting the scientists to distort the facts it becomes one groups word against another's. Political mayhem always ensues as they manipulate the facts around election years for votes, and then the subject becomes null."

"What's your point, Jim?" Ron pushed.

"My point is that if they are giving up on the world's leadership when it comes to climate change, maybe they are planning to go directly to the public?"

"For what? To put pressure on the politicians?" Luke blurted out. "Leaders are the only ones who can affect any change or put any plan for the future into effect!"

"No, by going around the politicians. They know things that we don't, but that's not what's at issue here. Maybe, just maybe, time is getting shorter than we have realized. Maybe it's running out?" Jim said seriously.

"Why not just go to the scientists, the way they've done things for millennia? If they believe the leaders are a waste of time?" Wayne asked.

"You know why Wayne, the scientists have little power these days. There's just too much politics in everything." Jim stated.

"I do agree that politics does seem to have everything going around in circles, and it doesn't help that news personalities distort the facts. If time is truly running out, they may do something desperate. But I don't know what they think they will accomplish bringing civilians like the Domern family into the mix?" Ron stated.

"I don't either, all I know is they have something in mind and my gut is telling me it's something big!" Jim exclaimed.

They sat in silence for almost a minute. "Okay. Let's call it a day. I think we all need a little down time." Ron stood and began to put papers in his briefcase.

Jim and Wayne looked at one another, then at Luke.

"We'll meet up tomorrow morning before you two resume your monitoring of the situation." Ron said.

"See you then." Jim answered, as he and Wayne left the office and headed toward the parking lot.

"I hope Jim keeps control of himself." Ron stopped collecting his belongings and looked over at Luke.

"He will." Luke replied.

"Yeah, you're probably right, I just worry sometimes that he will go off and do something out from the scope of our protocols. He's always been a rebel of sorts, even when we were kids."

"He knows his job. None of us are children anymore, we all know why we have to follow the rules. He's just a little frustrated, we all are." Luke acknowledged.

"We are, aren't we, I wonder if the other groups feel the same way. It would be nice to know."

"During vacation we can talk to them, where are we scheduled to go this June anyway, have you heard?"

"Ireland I believe. My dad said something about it last month."

"I hope your right, that's one place that I've never been to. Since there aren't any Aerthen's there I had no reason to go!" Luke said, resuming the gathering of his laptop and other items.

"Me either. Let's get back to the hotel, I'm beat."

21

"Where do you think Thomas is this morning?" Wayne asked, although he had a good idea. Thomas rarely deviated from his daily routine. He would most likely be going to the college to see Dominick or Wilson.

Jim watched as Wayne finished gathering his clothes and started to head toward the bathroom. "He'll either be at the college or his apartment I would suspect."

Turning and looking at Jim, "I get the feeling that Ron is concerned about you, after your outburst yesterday."

"Ron is too serious and he needs to relax a little bit . . . don't you think?" Looking up at Wayne, Jim continued. "Like I said, I have a feeling that whatever is going on is big, and I doubt we could even guess what it is."

"Are you going to disobey Ron and talk to Thomas?"

"I've thought about it." Jim said as he stood, "But I don't think that it would really get me anywhere. So no, I'm not planning on it!"

"I'm glad to hear it. The last thing we need now is your family and Ron's going at each other."

"Right, just because Ron is coordinator here means nothing. My family still calls the shots and would back me up."

"They may be on top, but your father abides by the rules and you know it!"

"He doesn't know the situation."

"Neither do we, Jim." Wayne snickered, "Neither do we."

"We will eventually, and then I'll decide what I'm going to do."

"You should consult with your father before making any move toward Thomas. Protect yourself . . . and your family from unnecessary conflict with Ron's family."

"What about your family? If we find out what their up to and it is as serious as I fear, we should talk to your family too. After all we're all equals in this, my family happens to be the ones who have always guided the course of our mission, but ultimately we are all equals."

"If things get serious I will, and so will you, do you agree?"

"I agree."

"Good, now I need to go and get my shower." Wayne walked into the bathroom relieved. He knew that Jim would keep his word. The last thing the four families needed was a conflict that would distract them from their mission at this apparent, crucial juncture. After all the fact that the teams were made up of a member from each family was done for a purpose.

+ + + + + + + + + +

After Jim showered, they ate breakfast and headed toward the college not finding Thomas's car at his apartment. They didn't have any trouble locating Thomas's car in the parking lot and parked a few rows behind. They walked around the campus and watched at a distance as Thomas and Dominick left the lecture hall, went to the cafeteria, then sat on a bench under a shade tree and talked. Dominick stood and walked away forty-five minutes later leaving Thomas alone on the bench. After a few minutes, Thomas returned to the lecture hall.

"Another exciting day!" Wayne remarked as they returned to their car and waited.

At three o'clock Thomas and Wilton came across the parking lot, they stopped and talked, then shook hands. Thomas continued to his car while Wilton walked to his.

When Thomas approached his car he unlocked the door, then turned and walked to the back and stopped just beyond the trunk, he looked a few rows back, then took a few more steps forward and stopped.

"What is he doing?" Wayne asked, surprised by his action.

"Looking at us!" Jim said in a monotone voice.

"I know . . . but what's he doing?"

Jim opened his car door and started to get out.

"WHAT ARE YOU DOING?" Wayne shouted.

Jim ignored him and stood outside the care facing Thomas.

The two men stood facing one another, eyes locked on one another.

Thomas smiled, threw his car keys up into the air, caught them, then he turned and went back to his car.

Jim watched as Thomas closed the car door and started his car. He then did the same and followed at a distance as Thomas drove to his apartment.

"What was that?" Wayne asked.

"I'm not sure. Maybe a first step."

"He knows we watch; but he's never acknowledged us before, not even slightly." Wayne thought aloud.

"Are you going to tell Ron and Luke?" Jim glanced over at Wayne as he faced forward staring out the windshield.

"No."

"Me either."

"I agree." Wayne looked over at Jim, "They wouldn't understand why he did it either, and certainly wouldn't be able to deal with it, especially Ron."

Jim shook his head and smiled, "You're right. He would probably accuse me, or both of us, of doing something that caused the situation, especially considering our discussion yesterday."

"It's better to just go on as if it never happened." Wayne remarked.

"Go on, yes, but not forget. He must have had a reason for what he did."

"I thought he was going to come over and talk to us." Wayne confessed.

"The thought crossed my mind too. Maybe he was and then changed his mind."

"You know what I think?" Wayne was dead serious. "I think you should report Thomas's behavior to your dad and see what he says."

Jim thought for a second, "That's a good idea. That way if it ever comes out Ron won't be able to accuse us of keeping it to ourselves."

"Yeah, and you know he would feel like you purposely kept everyone in the dark."

"He would, your right, unfortunately. I wish he wasn't so insecure about his position."

"He knows that someday you'll take your fathers position and be the head of the Council. The only reason he's in charge of you here is so that you can experience being a subordinate, and he knows that."

"He'll still have a position of authority; he's the oldest child in his family. That's why I don't understand him." Jim confessed.

"Who knows, I think it's easier for me and Luke because neither of us is the eldest!" Wayne said with a laugh, "Our sisters have that problem!"

++++++++++

That evening when they returned to their hotel Jim called his father in England. "Hi dad, how have you been and how's mom?"

"We're both doing well. We just returned home probably about a half an hour ago, we had our evening meal at Buckingham Palace with the Queen. How have you been?"

"I've been good, but I thought you might want to know about an incident that happened today."

Sitting forward in his chair, Jim Sr. felt a chill run down his spine. "What incident was that?"

"Thomas sort of approached us today."

"What do you mean, sort of approached you?"

"He walked toward our car, but stopped about twenty-five yards away, made eye contact, smiled, and then returned to his vehicle and drove back to his apartment. We both thought that he was going to talk to us, but he didn't"

His father fell silent, the only reason Jim knew that he was still on the line was by his breathing. Jim waited until his father finally spoke. "Keep this to yourselves, I'll set up a meeting with the heads of the other families, and then I'll get back to you."

"Why? What do you think it means?"

"It means that things are going to change, their mission is going to change, they're letting us know."

"How do you know that?" Jim asked getting upset. He didn't understand how his father could possibly deduce that from what he told him.

"Protocols, son, protocols. I'll get back to you!"

Jim hung up the phone and looked at Wayne.

Wayne looked pale. Jim was taken back. "What is it?"

"You turned white as a ghost! What did your dad say?"

"He said that Thomas's action means things are changing, that their mission is changing and he wanted us to know about it!"

"How does he know that?"

"I don't know? That's what freaked me out even more than what he said. He also told me that he was going to contact the other three family heads and get back to me."

"Wow, it's a good thing you called him then."

"Yeah, I'm glad you thought of it."

Jim thought for awhile. "You know, I'm tired of being kept in the dark. Our parents obviously know more than we do, and so does Thomas and his counterparts. We're between them and I think we should be told what's going on, don't you! I mean what if I hadn't called him? I had no idea that Thomas was sending us a message!"

"It would certainly help, and I think we could do our jobs better. After all who knows if anything has been missed in the past because we aren't told everything?" Wayne agreed.

22

"Hey, I really miss you."

"I miss you too, how was your day?" Bethany asked.

"Interesting. I walked toward one of the watchers cars today and he got out of his car. Then we just looked at each other."

"Really?"

"Yeah, I really felt like he was hoping or wanting me to approach him. I thought he wanted to talk with me."

"That's surprising. They usually shy away and keep their distance."

"I know! I really didn't expect him to do that. I just wanted to relay the message to them, and instead of looking from the car, he opened his door and got out! And I'm pretty sure that it was Jim Jr."

"You know, it sounds to me that maybe he wasn't aware of the message system that we use."

"Huh, you know, I didn't think of that. Do you believe it's possible that the ways of our families aren't being passed down?" Thomas questioned.

"I hope not. I mean, how will we function if that's the case?"

"I'm going to contact my father and see what he thinks. This could turn into a bad situation if our lines of communication have been eroded by time."

"I would be surprised if they haven't been passing these protocols from generation to generation. They're just too important." Bethany stated.

"I don't know, but I need to find out, or our plans could be in jeopardy. We're going to need them; we can't do this without their help!" Thomas was becoming a little worried. "I'm going to try and get ahold of my father. I'll talk to you later."

"Okay, I love you. Bye."

"I love you too."

Thomas went to his bedroom drawer to get his communication device. He knew it was early morning at home and he hoped his father would be awake. He pushed the appropriate combination of numbers to reach his father's personal communiqué. This was too important to go through a number of people to get to him.

"Is everything alright Thomas?" Tegan asked when he answered his device.

"I'm not sure. Something odd happened today."

"What could have happened that would cause you to call me directly?"

Thomas recounted the event to his father. When he finished Tegan was silent.

"Father? Are you still there? Father?"

"You're right, something sounds off. I'm going to need to contact the Council Headquarters in Ashford. After I speak to Suren in England, I'll get back to you as soon as I can. Keep me posted if anything else happens, okay."

"Okay." Thomas felt relieved after he hung up. Then he thought about how his father had reacted and could feel the anxiety rising in his chest. This could be a real problem for them.

After taking a few deep breaths, Thomas called Bethany. "I spoke to my father."

"What did he say?" Bethany wondered.

"He agreed with you. He's going to contact England and get back to me."

+ + + + + + + + + +

Thomas was sitting in the auditorium next to Dominick when he felt his device vibrate. He had brought it with him since speaking to his father so he didn't miss his call. "I'll be right back." He whispered to Dominick.

Dominick nodded as he continued to face forward and listen to Professor Walters. He glanced back a few minutes later and noticed Thomas pacing in the hall outside the auditorium as he spoke on what looked like a phone of some sort.

When Thomas returned to his seat, Dominick turned to look at him. His demeanor seemed different, more relaxed that he was earlier.

Realizing Dominick was concerned about him; Thomas smiled then looked forward not wanting to talk during Professor Walters lecture.

Once Professor Walters concluded his lecture and walked away from the lectern, Dominick turned to Thomas, "Is everything alright? I saw you pacing in the hall."

"Yeah, I was just talking to my father."

"Is he here too?"

"No, he's back home on my world. I called him a few days ago and he was just getting back to me."

Dominick felt like he was intruding so he didn't ask Thomas any further questions. "That's amazing that you can call each other, I mean, it's so far away!"

"It would really be difficult here if we couldn't."

"Yeah, I can imagine. But I don't understand? When we send messages to astronauts in space it takes a few minutes to reach them, and communication with our rovers on mars takes close to twenty minutes, so how can you talk on your phone as if your dad was here, on this world?"

"The communication devices we use for contacting back home are much different than the type you have here that use cell towers or even satellites. The signal they send opens a small bridge inside the device just big enough for sound waves to enter and travel to the receiver at the other end. So it's as if the two devices were only a few miles apart instead of light-years."

"Wow! I can't even begin to understand that, it's amazing!"

"So, what are you doing this weekend?" Thomas inquired.

"I don't have any specific plans at the moment, why?"

"Do you want to get together and do something?"

"Yeah, that sounds like fun. What do you want to do?" Dominick asked. He was starting to really enjoy Thomas's company and wanted to get to know him better.

"How about a trip to Virginia?"

"Virginia!"

"Yeah. We can stay with Bethany at my old apartment and find something to do Saturday."

"I would like that, I haven't had the chance to get to know Bethany and would like to."

"I'll pick you up Friday afternoon then and we'll head down."

"Sounds like a plan, I'll see you then." Dominick answered, excited about the thought of spending an entire weekend with Thomas . . . and Bethany.

Thomas walked to the parking lot and called Bethany once he was situated in his car.

"Hello."

"Hi, I heard from my father a little while ago."

"Oh, good . . . what did he have to say?"

"He told me that the families haven't forgotten our methods of communication."

"That's good, but why did Jim react the way he did then?"

"Because they haven't told the next generation everything they need to know yet. He said that the reason they didn't tell them was because they were relying on the teams to report back to the Council if and when anything happened."

"Why wouldn't they just tell them? I don't understand." Bethany questioned.

"Evidently, they didn't believe it was necessary for them to know all of the ins and outs. The plan was to tell the next generation when it came time for them to move up and take their father's places as leaders on the Council and other areas within the organization."

"That's a little scary. I mean what if something happened and they were never told about these things!"

"I agree, and so did the Administrative Service and the heads of the Projects on Aerthen II."

"So what's going to happen? Will the situation change?"

"They relayed their displeasure to the Council through Suren and now the Council is planning on informing everyone during their vacation this summer. Those who are followers will be told this week."

"That's good; but I think they should have known all along."

"Yeah, the people here still have a lot to learn and time is getting short."

With these new developments, Bethany wondered if this changed Thomas's plans. "Are you still coming home this weekend?"

"Oh yeah, not even an ice age would keep me from seeing you this weekend."

Bethany giggled, "You are such a romantic!"

"I hope you don't mind, I thought I'd bring Dominick along. I want to get closer to him before we go home the end of December."

"Of course I don't mind. That sounds like fun, I want to get to know him better too, I wonder if he's ever gone hiking in the Blue Ridge Mountains?"

"I'll ask him."

"We could pack a picnic basket and spend the day on the trails."

"I miss you!" Thomas said with a laugh, feeling the excitement in Bethany's voice.

"I miss you too. I can't wait to see you; it's lonely here all by myself." Bethany said in a solemn tone.

"I know it is. It won't be much longer." Thomas remarked, hoping to console her.

"I hope not."

"It won't, I promise." Thomas had regretted their decision to separate during his business in New York from the second it was made. They should have went through with their alternate choice to have her take a leave from her position, but Bethany felt the timing was too critical for her to leave.

"I'm really looking forward to this weekend." Bethany said, trying to lighten the mood.

Thomas smiled thinking about how great it was going to be to spend time together; it helped to brighten his mood. "Hey, make some of that mushroom salad for the picnic you made a couple months ago. That was fantastic!"

"Alright, and I'll get some of the fruit and nuts that you like too. How does that sound?"

"That sounds wonderful, my darling." Thomas said in a lower voice.

Bethany giggled. "You sound so passionate. I'll see you Friday night, please be careful driving down."

"I will. See you soon." Thomas hung up and leaned his head back against the headrest, he continued to smile thinking about their conversation. However, his smile quickly faded, it was truly hard for him to be away from her.

He tried not to dwell on their situation so after a few seconds, he started his car and began the drive to his apartment. As he drove he glanced out his rear view mirror looking for the car he knew would be there. They were a couple cars behind him, and they would follow him to his apartment and then leave him until the next day.

23

"Ron called. We have to go to the office before we follow Thomas today." Jim explained to Wayne who had been in the bathroom when Jim received the call.

"Did he say why?"

"Only that he had a call from the Central Council and there are some new protocols we have to learn."

"It must be because of our call to your dad. Don't you think?"

"I do." Jim replied. "I only hope Ron doesn't connect the dots to us, that's all we need. I really don't want any tension in our group."

"I doubt he knows. Our leadership's discreet when it comes to these types of things, they don't want any resentment among us or between our families."

"We better get going so we're not late." Jim said as he grabbed the car keys off the bureau and walked toward the door of their hotel room.

Luke was just arriving when Jim and Wayne pulled up. He had stopped at a coffee shop on his way to work and had four large coffees with him.

"Thanks Luke!" Jim said, he then picked up two of the coffees and handed one to Wayne.

"How did you know we hadn't stopped for coffee yet?" Wayne asked.

"I didn't. After yesterday, it was the least I could do. I'm not comfortable when we argue. I've had it drilled into my head since I was a child how important it is that our families band together for the good of everyone. So when we disagree . . . I just feel awful. That's all." Luke confessed.

"It's alright, man. None of us likes it when we argue, but I don't think it effects our relationship. Disagreeing is normal, don't you think?" Jim asked. They walked into the hangar and toward the office door that was already open with Ron waiting inside.

"I suppose that's true but I still feel guilty. It's like I'm letting our families and the entire world down when there's any words between us." Luke continued.

"Don't worry about it, Wayne. We've already forgotten what was said yesterday." Wayne added.

Hearing the three men nearing the door, Ron walked over to say good morning. He also regretted the tenseness of the day before. "Hey guys, everyone okay this morning?"

Luke handed Ron a coffee, "Yeah, I think so."

"We're both good." Wayne said, smiling. He then took a seat in the office along with another mouthful of coffee.

"So, what are these new protocols I hear we're getting?" Jim asked.

"You're dad called last night. He told me that he would send us some new information, that it was time for us to know more about what's going on. I received his email this morning with attachments containing the materials and made copies for each of you." Ron passed Wayne a stack of papers; he took the first stapled copy and passed the other copies to Jim, who passed the last copy to Luke.

The three men leafed through their copies. "Why didn't we know about this before? Did he say?" Jim asked.

"No. He just said it was time. He also said that the Council was given a message to expect communication to begin between us and the Others at any time."

"Oh, boy . . . what does THAT mean?" Luke asked.

Ron shrugged, "We'll have to wait and see I guess."

Jim and Wayne just glanced at one another knowing that communication had started the day before.

"We better get on the road; we don't want to miss Thomas when he leaves his apartment." Jim remarked, feeling a little uncomfortable, and not wanting Ron or Luke to sense that he and Wayne are not as newly informed as they were.

"Sounds good. Call if anything happens. Okay." Ron said, in a tone that was not a request.

"No problem." Wayne called back over his shoulder as he and Jim exited the office.

When they were out of earshot, Jim slowed his pace and waited for Wayne to catch up to him. "I get the distinct impression that my father was given a message from more than us."

"I was wondering that myself. It was odd the wording that Ron said he used."

"It was. Do you think someone there was contacted by one of the Others?"

"The thought crossed my mind." Jim said, getting into the driver's seat of their car. "I'm going to call my dad later and find out if they contacted him or the Council."

Wayne nodded without objecting to Jim's decision.

"This was a boring, non-eventful day." Wayne remarked, as he and Jim walked up the stairs to their hotel room.

"I was expecting something more myself after the last forty-eight hours." Jim sat on his bed staring at the floor with a blank expression. He then pulled out his phone, "Do you feel like pizza? I sure do."

"I could eat anything right now, I'm starved."

Jim ordered a pizza to be delivered to their hotel room and then dialed his father.

"Hello." Jim Sr. answered.

"Hi, dad. We got the new protocols you sent this morning."

"Good, they should help you if anything else comes up."

"By your message I thought you were expecting something to happen! We were waiting all day but nothing came about."

"It will in time, I wouldn't be surprised if you don't hear something in a day or two." Jim Sr. answered.

"Dad . . . I also have the feeling that there's more to it than that."

"I don't understand. More to what? The protocols?"

"No. It sounded like maybe the Others contacted the Council; it was the wording you used that Ron relayed to us."

Jim waited for an answer and wondered if his phone had lost the signal. "Dad, are you there?"

"Yeah . . . Listen son, I'm not able to tell you everything. Some of what we know has to stay within the leadership circle, that's just the way it is."

"One day I'll be apart of that circle and so will Ron. Don't you think we should at least be told when we ask? We obviously already know something if we're asking!"

"Alright, this one time I will, since you asked, but it CANNOT go past the two of us, not even Ron can know until his time comes. Do you understand?"

"I do, it won't go any further."

"Alright then, I'm only going to say this once and then it's a dead subject. You know that the Council has a representative from each of the four families."

"Yeah, everybody knows that."

"Well, there's a fifth Council member that no one knows about."

"What? Who is it?" Jim couldn't imagine who it could be. "Does one of the families have two representatives?"

"No, his name is Suren Samgi."

"Suren Samgi? That sounds like an Aerthen name."

"It is he's from Aerthen II. They have had a representative on the Council since its inception."

Jim was shocked. He had never even once imagined that as a possibility. He was also beginning to realize just how left out of the whole scenario he and the other members of the four families were who weren't on the Council.

"Why does the Council keep so many secrets from our families?" Jim shouted into the phone.

"For the safety of our mission, it's that simple."

"Sometimes I think we need to reconsider the times we live in. Our ways are antiquated don't you think? Our mission is being jeopardized by the Council not being honest with every last one of us."

"I hear what you're saying, but this is how we have always done things and it works. When the day comes that it doesn't work then we'll reconsider how to do our job." Jim Sr. stated sternly.

Jim realized that he had overstepped his bounds and that it was probably better to refrain from pushing the subject. It was becoming obvious that his father wasn't going to listen to him and nothing was going to change in the near future.

"I have to go. I'll talk to you later, tell mom I said hi."

"I will, take care and keep your eyes open!"

24

"Which path should we take?" Dominick asked, calling over his shoulder. He turned back around to face forward and contemplated the fork in the trail that was before him.

"It doesn't matter. They both end up at the same spot." Bethany called to him.

"Do you care if we go to the left then?"

"Nope, wherever you want!" Thomas answered, as he and Bethany caught up to Dominick.

They continued their hike to the summit of the mountain where they planned to eat their lunch. Bethany started to lay down the blanket she brought from her apartment as Thomas began to unpack the containers of food. Dominick helped by holding down the other side of the blanket until Bethany could place a rock to keep it from being tossed by the breeze.

Once they finished eating, Thomas laid on his back and relaxed feeling the sun on his face. "It'll be too cold to do this pretty soon; winter will be here before we know it!"

"Does it snow as much in Virginia as it does back home?" Dominick wondered.

"There have been years when it did, but it usually doesn't." Bethany answered. "It never gets as cold as Thomas said it was in New York last year. I'm glad about that!" She said with a giggle.

"Do you care if I walk around?" Dominick asked.

"No, but be careful." Thomas answered.

"I will." Dominick stood up and quickly walked over to the edge of the summit. As he stood on the rocks that overlooked the valley, he realized how breathtakingly beautiful the scene was. Most of the deciduous trees had started to change color leaving the evergreens, which consisted of mainly blue spruce, even more pronounced between the yellow, orange, and red leaves of the trees around them.

Dominick tried to imprint the scenery into his mind before he started to explore the paths around the peak of the mountain but found himself once again looking at the view from the edge a little farther down the path. He didn't hear Thomas and Bethany come up behind him, and jumped when he heard Thomas speak.

"Anything interesting?"

"This!" Dominick answered, while raising both of his arms and opening them as wide as he could, gesturing toward the view in front of him. He turned around to see Thomas and Bethany holding hands as they stood on the path behind him. "The view from up here is mind-blowing!" Dominick added.

Coming up to stand next to him Thomas pointed to the field far below them. "Do you see that field?"

"Yeah."

"That's where we're going to be lifting off from in a few weeks when we go visit Aerthen II."

"Really!"

"Yep. One of our shuttles will land down there and take us to the homeship that's in orbit behind the moon."

"Won't someone know that it's there?"

"It wouldn't matter if they did."

"It wouldn't? Aren't you afraid that the government will do something?"

"No."

Bethany thought it would be best to change the topic. "Are you looking forward to visiting our world, Dominick?"

Turning toward her, Dominick answered. "I am, but I'm also a little nervous. So I'm glad my dad is going with us."

"We are too. It will be exciting to show you both around and introduce you to everyone. The people back home are as excited to meet you as you are to go." Bethany said smiling.

Thomas looked knowingly at her realizing she purposely intervened in their conversation.

"How many people live on your planet, are there a lot more than we have here?" Dominick asked. It had been something he had been thinking about since Thomas explained how most of the population left Earth for Aerthen II so long ago.

"Actually there's less." Bethany said.

"Wow, I'm surprised! Since the majority of the population went to your world so long ago I would think that there would be at least three times the number of people than we have here!"

"Our population hasn't grown as quickly as yours, because our culture is different. We rarely have more than two children if we even decide to have any children. Many of us choose not to have a family." She explained.

"Oh. Doesn't everyone want children?" Dominick asked astounded by her answer.

"Only some of us do, we don't place as high a priority on reproducing as you do here."

"That seems weird to me." Dominick said without thinking, "I'm sorry, I didn't mean it that way!"

"It's alright. Like I said, our cultures are different." Bethany explained.

"We should start to head back down the mountain, it will be dark soon." Thomas mentioned looking toward the west and seeing the sun starting to dip behind the trees.

They packed up the picnic basket and blanket making sure not to leave anything behind, and then started walking back down the path.

"I really enjoyed the food you packed, Bethany." Dominick said smiling.

"I'm glad Dominick."

"Even though it consisted of fruits and vegetables?" Thomas asked.

"Yes, even though there wasn't any meat!" Dominick said laughing.

+ + + + + + + + + +

That night Thomas came out of the bedroom and into the kitchen for a glass of water, Dominick heard him and sat up on the sofa.

"I'm sorry; I didn't mean to wake you."

"You didn't. I was already awake, I couldn't help but think about the conversation we had today."

"Which one was that?" Thomas asked, walking into the living room and sitting on the chair across from Dominick.

"About having children. Don't you want any kids?"

Thomas laughed, "Why do you ask?"

"I don't know, I guess because it seems so strange to me, we think about having kids our whole lives, it's unusual for us to not plan on having a family. We look at couples who don't have children and wonder why they don't."

"You remember I told you how your part of the population changed after the flooding?"

"Yeah."

"Your survival was important which meant having children was a high priority. You've lived with that urge ever since, it's ingrained in you. The struggle to survive that your ancestors faced has never happened to us, we never had to cope with a catastrophe in the same way they did. Does that make any sense to you?"

"I suppose it does."

Thomas stood to return to his bedroom, "To answer your question, yes, Bethany and I have talked about having our own children one day."

Dominick smiled, for some reason he felt relieved hearing Thomas say that.

Noticing a look of relief in Dominick's expression, Thomas smiled. "I'll see you in the morning. Try to get some sleep; we have a long drive home." He rubbed the top of Dominick's head as he headed back toward the bedroom to tell Bethany about their conversation. He knew that she would appreciate it.

"I will goodnight."

"Goodnight."

+ + + + + + + + + +

Thomas dropped Dominick off at his dorm late Sunday afternoon, and then headed to his apartment.

He parked along the side of the road and stepped out of his car. As he headed toward the front door of his first floor apartment he looked back toward the street, he watched as the car driven by Jim drove past. The driver didn't look his way but the passenger did, their eyes met for a brief second before the car drove past and out of site.

Thomas turned and went through his door to the kitchen, where he poured himself a glass of orange juice and looked inside the refrigerator to see what he could find for dinner. He decided on some root stew he had left over from the previous week.

After he finished eating Thomas sat on the sofa to channel surf, when he couldn't find anything worth watching he turned off the television. It was only six-thirty so he decided to take a walk, as he went around the block he reflected on the interaction he had with the passenger in the watchers car.

He wondered if the two men, who seemed to be about his age, really understood their mission. They didn't know about the silent communication the groups had worked out hundreds of years ago, so it seemed logical that they may not know what their role would be in the not so distant future.

He was troubled by the prospect. He and the other teams around the globe needed the members of the four families and the influence they had within the world's governments. Their plan would fail otherwise.

Thomas decided the best course of action would be to see if he could speak with at least one of the members of the four families. He wanted to find out for himself exactly how much the members of the families knew who were not privy to the Council meetings.

When he returned to his apartment, he called Trent Tarbuk and explained his uneasiness with the situation.

"I understand why you are concerned, Thomas. I'll talk to Timothy and he can take it up with your father and the other Project Leaders. What did you say the name of the watcher was that you hoped to speak with?"

"Jim Jr.."

"Okay, I'll take care of this first thing."

"I appreciate it, Trent. By the way we're coming home in a few weeks; I hope we can catch up while I'm there."

"That would be great; Lana and I will be looking forward to it, take care."

Talking to Trent gave Thomas some peace of mind, he felt relaxed enough now to realize how tired he really was from the weekend and the drive home. It only took a few minutes for him to fall asleep once he laid in bed.

25

Jim heard his phone ring before he was even awake enough to realize what the sound actually was. He reached over onto his bedside table and felt around until he located his cell phone. "Hello."

"Good morning."

"Dad, is that you?" Jim asked. He was still trying to wake up and focus, he glanced over at the clock on the table next to his bed. "It's four in the morning, is everything alright?"

"I needed to reach you when I knew you would be alone."

Jim was more awake now and began to realize his father's call must be important. "How come?

"Thomas requested a meeting with one of you and we don't want it to become common knowledge. We felt it would be easier for you to get away and meet with him than anyone else."

Jim was now sitting up in bed. "A meeting with Thomas, for what?"

"He'll explain all that when he sees you. Do you know a place called Brannigan's, it's not far from your hotel?"

"Yeah, we've passed it a few times."

"He wants to meet you there at seven o'clock tonight, your time."

"Okay. I'll get back to you after I meet with him."

"Good, I have to go now; I have a meeting and I don't want to be late. Don't forget tonight at seven, and keep it to yourself."

Jim heard the click of their phones disconnecting as his father hung up on his end. He laid down but couldn't get back to sleep. He realized that this was unprecedented; the two groups just did not have contact with one another. He wondered what Thomas could possibly want to meet with him about?

The day seemed to drag by. They followed Thomas to and from the college campus, and returned to their hotel by five o'clock. Jim told Wayne he had an appointment but did not expound about where or with whom. Thank goodness, he thought, that Wayne was not a curious kind of person and didn't ask where he was going.

At six-forty five, he arrived at Brannigan's and took a seat at a booth near the back of the bar that seemed rather dark compared to the rest of the room. Thomas walked through the door and glanced around the room, when he saw Jim he headed toward him. It was one minute to seven. Jim felt the anxiety rising in his stomach, the thought of coming face to face with Thomas was quite nerve racking to him.

Jim stood when Thomas arrived. Standing next to the booth he was sitting at, he held out his hand. "Hi, I'm Jim."

The two men shook hands, "Thomas, you know I feel like I know you from someplace!" Thomas remarked with a knowing laugh.

Thomas's lighthearted gesture put Jim at ease. "I know what you mean. It does seem like we already know each other doesn't it."

Thomas moved toward the opposite side of the booth, and Jim returned to his seat, a waitress noticed the two men and came over to take their drink orders.

Jim noticed that Thomas ordered a ginger ale. "Is it true that you don't drink alcohol?" He asked.

Thomas suddenly felt as though he was with Dominick, Jim had the same curious nature. "It's true, our systems aren't use to the fermentation process like yours are."

"I was surprised to hear you wanted to meet with one of us. Is there something wrong?" Jim asked.

The waitress brought Jim's beer and Thomas's ginger ale. "Thank you." Thomas said waiting for the young woman to leave before he continued the conversation.

"I was concerned about the family leadership not relaying all they know to the members who aren't on the Council." Thomas explained.

"It concerns me too." Jim replied. He wanted to yell out all his frustrations to Thomas but held his tongue waiting to see where the conversation was headed.

"I really need to be sure that you understand what is going to be happening in the not too distant future."

Jim felt the anxiety building in his stomach again. "What do you mean, what's going to happen?"

"As you now know, we're changing our original plans. The governments and politicians around the world are too wrapped up in their own agendas to listen to what we are trying to get across to them. There is virtually no chance that they will cooperate with each other and prepare for the changes to come, and when they realize what's happening, it will be too late."

"We just found out that you were going to change things when I called my father and told him how you walked toward our car."

"I was worried because it was obvious that you didn't understand my purpose for doing that. So I just wanted to make sure that your leaders are preparing your team, and the other teams around the globe. We don't want them to keep information from you anymore. As a people we don't believe in keeping anyone in the dark or misleading them."

"I feel the same way. It's a relief to know how you see things. But what would they be preparing us for?"

"The evacuation of your populations."

Jim looked at Thomas, he was stunned and speechless. After his mind caught up with what he had just heard, he asked. "Did I hear you right? Evacuate everyone!"

"It's the only way to save you. We've had an alternate strategy in mind for a long time."

"The Council . . ." Jim realized he was raising his voice and lowered it. "knows this?"

"They should, Suren was supposed to brief them about it. We all agreed that the public leaders would never be able to cooperate and work together to move forward with a plan so we came up with one on our own."

"This is unbelievable. How can seven billion people be relocated?"

"You know as well as I do that not everybody will want to leave." Thomas stated frankly.

"Yeah, probably not. But there will still be an extremely large number who will."

"We have a few hundred ships that can carry around ten thousand people on each, and we plan on making numerous trips. If we have the time it should go smoothly, if not your guess is as good as mine."

"I was told this meeting is a secret, not to tell anyone!" Jim said, not knowing how to react to what Thomas was revealing to him.

"That doesn't surprise me. Suren will have to speak with the other four council members to get the word out."

Jim drank the rest of his beer in four large gulps, what Thomas was saying was huge, and unbelievable. "When will all this happen?"

"Within the next twenty years. The planet is starting to change faster than we expected."

"Will there be another flood?"

"No, there may be coastal flooding, but we don't expect another worldwide flood. The polar shift isn't the only problem that we are going to be facing either; we fear it will be accompanied by an ice age."

"An ice age with glaciers coming down into North America!"

"Not that extensive, but temperatures will be much cooler. The atmosphere is starting to accumulate ash and other particles from the swarm of volcanic eruptions that have occurred over the last few years. And since they are predicted to continue, the particles will eventually block the sun's warmth from reaching the surface of the planet. There is also something going on in the ocean that we don't understand."

He feared what he was going to hear, so after bracing himself, Jim decided to ask Thomas about the oceans. "What don't you understand?"

"The Sargasso Sea has been changing, the seaweed has been growing exponentially and is also mutating."

"Mutating into what?"

"We don't know exactly, the outer surface of the weed is almost impenetrable."

"I see." Jim called to the waitress as she walked by, "Can I have another beer, please." They sat in silence until Jim's beer arrived.

"I asked to talk to you specifically. Do you know why?" Thomas asked.

Jim looked at him a little perplexed. "I didn't realize that, my dad just said it was easiest for me to get away and meet with you."

Thomas could see the confusion in his eyes and wasn't surprised by his response. "I asked for you because I sensed that you are somewhat of a free thinker and not someone who blindly follows orders."

Jim smiled, "That quality isn't always appreciated, especially when I question what I'm told!"

Thomas put his hand on Jim's hand. "It makes me trust you more than any of the other watchers or Council members I've seen."

Jim nodded, showing he understood. "Can I share this conversation with anyone?" Jim asked, testing Thomas to see if his motivation was truly how he was portraying himself.

"Whoever you feel should know. I'll leave it up to your judgement." Thomas withdrew his hand and lifted his glass, swallowing the last of his soda. "Anytime you want to talk with me I'll make the time. I never totally liked this arrangement we have about no contact, I think it's silly."

Jim laughed, "I told my father that last week. It didn't go over very well though."

"I think it's time that we get to know one another better, not just you and I, but all of us. After all, when the time comes the four families will become the only government for your population."

Jim looked up at Thomas. By his expression, Thomas could tell he was not aware of the plans for their rise to power either.

"They're will be plenty of people who would disagree with that plan and put up a good fight to stop it." Jim exclaimed.

"Think about something, when your families step up when a situation occurs does any person or government argue?"

"No, I've never heard of there being a problem, but we don't interfere in their daily activities or the positions they hold either." Jim stated.

"That's true; but I don't think it will be any different when you do."

"We'll see, anyway that's a long way off . . . isn't it?" Jim asked.

"Let's hope, we don't want to be caught off guard like we were with the flood the last time. The elements do have a mind of their own after all."

"The elements?"

"Nature."

"Oh . . . yeah it certainly does." Jim agreed.

After a couple minutes of silence, Thomas decided to tell Jim about his upcoming trip.

"In December I'm going home for a few weeks. Dominick and his father are going with me."

"Really! That's amazing."

"It definitely will be a first. I know Dominick is excited about going."

"Why did you choose his family anyway? They aren't important in our world." Jim asked, having been wondering about it for weeks now.

"That was something that was decided two generations ago when our great-grandfathers met as teenagers. My great-grandfather came here to work with the Project and that's when he met the Domern's ancestor."

"How did they meet?"

"I've been told that my great-grandfather, Talbot, wanted to meet a few of his relatives, so when he wasn't busy with the Project he would search them out and then go meet them. When he met Dane Domern, they became instant friends and remained that way until Dane passed away. That's what led to the Domerns being the first family who would be told the truth."

"Did Dane know who he was?"

"No, I don't believe he even knew that they were related. In honor of their friendship my great-grandfather decreed that if we ever found it necessary to reveal who we are to the people on Aerthen that it would be Dane's descendants we would contact."

"Geeze, I have goose bumps." Jim said rubbing his arms. "They must have had quite a bond."

"I think they did." Thomas said, thinking of his growing relationship with Dominick.

The two men continued to talk and get to know one another not realizing how late it had become. Jim's phone buzzed, "Hello." . . . "Oh, hi Wayne." . . . "I'm fine, I just lost track of time, I'll be there soon." . . . "Okay, bye."

Jim put his phone back into his pocket, "That was Wayne. He was getting worried about me."

"I suppose you should be getting back, I didn't realize it was almost eleven." Thomas said, looking at his wristwatch.

+ + + + + + + + +

As Thomas drove home, he felt a real satisfaction with getting to talk to Jim. It felt right, after all this time knowing that he was always around, watching his back.

As Jim drove back to his hotel he tried to figure out how he was going to explain to Wayne where he was all evening. He knew Thomas didn't want him to keep their meeting a secret, but his father did. He felt caught between the two, leaning more toward Thomas's view on the situation.

Wayne was in bed when Jim arrived at their hotel room. He tried to get ready for bed as quietly as possible so he wouldn't disturb his partner.

When he came out of the bathroom, Wayne was sitting on the side of the bed. "Hey, where were you? It's not like you do disappear like that. You have a secret girlfriend or something?"

Jim laughed, "I don't think I have time for a girl, do you?"

"Unfortunately neither of us do . . . seriously though, what's up?"

"I had a meeting with Thomas."

Wayne looked blankly at Jim, and then laughed. "Seriously, what's going on?"

"I am serious! I had a meeting with Thomas. My dad called and told me to meet him at a bar a couple of blocks from here."

"Whoa . . . man, you really had a face to face with Thomas!" Wayne exclaimed standing and pacing back and forth realizing the magnitude of what he had just heard.

"Yeah."

"What for?"

"It seems that he's concerned there are important issues that we aren't being made aware of."

"That's an understatement!"

"Yeah, tell me about it. We haven't been told half of what our parents and leaders know."

"Like what?"

"Thomas gave me a pass to tell whoever I choose, but I know that my father wouldn't approve."

"I'm sure no one on the Council would!" Wayne agreed.

"It seems that the new plan is to relocate our entire population someplace else."

"Say that again." Wayne stopped pacing and stood looking at Jim in disbelief.

"He said that they have ships, and it will take a few trips, but they want to relocate everyone who is willing to leave here."

"That's huge!" Wayne sat back down on his bed and stared at Jim, his mind racing with a million thoughts and questions. "Relocate . . . wait a minute . . . because of what?"

"Climate change and something that's going on with the seaweed in the Sargasso Sea."

"Did he give you any details?"

"Only that there might be an ice age coming in about twenty years."

"Oh, is that all." Wayne answered sarcastically.

"He said it gave them plenty of time to relocate people."

"When is all this going to start?"

"I don't know. But he's going back home in a couple weeks and taking Drew and Dominick Domern with him for a visit."

"Are you kidding me? That's unprecedented!" Wayne stood back up and began to pace once again.

"I know, tell me about it!"

"I think I need a drink, let's go down to the bar by the lobby." Wayne said. He grabbed his wallet and room key and headed for the door.

26

"Dominick, are you ready?"

"I'll be down in a minute dad." Dominick answered, then returned to the conversation he was having on his cell phone. "I only have a minute Patrick, but I want you to know that I won't be around for a couple of weeks."

"Are you going on vacation?" Patrick wondered.

Aerthen

"Of sorts. My dad and I are going with Thomas to his world. I wasn't supposed to tell anyone but I really felt that I had to tell you."

Patrick was silent; he couldn't believe what he was hearing. "For real?" He asked.

"Yes, we're meeting him in a half hour and driving to Virginia. We leave from there with his girlfriend, Bethany, and Professor Walters."

"Your professor was invited too?"

"No, I never told you, but he's one of them; I forgot I didn't tell you about that. I'm sorry man!"

"That's crazy, who else is one of them?"

"No one else that lives around here." Dominick said, thinking that he wasn't quite sure if he really believed that was true.

"Just come back, I would miss you if you didn't."

"I will, don't worry. My dad's calling again I have to go, don't tell anyone okay."

"I don't think you have to worry about that, it's too crazy. Be safe."

"Okay, bye."

Dominick picked up his suitcase and went down stairs.

"What took you so long?"

"I just had to pack a couple of last minute things."

Rebekah was standing next to her husband, visibly upset. "Come here." She said motioning to Dominick, "You better be safe do you hear me!" She said hugging her son.

"I will mom. Thomas says that his planet is peaceful and that the ships are in good shape. Please don't worry, okay."

"There is nothing you can say that will stop me from worrying." She let go of her son and reached to hug her husband.

"Everything will be alright, I promise. We'll be back before you know it." Drew stated trying to comfort his wife.

"Yeah, for you it will go fast, for me I'm sure the hours will drag. I can't even contact you! That's what bothers me the most I think."

"Maybe we can find a way, Thomas talks to his father and brother from a special phone that he has, maybe we can call you the same way!"

"If you can please do, even if it's only for a minute." Rebekah said.

Drew gave his wife a kiss. "We have to leave so that we aren't late." Drew opened the door for Dominick to go out and followed him to the car.

Rebekah stepped forward to hold the screen door open, and watched as her husband and son left their home, walked to the car, and drove off. She couldn't believe they were really going to another planet.

Thomas waited at the college for Drew and Dominick, he felt nervous, and worried they might change their mind at the last minute and not show up. They were supposed to meet him at seven that morning and it was now three minutes after. He gazed at the entrance to the college parking lot, running his hand back and forth on top of the steering wheel. Finally, he noticed Drew's car come down the road leading to the parking lot. He breathed a sigh of relief and got out of his car so they would see where he had parked.

Thomas reached inside and pushed the button on the door to pop the trunk for Drew and Dominick to put their luggage into his car.

Drew pulled up and parked next to Thomas, then he and Dominick placed their luggage in Thomas's trunk.

Once their belongings were transferred, Drew took a seat up front next to Thomas and Dominick sat in the back.

They hadn't gone very far when Dominick took out his phone and put earphones in his ears to listen to music.

Thomas glanced in his rear view mirror and smiled, he enjoyed seeing Dominick act like a teenager. He worried that all he had been privy to may have overburdened him. "Dominick doesn't seem to be effected to badly by the revelations over the last few months."

Drew glanced back at his son. "No, he's resilient. I think it would take alot to shake him up."

"I'm glad; I've grown rather fond of him." Thomas laughed a little to lighten the mood.

"I thought Dominick's professor was going with us?"

"He is. He went to Virginia ahead of us to take care of some business he's working on. He has information he needed to pick up from a colleague before we leave." Thomas explained.

"What exactly are we flying in?"

"We'll leave on a small shuttle that will rendezvous with one of our home ships."

"Why do you call it a home ship?" Drew wondered.

"The name just stuck from when we considered them our home away from home when we left for Aerthen II."

"Oh, I see. How long will the trip take again, I think you told us before but I was a little shocked and can't remember." Drew explained, laughing to hide his feeling a little foolish for not remembering.

"From the ground to the ship will be about forty minutes, to the outskirts of the solar system another five hours. Once we open the bridge it will take us about fifteen minutes to reach our solar system, then the final stretch to Aerthen II will be about two hours."

"I suppose we can't complain about that, now can we! How long did it take you when you left her originally?"

"Twelve years at light speed."

"Well, thank goodness those days are over. Don't you agree?"

"You better believe it; I would not want to go back and forth if I had to lose twelve years of my life like that!"

"I don't blame you."

They continued with small talk on and off until they reached Virginia. At Bethany's apartment they joined Wilton Walters and another man that neither Drew nor Dominick had met before.

"Drew, Dominick this is one of our pilots; Sully Samgi."

Sully held out his hand and shook Drew's hand and then Dominick's. "Nice to meet you both."

"Likewise." Drew answered.

"Is it hard to fly the space ships?" Dominick asked.

"Once you learn what all the buttons do, it's not too bad." Sully answered. "You can come into the navigation chamber if you want once we're out of the atmosphere and take a look for yourself."

"I would love too." Dominick looked at his father. "Is it alright?"

"Of course, just don't crash us, okay!" Drew laughed.

Dominick laughed too knowing his father was joking with him. "I'll try not to."

"If everyone's ready we should go get something to eat and then be on our way." Thomas said taking command.

"I just have to get my bag." Bethany said.

The six walked to their cars, Sully and Wilton headed to the professor's car and followed Thomas to a local pizza restaurant.

"Bethany called ahead and ordered pizza for you and Dominick and tomato pie for the rest of us to save some time." Thomas said to Drew as they entered the restaurant.

The group sat in two booths and ate their fill. Then they set out for the shuttle that was waiting in the field Thomas had showed Dominick during their hike. They parked their vehicles, removed their luggage, and walked down a path to an open field.

"Where's the shuttle?" Dominick asked.

Bethany reached into her purse and took out two pairs of what looked like sunglasses. "These are for you and your dad." She said, and handed them each a pair.

Dominick and Drew watched as Thomas, Professor Walters, Sully, and Bethany all put on sunglasses that were identical to the ones that they were just given. They glanced at one another and then followed suit. When Dominick looked back out into the field, he saw the ship. It was metallic, oval shaped with windows along the side and a large window at the front. There were slight projections at the sides, too small to be wings.

"It's invisible." Dominick blurted out.

"Not really. The hull just reflects the sunlight so that it can't be seen with your naked eyes." Thomas remarked.

"It can't be picked up on radar either." Sully said; smiling in a way that Dominick felt showed how proud he was of his shuttle.

"That's amazing!" Drew stated gawking at the ship with the glasses on, then removing them, and putting them back on. "Just, amazing!"

Sully took out a hand held instrument and pushed a button, a door slid open on the side of the ship facing them. They walked over to the ship and one at a time, they climbed the three steps to enter.

The interior reminded Dominick of an oval shaped bus; it had seats on either side with windows next to each seat. He also noticed that there wasn't a partition between the seats and the cockpit where Sully took a seat and started to push buttons.

Dominick heard a low hum, and felt a slight tremor as the shuttle engines started.

"Let's all get buckled in until we're in orbit." Bethany stated taking the lead and sitting in one of the seats directly behind Sully.

Dominick and Drew sat across from her in the two front seats on the right side of the craft, while Professor Walters sat behind Bethany.

Thomas was next to Sully looking at the instruments and having what appeared to Dominick as a serious conversation.

"What's going on?" He heard Wilton ask.

Glancing over his shoulder, Thomas answered. "We need to take a little detour from our scheduled route. There's an electrical storm over the North Atlantic so we'll have to go a little further south, that's all."

Thomas and Sully continued to talk for a few more minutes. Thomas then took a seat next to Bethany and buckled himself in as the shuttle started to lift straight up into the air.

Dominick looked out the window as the trees became smaller the higher the ship soared. The shuttle hovered for a second and then began to fly parallel to the ground. It didn't take long before they were out over the open ocean.

"We have a problem Thomas!" Sully called over his shoulder.

"What is it?" Thomas asked.

"Look out the window to your left."

Thomas leaned over Bethany as they both looked out the window. "We'll have to call your brother and let him know." Thomas replied to Sully.

"Everyone hold on!" Sully announced as the shuttle suddenly swerved to the left.

Dominick slid sideways in his seat but the seatbelt kept him in place. He glanced out the window just as what looked like a missile flew past the shuttle. "Look!" He yelled pointing toward the object.

Drew looked but it was too late, the object was out of sight. "What was it?"

"I think it was a missile!"

Drew looked at Thomas, concerned for their safety.

Shrugging his shoulders with apparently no concern over the incident, Thomas smiled, "These things happen once in awhile when we take a route that we were unable to get cleared ahead of time."

"I thought the shuttle wasn't able to be seen by anyone who wasn't wearing those glasses!" Drew remarked in an irritated tone more concerned for his son's safety than his own.

"When it's on the ground that's true, but while it's in flight the reflection of the light particles aren't as efficient. The shuttle appears to blink in and out randomly. One of the crew members must have noticed." Bethany remarked.

"Don't worry they can't hit us! The ship is programmed to automatically evade any incoming objects." Sully called back to Drew and Dominick.

"That's comforting." Dominick replied looking up at his father who was still not pleased with the situation.

A few minutes later, Dominick watched Sully direct the shuttle upward. The ship accelerated and soon they were through the atmosphere and into the darkness of space. The shuttle leveled off and slowed.

"Look dad!" Dominick remarked staring out the side window. "I never realized how beautiful the Earth was!"

The shuttle was now orbiting over Europe and Northern Africa, the cloud covering wasn't heavy and the outline of the continents was easily seen. Between the white clouds was a very blue ocean along with shades of green and brown from the different land topographies. "It's just like the pictures from the astronauts!" Dominick exclaimed.

"It certainly is breathtaking; it seems so tranquil, so serene from up here." Drew reflected.

"I can never get enough of that peaceful feeling that comes with orbiting the planet!" Wilton added. "Wait until we get to Aerthen II, it's magnificent in its own way."

"Does it look anything like this? You can't even tell that there are people living there during the daytime. I bet when night falls the lights from the cities are amazing!" Dominick continued.

"The land configuration is different, and the oceans are more green than blue, but they are alot alike." Wilton answered.

"I bet it's impressive." Drew answered.

Dominick watched as Sully reached into a panel to his left and pulled out what appeared to be some kind of phone. He pushed a button and held it to his ear.

"Suren, hi it's Sully." . . . "We had to reroute because of a storm and encountered a problem in the Atlantic." . . . "An aircraft carrier spotted us and fired a missile." . . . "Alright, I sure will. Talk to you soon."

Dominick was mesmerized by Sully's conversation, wondered who Suren was, and what he could possibly do about an aircraft carrier firing at them.

He was still watching as Sully turned around to get Thomas's attention, "It's taken care of."

"Good, let's be on our way then, are you two ready?" He asked looking toward Drew and Dominick.

"I believe we are!" Drew answered putting his arm around his son's shoulders.

Dominick began to realize how Thomas seemed to be the one that everybody else looked to for direction; even Professor Walters. He had overlooked it before because of Thomas being so close to his age, it just hadn't occurred to him.

As Sully turned the shuttle toward the moon, Thomas pointed out the front window, "Take a look at this!"

Drew and Dominick watched out the window as the moon grew larger the closer they came. "Wow, no one will ever believe this!" Dominick remarked.

Drew pulled his son closer as they continued to look forward at the moon. "It's fantastic, I'm really glad we came."

"Yeah, me too." Dominick answered as he continued to stare out the window.

The shuttle pulled to the right in order to circle behind the moon. Dominick followed as the image in front of him moved from the front to the side windows where Bethany and Thomas were sitting.

27

Jim and Wayne decided to stay in Virginia rather than return to New York until Thomas returned. They were booking a hotel room when Jim's phone rang.

"Hello." . . . "Hi dad, what's up?" . . . "Yeah, we're still in Virginia." . . . Jim glanced at his watch. "Okay, we'll meet you there." . . . "Ron will be coming too, oh alright." . . . "Bye."

Wayne finished the transaction with the clerk and joined Jim at the elevator. When they were inside the elevator alone and heading toward the fourth floor Jim turned to Wayne. "My dad, Ron Sr. and Ron Jr. are coming into the airport tomorrow, we'll have to go and get them. After that I have to go with them on official business."

Knowing what that meant Wayne asked, "What happened?"

"A Navy aircraft carrier took a shot at the shuttle and they found out that some of the sailors also took photos."

"Great, another fine mess we have to deal with!" He said laughing.

"It is sort of funny isn't it; I mean the look on their faces when we show up!" Jim said also laughing as he recalled other times they had to fix similar problems.

"I know the one time I went I almost started laughing right then and there; I swear I could read their thoughts by the expressions on their faces as they began to realize who they were looking at!"

"You definitely get a feeling for who is into conspiracy theories and science fiction, as well as who doesn't have a clue!" Jim concluded as they entered their room.

+ + + + + + + + + +

Ron Jr. coordinated his flight to land within the same hour as his father and Jim Sr. were due to arrive from England.

Jim Jr. and Wayne met them all at the airport. They then drove back to the hotel to change into their official uniforms.

"Wayne, when we're ready, you will need to drive us to the base where there will be a helicopter waiting to fly us out to the ship." Jim Sr. said.

"Not a problem." Wayne answered, knowing that the Council members always handled this type of official business in person. When it involved Jim and Ron, they also went along for experience, because they would both be Council members one day as the oldest children within their families. In some ways Wayne envied them, his sister Wilma would be the representative from his family to sit on the Council, he was third in line behind her and his brother Warren.

Wayne drove; Jim Sr. sat up front, while Jim Jr., Ron, and Ron Sr. sat in the back seat. They pulled up to the gait at the Air Force Base and Jim Sr. flashed a badge to the soldier who was stationed at the gate. He immediately saluted and let the car pass.

"We need to go to Hangar F; it's located around the back of that large building up ahead." Jim Sr. stated, as he pointed out the windshield.

The helicopter they drove up to was large enough to carry a tank and was sitting where Jim Sr. said it would be in front of the Hangar marked F with a pilot and co-pilot standing at attention waiting alongside.

Wayne watched as his four companions, who were dressed all in black and wore dark glasses that made it impossible to see their eyes, walked toward the helicopter, and climbed aboard. The pilots then started the engines and the large machine lifted into the air and out of site.

Jim Jr. looked out the window of the helicopter at the rolling ocean waves; he watched the white caps breaking at the top of the occasionally larger wave. The water seemed to have no end; there wasn't anything else in sight as far as the horizon. A few hours later, he felt the helicopter start to slow and he noticed the aircraft carrier become larger as the helicopter descended. Once they landed on the deck, the copter's engines were turned off, and the propellers became still, the door was opened and the four men walked onto the deck of the ship.

Every sailor on board was standing in front of them at attention, along with their senior officers. The crew saluted. They then saluted back.

Jim and Ron couldn't help but watch the looks passing back and forth among the sailors, along with a whisper here and there. Jim Jr. nudged Ron's arm inconspicuously and felt him reciprocate also revealing his enjoyment of the situation.

"At ease." Jim Sr. commanded.

"What brings you to the Minnesota?" The Captain asked.

"We came to resolve an incident that occurred almost forty-eight hours ago, when your ship fired upon an unidentified aircraft. It is of the highest priority that we confiscate any pictures that you may have from the encounter with the unknown ship." Jim Sr. commanded in a voice that left no room for question.

"Yes, Sir." The Captain replied. He then turned to his men, "Any photos, negatives, or other evidence of the encounter are to be brought forward immediately! Dismissed!"

The sailors turned and walked away. After a few minutes, one by one they returned with cameras, film, and phones that contained pictures. Ron Sr. and Jr. along with Jim and his father took turns checking the devices they were handed, removing the sim cards and deleting the evidence. They placed any photos or film in a suitcase that they had brought along with them. The whole while remaining silent and without making any type of a gesture that could be interpreted by the sailors in any way but authoritative.

When the last of the crew handed over their evidence, and took their position back in line, the Captain asked, "Is there anything else . . . Sir?"

"The incident, along with our being here today is not to be spoken of after we leave, none of you are to talk to anyone about it, or speak of it among yourselves. If it is found out that you have done so, you will be charged with treason, and court-martialed. Does everyone here understand what was just explained?"

Unanimously and at almost the exact same moment, they answered Jim Sr. "Yes Sir!"

"Is there anyone who does not?"

There was silence.

The four men then saluted, turned, and returned to the helicopter.

Jim Jr. watched out the window as they took off, not one of the sailors moved out of place.

28

When they arrived on the far side of the moon, the shuttle docked with a larger ship that Dominick could only catch a glimpse of since they approached from underneath. As they entered the ship through the cargo hold, they came to rest on top of the doors after they closed.

Sully pushed a few buttons, checked his gages, and then announced, "The atmosphere is stable, we can exit the shuttle."

The shuttle door opened, Thomas and Bethany led the way out followed by Drew, Dominick, and Professor Walters. "The entrance to the main deck of the Traveler is this way." Bethany said, as they walked around the shuttle and to the left.

When they were halfway to the door, it opened. A tall dark haired woman walked through, "Welcome aboard!" She said, with a smile.

"Good to see you again." Thomas replied. They took turns hugging one another before Thomas introduced everyone. "Ginny I'd like you to meet Drew and Dominick Domern."

Drew held out his hand, "Hello."

Dominick followed his father's lead. "Hi, how are you?"

"I am doing much better now that I have company." She answered, chuckling slightly. "Come this way, I will show you to your seats for the second part of your journey."

Drew and Dominick followed Ginny to the door that had opened. As they came closer, they realized that it was an elevator. Dominick watched as Thomas and Bethany walked back toward the shuttle, and Professor Walters walked toward a set of stairs. "Where's everyone else going?"

Ginny pushed the button labeled M-B that was next to a button labeled M-A on the elevator, then turned to face a set of doors behind them, as the door closed she answered Dominick. "Wilton likes to take the stairs for exercise. I think Thomas and Bethany went to help Sully."

"Why would they have to help him?" Drew asked.

"They want to make sure the shuttle will be ready to take you down to Aerthen II when we arrive. The atmosphere there is slightly different from what you have been accustomed. The Traveler is programmed to change the makeup of the atmosphere slowly between trips so that by the time we arrive everyone will be acclimated. However, the Shuttle has to be programmed manually."

"Oh, I didn't think about that! How different are we talking?" Drew asked, with concern in his voice.

"The pressure at sea level is greater, and the atmosphere is slightly thicker. You will not notice once we get there, your bodies will become adjusted over the next six hours."

"That's pretty cool, don't you think dad?"

"It is." Drew answered trying to hide his apprehension so Dominick wouldn't become uneasy about the situation.

The elevator doors that were now in front of them, opened onto the level marked M-B. The three walked into a room that was shaped like a semi-circle. There were comfortable cushioned seats with tables between them making it seem more like a hotel lobby than a space ship.

"This is where you can sit while we travel. There are refreshments over on the counter to the right, and if you need to . . . what is your word . . . use a room?"

"A bathroom?" Dominick asked.

"Yes, sorry, I am not as fluent as the others and have not learned to shorten my words either."

"What do you mean shorten your words?" Dominick asked.

"When you use one word instead of two." Ginny explained.

Drew and Dominick looked at one another not sure to what she was referring. Then Dominick realized what she meant. "Oh, you mean using a contraction like it's instead of it is?"

"Yes, a contraction, Bethany says that I will pick it up once I spend time on Aerthen and not to worry about it."

"So when we get to your world no one will be using contractions?" Dominick asked.

"No, only those of us that frequent Aerthen use them. Thomas tells me that when you hear them enough you just start to use them."

"That's probably true, like an accent that you pick up from being around people from different parts of the world." Dominick added.

"That sounds right." Drew agreed, he then turned to Ginny, "Don't worry about it . . . will Thomas be joining us soon?"

"Yes, everyone will travel here except Sully and myself, we will be at the helm one level up on H-B."

"Ginny? Why aren't the levels marked 1, 2, 3 or A, B, C? It seems confusing." Dominick asked.

"The letters stand for what is on each of the levels. M is for the Main Area, where we sit and eat. The top level is H for the Helm. Directly below us is Q for Quarters, where we sleep, and the lowest level where you arrived is A for the Alcove, where we dock our ships and keep storage."

"What about the A and B?"

"Oh sorry, the A is Astern for the back of the ship and the B is the Bow or front of the ship."

"That's similar to our terms for a ship." Drew remarked.

"Yes it is! We also call the right starboard and the left side port."

"That's very interesting, why is that?" Drew wondered.

"Well, it started when members of the Aerthen Project used the terms while they were visiting your world and it stuck with your sea farers many years ago."

"I wonder how many of our words and how much of our culture you guys have influenced. Thomas told us about the electrical wars with AC and DC." Dominick said.

"Thomas knows more of them than I do, but I do remember one, the one where we did not get our way."

"Really! I thought you guys always got what you wanted." Dominick was surprised at her remark.

"I would not say that we do, we cannot force you to do anything, we can only influence you and hope you listen."

"What was it?" Dominick asked, dying to find out.

"It was our biggest let down. Did you learn about the big war?" She asked.

"We've had lots of wars." Dominick said.

"You mean one of the world wars?" Drew asked.

"Yes, that is what it was called, the second one."

"Yeah, we all know about that, we won!" Dominick said.

"We were very happy about that. But we tried to stop you from making the bomb."

"The Atomic Bomb?" Dominick asked.

"Yes, the whole thing was horrifying for so many reasons. No matter what we tried, no one would listen to us. Our greatest asset at the time was Nikola Tesla who tried to persuade the government to wait for his particle beam weapon. The bomb was built first and our efforts then turned out to be a gaffe for us and ruined Mr. Tesla."

"Without it we might not have won." Dominick remarked.

"Who knows, but at least that was the only time you were able to use it." Ginny said in a solemn tone.

223

"What do you mean?" Drew wondered. Her tone gave away something he was sure of it, and felt that whatever it was, it was not common knowledge.

"There were times when we had to interfere." Ginny looked at Drew. "I probably should not say."

"Why?" Dominick asked.

"You might not like it." She said.

"I don't think whatever you tell us will really affect us either way." Drew commented. He glanced at Dominick who just shrugged not really understanding what there would be to bother him.

"All I know is that there was a few times that if we did not disable your electronics that it is very likely you would have used them again."

"You are able to do that?" Dominick blurted out.

"Then why didn't you stop us from using them on Japan?" Drew asked.

"That was different, you dropped them. The ones we could interfere with were in silos in the ground and could fly to their target. It was not very recent anyway."

"When was it?" Dominick wondered.

"In the 1950's or 60's your time. I think."

The elevator opened and Thomas, Bethany, and Wilton emerged laughing. "Sully will be up in a minute." Thomas mentioned to Ginny. "How are you two making out?"

"Good, Ginny was showing us around." Drew stated, as he smiled knowingly toward her. He wasn't sure she wanted him to share their conversation.

"I better go find Sully." Ginny said. "He is going to want to leave shortly, I will see you later." She was waving as she walked toward the elevators.

"Did you get anything to drink?" Bethany asked seeing Wilton head to the juice bar for a drink.

"No we were mostly talking." Dominick answered.

"Let me show you what we have." They walked over to the counter and Bethany showed them the water and juice machine. "We have water, of course." She said smiling, "Then there are all types of juices. We don't drink alcohol or soda on our world, but I think you will enjoy the juice. The first one is a type of carrot and apple, then there's orange, apple, and a fruit that is from our world. We call it liming, here take a taste." She pulled the last lever and a greenish juice came out of the spout and into the glass. Bethany handed the glass to Drew.

After taking a sip, Drew smiled. "That's pretty good . . . here try a sip." He handed the glass to Dominick.

Dominick took a sip, "That is good. It's sort of has a lime flavor, but has a sweetness too."

"It's one of our favorites back home." Wilton added, as he drank a cupful of the liming.

"I'm glad you like it." Bethany said.

Joining them for a drink Thomas pulled the combination of carrot and apple lever on the juice machine and filled his cup. "Sully will ring a bell five minutes before we set out. You don't have to buckle up but you should be seated so that you don't lose your balance."

"Thanks, we will." Drew said.

"If you will excuse me, I'm going to rest while we travel. I have a presentation to make when I get home." Wilton stated as he placed his cup into a hole that was in the counter top and led to a bin underneath.

"We'll see you later then!" Drew said.

"Have a nice rest." Dominick remarked, knowing he was much too excited himself to relax during their flight.

Drew and Dominick helped themselves and tasted a few more of the juices available at the drink bar. There was a juice that had to be apple juice, and another that was foreign to them. It was yellow and tasted sour.

"I don't care for the yellow juice." Drew mentioned.

"It reminds me of sour candy. You know the kind we use to get when I was younger. It's not bad." Dominick said smiling, he had always enjoyed the sour candy from the corner store, the sourer it was the better he liked it.

Dominick heard the ringing Thomas had mentioned. He and his father took seats as close to the front of the ship as they could find in order to see out the window. When Thomas and Bethany took seats next to them, Thomas and Dominick ended up sitting next to one another.

Dominick leaned over to Thomas, "I am so glad you asked us to come with you."

"Wait until we get to Aerthen II, I think you'll like it there alot."

"Is it like Earth on the surface?" Dominick wondered.

"In some ways it is, yes. But it also is very different, I can't explain it, you have to see it for yourself."

The ship started to move, the only way Dominick knew that it was moving was because the moon started to get smaller as the ship pulled away. "Wow, you can't even tell it's moving!"

"Is it always this smooth of a ride?" Drew asked.

"Most of the time, you'll feel the ship lurched slightly when we go to light speed, and then when we decelerate." Thomas stated.

Dominick looked out the window as Sully and Ginny maneuvered the ship so that it was facing away from the Earth and Moon. Suddenly he felt as though he was being pulled gently back into his seat, then the feeling left. "Was that it?" He asked.

"Yep, that was it." Bethany said with a smile.

Thomas waited; he knew they would be passing Mars in about four minutes. He pointed out the window, "Look to the left, you can see Mars."

"It really is a red color! That's amazing!" Dominick was bouncing in his seat with excitement. "Will we see Saturn?"

"Yeah, in about a half hour we'll pass Jupiter, then Saturn an hour later."

"This is unbelievable!" Drew remarked.

"Are you hungry? Thomas and I were going to get something to eat because it might be awhile before we get a chance once we land." Brittany remarked.

"That would probably be a good idea since we haven't eaten for awhile." Drew answered.

"What do you have?" Dominick asked.

"We have sandwiches, salad, fruit, and some muffins. I'll put them on the counter then you can pick out what you want, okay?" Bethany asked.

"That sounds good, thank you." Drew said.

Bethany walked to the cabinet and took out a few baskets full of different types of fruit and muffins. Then she opened another door that resembled a refrigerator and placed wrapped sandwiches and salad on the counter. "Here you go; the utensils are in the middle drawer. Help yourself!"

Thomas led the way over to the counter where they chose their lunch, then sat back down to eat.

"Look Dominick, to the right of the window, it's Jupiter! Look how big it is!" Drew exclaimed.

"You can see the spot too! How cool is that." Dominick added, he then stood and walked to the window staring out at the largest of the planets not believing his eyes. "It doesn't even look real." He remarked. Dominick wanted to remember everything about the planet's distinct color bands that the clouds created. He counted nine of the larger stripes, brown, reddish, light blue, and grey colors that were almost perfectly segmented. The red spot was evident to the lower left of the planet right above a light blue segment inside a reddish brown one. He then noticed a couple of Jupiter's moons. "Which moons are those, do you know?" He asked in general to anyone who might know the answer.

Drew pointed to one of the larger moons, "The one over there, that's mostly brown with craters, keep watching. If we're lucky you might get to see one of the sulfurous eruptions. It's called Io and it's extremely volcanic."

Dominick watched and a minute later at the far left side there was suddenly a fume of bluish color against the black backdrop of space. "Look, there's one there!"

Thomas also came over to see the eruption, "I never took the time to watch for them, I'm glad you were able to see one." He said putting his arm around Dominick's shoulders.

"Wait until you see Saturn, it's even more beautiful." Thomas remarked.

"I can't wait." Dominick commented excitedly as they walked back to their seats now that Jupiter was out of site.

Dominick waited patiently for the next half hour until Saturn came into view. Once again, he walked over to the window to get a better look. His father, Thomas, and Bethany joined him this time.

"Saturn is my favorite planet." Thomas remarked.

"How come?" Dominick asked.

"Just look at it . . . there's a glow that comes up from the planet itself, the luminosity can be seen underneath the clouds. Look over there do you see the spots without clouds?" Thomas said as he pointed toward the spots. "See how they look like a string of pearls because of the glow, they're always there every time we pass by. I think it's more amazing than the great red spot of Jupiter!"

Dominick was fascinated by the site; there really was a light than came out from the planet. "I think we spend too much time looking at the rings. The planet is more magnificent than they are."

"I was hoping we could see it's moon Mimas." Drew mentioned. "It has a crater that is almost half the size of the moon itself. I would have liked to have seen that close up."

"I've seen it." Bethany stated. "It has craters all over it's surface and the largest crater has a mountain in the center of it. It's an impressive site, maybe on the way back it will be on the side we fly by."

"That would be nice. Will we pass any of the other planets?" Drew wondered.

"Just Pluto." Thomas said. "Then once we are past the Kuiper Belt we will be out of the solar system. When we get there, Sully and Ginny will open the bridge. We'll have to be seated for the entire time we travel through that, it can be a bit rocky at times. Make sure you watch out the window though, it's quite a site."

"What do you see?" Drew couldn't even imagine.

"Lights and color bursting all around, it's better than fireworks!" Thomas declared.

Dominick was relaxing with his head back leaning on the cushion behind him when his father nudged him. "Look Dominick there's Pluto!"

Dominick sat up and looked out the window, the planet was a tan color with craters and a lighter area in the southern hemisphere that was shaped like a heart. "It's incredible! It has a character all its own even though it's the smallest planet!"

"You can say that again." Drew remarked as they watched until the last planet in the solar system was out of sight.

29

A few hours later, they arrived at the outer edge of the solar system, Sully and Ginny slowed the Traveler until it was at a standstill, floating in space. "Go ahead and ring the two minute warning bell." Sully remarked to Ginny.

"I wish I could see their faces, the first time crossing the bridge is always so astonishing!" Ginny said as she reached for the button for the warning and pushed it.

Dominick heard the buzzing sound and knew exactly what it meant, "How long before we go?"

"It's a two minute warning so probably about a minute and a half from now." Bethany answered.

"This is exciting, isn't dad?" Dominick said, looking over at his father.

"It certainly is son." Drew reached over and pulled Dominick toward him. "Are you ready for this?"

"As ready as I can be, I suppose." Dominick answered with a smile just as a light appeared at the window, it turned into a red ring with brown fog at the center.

"Here we go!" Thomas announced. "Hold on!"

The Traveler slowly moved toward the center of the ring, suddenly the ship lurched forward causing Dominick to be thrown back into his chair by the force. He felt himself become pinned against the chair for a few seconds then he was able to sit forward again once the force lessened.

"Wow!" Dominick exclaimed, looking out the window. He watched as bright flashes of white, blue, a green-blue, and yellow danced across the screen. The ship shook, then there was a bright orange flash, another shake and a red flash.

"Is this normal?" Drew asked, unsure of what he was experiencing.

"Perfectly." Thomas answered. "Hold on, the peak is approaching."

"What's the . . ." Drew couldn't finish his sentence, the ship lurched forward, then sideways, right and left before settling down.

"Look away from the window and down at the floor." Thomas announced loudly.

Drew and Dominick looked toward the floor, they could see the reflection of white shimmering, and then it was gone.

Dominick looked back at the window, the bright flashing had ceased. In its place was the brown fog with hues of red running through it and around the edge. The ship gave a final lurch pressing him to the back of his chair once again and then they were at a standstill in the blackness of space.

"Are we in your solar system?" Dominick asked.

"We are." Thomas answered. He then stood and walked to the window. "Come on over and see." He said beckoning Drew and Dominick to follow him.

The two men walked over to the window followed by Bethany and watched as the ship began to move forward, passing a small rocky planet.

"There's our star. It's more orange than yours but just as bright on our world." Thomas said, nodding in the direction of the brightest star in site. We have three hours until we arrive at our world, in two I'll show you the other inhabitable planet in our system."

"There's a comet passing by up ahead, it orbits our star every ten years." Bethany explained. "It has two tails one is white and the other blue. I love to watch it travel across the night sky."

"I don't see it!" Dominic said, as he peered out the window looking back and forth.

"Give it a few minutes . . . There, to the far left it's starting to come into site." Bethany pointed.

"I see it now! That's awesome, look at that!"

"I can't believe it, it's amazing." Was all Drew could say as they passed the comet, it really had two tails one that was bright blue and the other white.

After passing the comet, they relaxed. Drew and Thomas went to get something to drink while Dominick talked to Bethany.

"When we arrive you and your dad will get to meet our families." She explained.

"Do you have any brothers or sisters?" Dominick wondered.

"No, but my parents will be there, Thomas has a brother who works at the Project Headquarters so he'll be there along with his father. His mother isn't well so she will probably be at home."

"What's wrong with her?" Dominick asked, concerned for Thomas.

"She was injured years ago and has never been the same since it happened. She has a hard time getting around so she stays home most of the time."

"Oh, I'm sorry."

"It's alright she's a strong woman and will want to meet you when you have time to visit her."

"Wilton's wife and daughter will probably be there too."

"Professor Walters has a daughter, he never mentioned her."

"He and his wife waited to have a child; they were older when she was born. I believe she's your age now."

"Really, that's interesting." Dominick said.

"What's interesting?" Drew asked.

"Bethany was telling me that Professor Walters has a daughter about my age."

"Is she his youngest?" Drew asked knowing Wilton had to be in his late sixties.

"She's his only child." Dominick answered.

"That's right." Bethany replied. "They didn't decide to have a child till later in life, he and his wife are both professors and were very much involved with our university. They were fulfilled in that role for a long time."

"I see." Drew remarked not really understanding their culture.

"In another minute or so the first planet should be in site." Thomas said, joining the conversation.

They walked over to the window and watched, waiting. It didn't take long before a large green planet came into view.

"How beautiful!" Dominick remarked staring out the window. "It looks like a giant emerald."

"Did you say that this planet is uninhabited?" Drew asked.

"That's right, there are no permanent inhabitants living there, however, there are usually some vacationers visiting, so someone is on the planet most of the time. We like to watch the wildlife and relax there, but no one actually lives on the planet." Thomas explained.

"It doesn't look like there are any clouds or oceans down there." Dominick noticed.

"Interesting. Is there water on the planet?" Drew asked.

"Yeah, there are rivers, streams, and lakes of all sizes but they're hidden by the foliage." Bethany interjected.

"That world seems so different from ours. Does yours have an ocean?" Dominick asked Thomas.

"It does, but it isn't as large as yours and it's made of fresh water not salty."

"This is unbelievable; I can't believe we are actually experiencing this." Drew stated as he stared at the planet below them watching as they passed by and continued to their destination that was now less than an hour away.

"What are we supposed to do when we arrive at Aerthen II?" Dominick asked.

"I haven't talked to my father about the details, but I think they're having a dinner later on for a meet and greet. After that, we'll show you the apartment you'll be staying at while we visit, and you don't have to worry about your suitcases someone will put them in your apartment before you get there."

"They don't have to go to all that trouble for us." Drew said.

"It's no trouble everyone is extremely excited to have family from Aerthen finally coming to visit!" Bethany said with enthusiasm in her voice.

"She's right; we have waited for this day for thousands of years." Thomas added.

"That's alot of pressure! We didn't even know you existed till a few months ago!" Drew said, feeling nervous.

"Don't worry; the whole planet won't be there. Just our immediate families and the workers at the Project." Thomas clarified.

"Is that all." Dominick said sarcastically.

"What Project?" Drew asked. "I've heard you mention that before."

"The Aerthen Project. It's the name we gave to our mission of visiting your world." Thomas explained.

"Oh, it sounds so official like it was quite an endeavor." Drew stated.

"Then I suppose it's official because it has been quite the endeavor, we probably should have called it the Aerthen Endeavor." Thomas said, laughing at his humor that went over Drew and Dominick's heads.

They glanced at each other, both wondering what exactly Thomas meant. Neither wanted to ask fearing what his answer might be.

"There she is!" Thomas exclaimed as he pointed out the window. "Aerthen II"

Drew and Dominick both turned and looked out the window, coming into view at the left of the screen was a large blue-green sphere.

"It's beautiful." Dominick said gazing at the planet. Aerthen II was enormous compared to Earth; the fresh water ocean Thomas had spoken of was facing them. It looked almost clear with a light blue hue. As they continued to approach, land started coming into sight, green, brown, and tan swirls that intermingled far below. Dominick noticed that there weren't any clouds on this planet either.

"Once we enter orbit we'll head down to the shuttle. From there we'll go to the surface." Thomas said.

Aerthen

"Are Sully and Ginny coming down?" Dominick wondered.

"Yes they are. The ship will orbit on auto pilot till we return."

The door opened and Wilton walked onto the viewing deck. "Are we in orbit yet?" He asked.

"Almost." Thomas answered.

A few minutes later Sully and Ginny poked their heads into the door, "You ready?" Sully asked.

"We sure are it's good to be home." Thomas said, he held his hand out motioning toward the door, "After you."

Drew and Dominick followed Sully and Ginny to the elevator and then to the shuttle. When everyone was seated, the shuttle left the Traveler and began its descent to the surface.

Looking out the side window, Drew and Dominick watched as they approached the surface. After a few minutes, the buildings started to come into view. They appeared to all be made from grey stone.

"Is everything built out of stone here?" Dominick asked.

"That's all we have ever used, even back on Aerthen." Bethany said.

Dominick thought about his archeology course and the ruins that were unexplainable. The large stone shapes whose builders were unknown, and realized that they were what was left of the civilization Thomas's ancestors left behind when they escaped the disaster so long ago.

As Dominick watched, the large stone structures grew closer; they landed on the flat roof of one of the larger buildings. They walked from the shuttle to a door that looked like it belonged to a shed on the rooftop. Sully opened the door and Dominick noticed that it led down a staircase, also made of stone.

Sully led the way down the stairs until they came to a second door where he waited for everyone to arrive and then asked, "Are you ready?" Smiling from ear to ear.

Drew shook his head yes, unable to speak at the moment, not sure if he was ready for what was waiting for them behind the door at the bottom of the staircase.

Dominick whispered "Yes." His nerves seemed to have taken his voice away.

Sully opened the door that led to a room full of people. They started to clap and shout as Drew and Dominick entered.

Thomas and Bethany escorted them to the center of the room where Tegan, Timothy, and Trent were waiting.

"Drew, Dominick this is my father Tegan, and my brother Timothy."

"Hi, it's so nice to meet you!" the older man with greying temples said as he approached Drew. They shook hands then he turned his attention to Dominick and shook his hand. Timothy followed suit.

240

"This is Trent. He has to put up with me when I call from Aerthen." Thomas said with a laugh.

"It's nice to finally meet you. I've heard your names so many times I feel like I already know you." Trent said, smiling.

After their initial introduction, everyone started to introduce themselves and shake Drew and Dominick's hands. Dominick felt like a celebrity being the center of so much attention.

Once the initial commotion calmed down Dominick started to look around at the room. It wasn't very extravagant, the windows had shutters but no curtains and the walls where different shades of light pastels painted over the stone. He felt awkward around so many strangers; his father was busy talking to Tegan and Timothy so he tried to find Thomas. It took a few minutes but he finally found him with Bethany talking with a group in the corner. He started to walk over making his way through the crowd when he noticed Professor Walters.

The professor saw him as he approached, "Dominick, come and meet my family." He called, waving to him.

Dominick started to head toward Professor Walters, who stepped aside revealing his wife, she was slender with thick blond hair that hung below her shoulders. Dominick had expected her to be older than his mother, considering his professor's age, but she appeared younger. Next to her was standing his daughter, Dominick almost tripped over his own feet, seeing the girl took his breath away, she was the most beautiful site he had ever seen.

241

Thomas had been watching Dominick start coming his way and then be called away by Wilton. Dominick's reaction to Willow Walters didn't escape him. He glanced over at Willow who seemed to be mesmerized by Dominick as well. He decided to go to Dominick's rescue.

Thomas met up with Dominick who was frozen a few feet away from Wilton's family, "Let me introduce you."

Still unable to take a deep breath, Dominick nodded then managed to answer, "Okay."

"Lorna, let me introduce Dominick to you." He said realizing Wilton and Lorna were now aware of the attraction between the two young people.

"It's nice to meet you Dominick." Lorna said, watching him closely.

"It's ni . . ." Dominick cleared his throat. "Nice to meet you too. Professor Walters is one of my professors at college."

"Yes, that's true. He's a good student and very interested in archeology."

Dominick barely took his eyes off Willow, "This is Willow, Wilton and Lorna's daughter." Thomas continued.

"Hi." Dominick managed to say.

Shyly smiling Willow asked, "Do you really come from Aerthen?"

Dominick stared at her long blonde hair and green eyes, "Yes, we just arrived. I can't wait to see your world."

"I can show you." She answered, not looking away from him.

"I'd like that." Dominick felt like they were the only two people in the room. "It's so hard to grasp that we're really on another planet."

Willow giggled. "I am glad you came."

"Wilton, why don't you and your family join our table for dinner?" Thomas suggested.

"What do you think Lorna?" Wilton asked, knowing Thomas asked them so that Willow and Dominick could get to know one another.

"I think it is a very good idea." Lorna answered with a smile, glancing at Willow and then Dominick.

Bethany watched Thomas as he quickly left her and walked over toward Wilton. Realizing what was taking place she walked over to Drew. "Let me introduce you to Wilton's family."

"Sure." Drew turned to Tegan whom he had been having a lengthy discussion with, "Will you excuse me?"

"We can talk further at dinner, go ahead." Tegan said.

Bethany led Drew over to where Thomas and Dominick where talking to Wilton and his family. After introductions, Thomas poked Drew in the side and nodded toward Dominick and Willow.

It took Drew a minute to realize what Thomas was getting at; the thought of his son and Wilton's daughter was the farthest thing from his mind in all the excitement. When he realized he began to wonder how this would complicate their visit. He leaned over to Thomas, "Is this a problem?"

"Absolutely not, it's more that we could have asked for!" He answered.

Drew looked at Wilton and his wife, thinking that they would be disturbed by the attraction, but they seemed to be giving Dominick and Willow room to be near one another. Drew, however, was starting to become extremely uncomfortable with the situation. He didn't understand why they would be so accepting of their daughter's attraction to Dominick. If circumstances were reversed, he knew he would not be so understanding of his daughter and a boy from this planet.

30

That evening dinner was served at an eatery near the building they had landed on top of earlier that day. The group entered the stone structure and Tegan introduced Drew and Dominick to Karaka Kaunda who ran the restaurant.

"Karaka has the finest food this part of the living zone." Tegan said as Drew and Dominick took turns shaking hands with him.

"It is an honor to meet you both." Karaka said, excited. "I am so glad you chose to come here and dine tonight."

"It's nice to meet you too." Drew said.

"I hope you find something on the menu that interests you, we eat a little differently here than I have heard you do on your world." Karaka said.

"I'm sure we'll find something that we're interested in trying." Drew said. He found himself smiling at the handsome middle-aged man in front of him. Karaka was unassuming and wore a white outfit surprisingly similar to the chefs back on Earth.

The group followed Karaka as he led them to a table in the back that was large enough to seat their entire group.

Drew watched as Thomas and Wilton made sure Willow and Dominick were seated next to each other. He thought it was strange how eager they seemed to want this relationship, but kept from saying anything. He wanted to talk to Dominick alone about the situation once they were settled into the apartment they would be staying at.

"My wife will be over to take your orders, in the meantime would you like anything to drink?" Karaka asked.

Tegan leaned over toward Drew, "Is fruit punch alright with you two?"

"Sure." Dominick answered.

Drew nodded yes.

"We'll all take your fruit punch, Karaka." Tegan stated.

"My pleasure." Karaka turned to prepare their drinks; he motioned to his son, Kerri, to assist him.

Tegan turned back to Drew, "It's his own recipe, and it is extremely delicious."

"Do Karaka and his family run the restaurant alone?" Drew wondered not seeing any other employees.

"Yes, he has an apprentice chef come and learn every once in a while, but other than that it is just his family." Tegan answered.

Dominick didn't care what they ate, drank, or who served it. All he was interested in was being near Willow. She was not only beautiful but also smart and funny. She was perfect, he tried not to stare at her too much but found he couldn't help himself.

After a dinner of vegetables, fruits, and nuts, Dominick whispered in Willow's ear when he felt everyone else was busy with their own conversations, "Do you want to take a walk?"

Willow smiled, "That is a great idea!" She wrapped her arm around Dominick's and squeezed his arm pulling him close to her." She then turned to her father, "Father, may we be excused; we would like to take a walk."

"Don't take too long; be back in time to leave with me and your mother." Wilton said.

Dominick looked at Drew who had a scowl on his face. "Is it okay dad?" He asked, suddenly realizing his father was not happy with what was going on between him and Willow.

"Don't be long, and be careful." Drew then looked at Tegan, "Is the neighborhood safe?"

Tegan had a strange expression for a few seconds, and then he relaxed. "I keep forgetting that you are not from here, I'm sorry. Yes, it is safe. Nothing will happen to them if Willow wants to show him around the zone."

"Still be careful, okay." Drew said to Dominick.

"We will." He stood and helped Willow from her chair. Willow led the way as they walked silently out of the eatery.

When they were on the street Willow started to giggle, "I am so glad to be away from everyone so we can talk."

Dominick reached over and picked up her hand as they walked, "I know, it was hard to really say anything with everyone around."

"Do you want me to show you the park? It is really nice there." She said.

"I would like that. Are there any animals there, we have all kinds back home."

"Oh yes, there is a small pond with fish, and there are birds and all different kinds of creatures. If they have the time they will come and see us."

"What do you mean, come and see us? Are they friendly?"

"They are all friendly, and if they are not doing anything they will come over so that we can hold them."

"Oh, aren't they wild and afraid of you?" Dominick wondered thinking of what the animals were like at home.

"Why would they be afraid of us? I do not understand." Willow stopped walking and looked at Dominick with a concerned look on her face.

"Back home the animals don't come near us unless they're our pets because they're afraid of us. I suppose they think that we might hurt them."

"Would you hurt them?" She asked not sure if she wanted to hear what his answer was.

"No, of course not, I wouldn't hurt them." Dominick hesitated, "There are people who would though."

Willow looked horrified, "Why would anyone want to hurt them?"

Dominick couldn't help it, he hugged her tight, she was so innocent and sweet. "People are different where I live, they do terrible things sometimes." He whispered in her ear.

"I never knew that." She whispered back.

Dominick held her tightly not wanting to let her go, she felt so good and it seemed so natural to be near her. It was hard to explain, but he was very comfortable around her, as though they had known each other forever.

"I like it when you hold me." Willow said, she then buried her face into his chest and hugged him as tight as she could.

They gave each other one last tight hug and then let go. Continuing to hold hands, they walked to the park that was three blocks away from the restaurant.

Willow led Dominick to a cluster of rocks that were next to a pond, they sat next to each other, and Dominick put his arm around her keeping her close.

"This is one of my favorite places." Willow told him. "We live over there, you cannot see our home from here, but it is down the street on the other side of the park." Willow pointed toward the opposite side of the park from where they were sitting. There was a spot where the grass stopped and a street began. Dominick could see smaller stone buildings on either side of the street with trees scattered between them.

"It looks like a nice place to live."

"I think so. We have lived there since I can remember." They sat in silence for a couple of minutes enjoying each other's company. "Dominick, can you tell me about what it is like on Aerthen? We are taught about how we left and how your families stayed behind and then rejected us when we returned. I also know that we send members of the Project back to be there and help you when you need us. But that is all I really know, except what I hear people say every once in awhile."

"What do they say?" Dominick wondered, not sure what he should really tell her.

"That you have all fallen, and that our creator had to recover you Himself. I do not completely understand what that means?"

"Wow!" Dominick was shocked by what she just told him, he didn't expect to hear anything like that. "I don't really know exactly what that means either. But I know from what Thomas told me that you don't have wars or the problems that we have."

"What is war? I have never heard that word."

She was more innocent than Dominick realized, he didn't want to scare her. "War is when one group of people doesn't like another group so they hurt each other. A better example would be when one group of people wants the land another group lives on so they fight with them until they win and take the land for themselves."

He felt her shiver. "Why do they not just share the land?"

"I don't know, I suppose that isn't how they want it to be."

"How do they hurt each other?"

"Usually they kill each other until one side gives up."

"Kill each other! How do they do that?"

"With any weapon they can find, like knives, guns, bombs, you know that kind of stuff."

"Oh my, that is horrible." Willow sat up and looked at Dominick, "I do not think I would want to go to your world. I am sorry."

"I wouldn't want you to go there either, you're too special."
He leaned over and kissed her tenderly on her lips. When
she kissed him back, a warm feeling grew inside him; he
knew that he had to protect her. He feared he was in love
with her despite just meeting her.

As they sat holding one another, Dominick began to rethink
the last few hours from when he met Willow until now.
Suddenly he realized how everyone on Aerthen II was
being awful supportive of him and Willow being together,
they seemed to be encouraging them. Then her
remembered the look on his father's face. "Why do you
think your dad and Thomas seem to want us to get to know
each other?" He asked.

"They probably just noticed that we liked each other."

"Is that the way it works here?"

Willow was quite. After a few minutes, she answered. "I
was so consumed with you that I did not really think about
it, but you are right they did seem a little eager for us to get
to know each other. Does that bother you?"

"No! I'm glad it's what they want because it's what I
want." He pulled her to him to express physically what he
was expressing verbally. "I just thought it was weird, that's
all."

"I would not worry, my father and Thomas are very
involved in the Project, and knowing we like each other
probably excites them. They most likely see us as our two
parts of the family getting back together again. You do

realize that you and your father are the first from your world to ever come here?"

"Yeah, I figured that from what Thomas said."

"It is something they have wanted for a very long time."

"To bring us here?"

"Just to be able to tell you about us, we would rather we all lived together like we used to thousands of years ago. But we all know that it is not possible with how different we have become."

"Do you think that we're that different?" Dominick asked wondering what she thought about a relationship between them.

"I do not think you are, no. I am sure a lot of you are like us, but there are many who are fallen too far from what they once were. Those are the people we could not live with and co-exist peacefully."

"Well, the truth is people like my family stay away from the violent people on our planet."

"Maybe just the redeemed can get to know us. That would work, right? Do you not think so?"

"I do." Dominick watched as a bright red bird flew past them and landed at the edge of the pond to drink. "What a pretty bird!" He said pointing toward it.

They watched as the bird finished and flew away. Suddenly Willow stood and started to walk toward the tree

Aerthen

line to their left, "Come with me, I just saw the mother cat walking through the trees."

Dominick followed expecting to see a house cat. To his horror, a jaguar came out from between the trees. Willow was heading directly toward the great cat, "Willow stop! What are you doing?" He ran and stood in front of her between her and the big cat. "Let's back away slowly." He said scared for Willow's safety.

"It is alright Dominick, she will not hurt us." Willow stood next to him, "Look there are her three cubs coming out of the woods following her."

The mother jaguar snarled and made growling noises as she turned and looked at her cubs. Dominick was scared, "I don't know about this." He said fearing for their lives. "Please, Willow let's just go back to the rocks."

Willow walked around him and toward the mother jaguar and scratched the top of her head. The great cat rubbed against her and started to purr. The cubs came running over and one jumped up on her leg. She picked it up and walked over to Dominick. "Here you go." She said handing the cub to him.

Dominick reluctantly took the smaller version of the mother cat into his arms; it smelled his face and rubbed against his cheek. "I think he likes me." He said keeping one eye on its mother.

Willow giggled. The other two cubs were wrestling and then ran toward them stopping at their feet. Willow picked up the smaller of the two and hugged it, then placed it back on the ground and picked up the larger cub, hugging him. "I do not want them to think I do not care for each one." She said.

The mother jaguar called to her cubs, the one Dominick was holding started to wriggle so he placed it on the ground, the three ran to their mother who led them to the pond to drink.

"That was amazing!" Dominick stated as he watched the family of cats.

"We should start back to the eatery, it is getting late, and I told my father I would be back before dark." Willow remarked.

They walked arm in arm until they were a block away from the eatery. Willow stopped, pulling Dominick toward her and looking into his eyes. "I wanted a few more minutes alone with you."

Dominick smiled and pulled her to him. "Do you think I can see you tomorrow?"

"I am sure you can, I want to spend every day that you are here together."

"I'm not sure I want to go back home. Maybe I could stay here longer than we planned."

"I would like that." She said, smiling at Dominick. She thought he was the strongest and cutest boy she had ever met. She ran her hand up his arm and over his muscular upper arm, the boys on Aerthen II didn't work out the way Dominick did and the difference excited her.

Dominick leaned down toward her and they kissed, this time more passionately. Dominick felt a hot flush throughout his body and wanted to hold onto Willow even more tightly, but he feared scaring her.

After holding one another tightly a few minutes longer, silently expressing their desire for one another, they relaxed. Willow placed her head on Dominick's chest, and Dominick rested his chin on her head. They stood for a moment longer before walking the remaining block to the eatery. Their group was still sitting at the table in the back talking. Dominick heard a few laughs as they approached. Thomas and Timothy seemed to be joking about something.

Drew looked up as the two approached, looking into Dominick's eyes as if searching for something. Dominick knew his dad wasn't as approving of him and Willow as her people seemed to be. He was worried about what he would say later when they were alone in their room.

"How was your walk?" Wilton asked.

"It was wonderful." Willow said. She smiled and put her arm around Dominick's as they approached their seats.

Dominick pulled a chair out for her to sit down. Then he sat down in his chair trying to avoid looking at his father.

"What do you think of Aerthen II so far?" Tegan asked.

"It's amazing! We met a family of jaguars at the pond and I couldn't believe how friendly they were. The cubs let us hold them before their mother called them away to drink from the pond."

"Jaguars?" Drew asked.

"They live in the woods outside of town. There must be at least ten of them out there wouldn't you say father." Thomas said looking over at Tegan.

"Easily, and they are doing very well there."

Karaka walked over to their table, "Is there anything else that I can get for you?" He asked.

"I think we have had enough, everything was as delicious as ever, I don't think we could eat another bite." Tegan laughed.

"That makes my family and myself very happy. I will say goodnight then, and hopefully I will get to see you and your son again before you leave." Karaka said turning toward Drew and Dominick.

"I wouldn't be surprised if you do. Your food is definitely worth coming across the galaxy for." Drew stated and he wasn't exaggerating, his meal had been delicious.

Karaka smiled, "I will be sure to relay your kind words to my family."

The group exited the eatery and began to go their separate ways. Tegan, Thomas, and Timothy escorted Drew and Dominick to the apartment they would be living in during their stay. Dominick walked behind the group with Willow, Wilton, and Lorna. Willow held his hand keeping him close.

"Willow, say goodnight to Dominick, we're going to head home now." Wilton said when they arrived outside the entrance to the apartment building.

"I will find you tomorrow, okay." Willow said.

"I'll be looking for you." Dominick answered, he pulled her to him and gave her a quick kiss on the lips. Willow giggled realizing everyone was watching them. She walked after her parents with a spring in her step revealing her excitement over the day's events.

Dominick watched until Drew called to him, "Let's head inside, son."

Dominick turned and followed his father into the stone building and up the stone stairway to the door at the top of the short flight of stairs. The apartment felt cozy, it consisted of four rooms, a living space separated into a living room and small kitchen, two bedrooms, and a bath. Their luggage was sitting in front of the chair in the living space waiting for them.

Drew shook Tegan's hand thanking him for the warm welcome and they made plans to pick them up early the next day for a tour of the zone.

Once everyone left the apartment and Drew was sure they had left the building he turned to Dominick. "What do you think you're doing with that girl?"

"Nothing dad! We just like each other and had a good time tonight."

"I'm worried; they seem to be a little too accepting of the relationship. How would it even be able to work, you can't expect to come back here very often."

Dominick felt it was best to just tell him how he felt. "I was thinking of staying here with her."

"What!!! Your mother would kill me! She would be devastated if I left you here, that is not going to happen do you hear me!"

"Dad, I really like her, more than I have ever liked any other girl. I can't just forget about her."

"Well, I think they're up to something, I don't like it."

"What could they be up to? You know that they're not like us, right."

"That's even more of a reason for you to stay away from her!"

"Dad . . . I'm not going to stay away from her." Dominick looked defiantly at his father.

Drew realized he was getting nowhere. Dominick was really taken with Willow and there was nothing he could say to make him see the situation any other way at this moment. He wanted to be with her and that was the bottom line. Drew knew he was doing more harm than good the way he was going about the situation so he backed off for now. "Alright, if that's what you really want."

"It is."

31

The next morning Tegan and Thomas arrived on time. Dominick heard the knock on the door as he finished getting dressed.

"Good morning, I hope you slept well." Tegan said, as Drew opened the door.

"As of a matter of fact we did." Drew answered. "Are you ready Dominick?"

"Coming." Dominick came out of his room with his sneakers in his hand. He sat and started to put them on.

"Are you hungry?" Thomas asked. He then sat in the chair next to Dominick sensing he was a little too quiet.

"Starving, have you eaten yet?" Dominick asked.

"No I haven't. I thought we could spend the day together, while our fathers get to know one another."

Dominick looked at his father. Drew nodded his approval; he wanted to speak with Tegan without Thomas or Dominick around anyway.

"That sounds like a good idea." Dominick said, glancing back at his father who was now in a conversation with Tegan.

The look did not escape Thomas. "We might end up taking a swim; do you have a swim suit with you?"

"Yeah, my mother told me to pack one, just in case. I'll go put it on." Dominick headed back into his bedroom to find his swim trunks. He could hear the three men talking in the other room, something about visiting the Science Center to show Drew their plans.

Dominick came out of the bedroom just as their conversation finished. "I'm ready."

"Let's go then." Thomas said.

The two friends walked down the stairs and out the door. Dominick still had not spoken a word except when Thomas asked him something.

"What's wrong, you aren't yourself this morning."

"My dad and I had a disagreement, that's all."

"Oh, I hate that. Do you want to talk about it?"

"No, not right now. Where are we going?"

"I thought we could go on a double date, me and Bethany with you and Willow."

Dominick's mood changed instantly, smiling he looked up at Thomas who winked at him.

"Everyone here seems to be really excited that Willow and I like each other. How come?"

"Your right we are, no one here would have tried to set you up with each other, we didn't even think about the two of you getting together to be honest. Then when we realized you were attracted to each other, well, it's just more that we could have asked for."

"Is it because you want to reunite with us back on Earth?"

"In a way I suppose. You two just give us hope that at some point in time we can be one people again."

"I think I would like that too, so many back home would love to know that you exist. It would change everything. Do you realize that?"

"We do, and I would like to think that it would be for the betterment of your people. Maybe someday, the Riven between us is complicated and goes back a long time." Thomas noticed Bethany and Willow waiting for them in Bethany's rambler, "There they are!" Thomas pointed at the silver vehicle parked along the road. Bethany opened the front door of the car and came out to greet them, Willow followed coming out of the passenger side.

Seeing her Dominick sped up his step and Willow headed quickly toward him, too. When they met they hugged, then kissed lightly on the lips. "Are you surprised?" She asked him.

"Pleasantly." He said, smiling.

"I was too, Thomas called me this morning."

Dominick and Willow sat in the back of the vehicle cuddled up so close that Willow could feel Dominick's heart beating. Periodically they would kiss between conversing with each other and talking to Thomas and Bethany. Neither even asked where they were going, they were just happy to be together.

"We thought spending the day in Westeros Park and having a picnic would be fun. What do you think?" Bethany turned around and looked at the young couple. Noticing how closely the couple seemed to be, she thought that Thomas should have a talk with Dominick so that he understood their culture a little better.

"That sounds nice." Willow answered, putting her head on Dominick's shoulder.

Dominick kissed the top of her head, "I like that idea, too."

It didn't take long before they pulled up to their destination and parked.

"Why don't you two go and find a nice spot for the blankets while Thomas and I unpack the car." Bethany said.

When Dominick and Willow were out of earshot, Bethany approached Thomas. "I think you should talk to Dominick about how relationships work here. I'm sure he doesn't understand and I would hate to see either one of them get hurt."

Thomas glanced over at the young couple. They were walking with Dominick's arm around Willow's waist and she had her arm around his as they headed toward the lake. "I think that's a good idea, I will."

Bethany carried the blanket down to the spot on the sand that Dominick and Willow picked out. It was a good choice, far enough away from the lake so that it wouldn't get wet. "Dominick, can you help Thomas carry the baskets over?"

"Sure." He turned to Willow, "I'll be right back."

Willow helped Bethany lay out the blankets. They placed small rocks on the corners so that they wouldn't be blown away by the light breeze that came off the lake.

Dominick headed back to the vehicle where Thomas was starting to unload the trunk.

Thomas was waiting behind the vehicle with the trunk open blocking his view of the lake. "Oh hey, do you want to take the brown basket? I'll get the grey one."

"Okay." Dominick said reaching into the trunk to lift out the basket.

Thomas put his hand on Dominick's, "Hold on a second, Bethany thought we should talk."

"About what?" Dominick asked putting his guard up, expecting him to say something about him and Willow similar to what his father had been saying to him the evening before.

"We just want to make sure you understand our culture and how things work here when it comes to relationships."

Dominick relaxed a little, "Oh okay, I suppose that would be a good idea. I really like Willow and don't actually know what she expects from me."

Thomas became more serious, "First of all, you know we don't have the rituals or legal issues that you have when it comes to relationships."

"Yeah, I remember you telling me that you don't have marriage like we do with a ceremony or celebration for others to witness your joining together as a couple."

"That's true, we join ourselves to one another by consummating our bond, we're much more private when it comes to our intimate relationships. Once we have a physical relationship with each other we're bound to one another for the rest of our lives. I know it isn't like that on Aerthen . . . or Earth. Willow won't ever be able to understand a casual physical relationship like a girl from your culture might. She would be devastated if you didn't look at your relationship with her the same way as she would after you two have been physical with one another."

Dominick looked at Thomas and became a little distraught, he had actually thought about how great it would be if he and Willow were more physical with one another, she was very affectionate and seemed to want him to touch her.

"Are you alright?" Thomas asked fearing their talk might have come too late.

"Yeah . . . uh . . . I'm glad you told me that before we did anything! I would never have realized how different she would see it, what it would mean to her. I don't ever want to hurt her."

"You really care about her, don't you?" Thomas thought aloud after seeing Dominick's reaction.

Dominick looked into Thomas's eyes. He trusted him and knew he could tell him anything. "Thomas . . . I think I'm in love with her . . . and I don't want to go back home if it means leaving her."

"You have to go home!" Thomas blurted out without thinking.

"Why? I can't expect her to leave her home! It would be too hard for her on Earth." Dominick exclaimed a little agitated.

"You just do, how would your disappearance be explained?"

"Does it matter? My parents will know where I am and they can tell my friends so they don't worry!"

"That might not be enough, if the authorities start asking we can't just tell them where you are. And even if we did they would never believe it! Your parents could even be accused of killing you or something crazy like that!"

Dominick didn't want to listen to what Thomas was saying, but he knew deep down that he was right. He felt like crying; he was becoming terrified at the thought that he might have to be separated from Willow. "What am I going to do then?" He asked looking at Thomas with the desperation showing in his voice and expression.

"It'll work out, you two are meant to be together, I can see that and so can everyone else. Don't worry about it. Let's just enjoy the day, and take it one step at a time, okay!"

Dominick nodded his head as Thomas grabbed him and gave him a hug. He then patted him on the opposite shoulder before releasing him. He then reached into the trunk and handed Dominick the brown basket. "The girls are going to wonder what's keeping us."

Dominick smiled and carried the basket over to the blankets where the girls where giggling together about something.

"Oh, you two finally decided to join us!" Bethany said scooting over to the second blanket so that Thomas could sit next to her.

Thomas put his basket down and then tackled Bethany. They were rolling around on the blanket and Bethany was laughing. They stopped rolling with Thomas lying on top of her; he leaned over and kissed her on the lips, "Did you miss me?"

Laughing again Bethany answered, "I always miss you."

Thomas and Bethany sat up on their blanket after another quick kiss. "Should we take a swim before we eat?" Thomas asked.

"I would love too." Willow answered.

"Me too. I'll race you to the water." Dominick said looking at Willow.

They quickly stood, took off the clothes over their swimsuits, and ran to the water's edge. Willow ran past Dominick and dove into the lake head first, seeing her Dominick did the same. He surfaced a few feet away from her and then swam to where she was bobbing up and down in the water.

They were treading water, dunking under and coming back up when a couple of birds that looked similar to ducks started to make their way toward them as they swam on the surface of the lake. Dominick noticed them first, "Bethany what are they called?" He asked nodding toward them as they swam closer coming up behind her.

She turned and looked, "Oh, there called skimmers."

The two birds swam around, and then between them. The one had all brown feathers and swam up to Dominick touching his face with it's flat beak, it then started to pull lightly on his hair. Dominick laughed, "What is it doing?"

"I think she wants your hair for her nest!" Bethany said, giggling.

The other skimmer, that had red and bluish colored tips to its brown feathers, swam over and nudged the skimmer near Dominick. The two then continued on their way over to the shore. Dominick and Willow watched as they waddled out of the water and disappeared in the underbrush.

Willow splashed Dominick in the face and swam underwater toward the shore.

Dominick watched to see where she would surface. Finally, she came up near shore and stood in the knee-deep water. He laughed and swam over to her. When he stood, he picked her up holding her above the water with one arm under her knees and the other across her back.

They both started to laugh and touched foreheads. Dominick then carried her to the blanket and set her down.

He sat next to her and then turned her face to him by placing his hand on her chin. He kissed her passionately before stating to pull away but Willow reached out and continued to prolong their kiss.

She then put her arm around his neck and pulled him down with her as they continued to kiss passionately until they were lying side by side on the blanket. She placed her leg across his and looked into his eyes while brushing his cheek with her fingertips. "My father said I could go back with him to Aerthen, and my mother is going to come too."

"Really, you're not afraid to go there?"

"Not if I am with my parents. My father said that it is not as bad where you live and go to school the way it is in other places on Aerthen. My mother is going to make sure that I am safe." She said giggling.

"You have made me the happiest boy on any world!" He said as he kissed her again and pulled her as close as he could. "I love you." He whispered in her ear.

"Oh Dominick, I love you too." Willow answered, holding him as tight as possible.

"What are you two up to?" Thomas asked as he and Bethany came back from their swim along the lakeshore. Noticing how intimate they were Thomas felt he needed to speak up before they were close enough for the two young lovers to hear him and Bethany coming. He didn't want to surprise them.

Willow and Dominick rolled over and sat up, "I was telling Dominick that my father said I could go back with him when he returns to Aerthen."

Thomas grinned, "That's good news, isn't it Bethany?" He looked over at Bethany who was also smiling.

"It certainly is, and I know that makes you both very happy." She said.

"Yes, it does." Dominick said, smiling at Willow and then lightly kissing her lips.

32

That evening when Dominick returned to the apartment, he found his father sitting at the table in the small kitchenette area of the apartment. He had a cup of juice in his hand that he was taking sips from and he looked horrible. His hair was messed, and he looked like he had lost his best friend. Dominick immediately thought that it was because of his relationship with Willow.

Slightly shaking he asked, "What's wrong dad?"

Drew looked up. "Do you know that there is not a drop of alcohol on this planet! They couldn't make it if they wanted to, there's no fermentation, no rain, only some mist that comes up from the ground when the sun goes down."

"Why would you need a drink?" Dominick held on waiting for the hammer of his father's anger to strike.

"I had a long meeting with Tegan and Timothy today."

"Yeah?" Dominick held his breath.

"It seems that our planet is going to go through some disaster in about twenty years."

"Twenty years, that's a long way off. Why are you so upset about that now?"

"They want to take everyone, who is willing, to another planet somewhere light years from Earth! They want to do it soon so it's controlled and not rushed."

"But nobody knows about them, how would they work that out? No one would trust them!"

"Your right the public doesn't know about them, but evidently governments do!"

Dominick was surprised, "Really? But that Navy vessel fired a missile at us when we took off from Virginia! That doesn't seem like they know about them." Dominick suddenly remembered the conversation he was having with Thomas in Virginia, "You know dad, I asked Thomas once if he was worried about the government finding out about them being here and his answer was no. Then Bethany changed the subject before he said anything else."

"Well, it seems that there's more to all of this than we know about, and I don't believe Tegan told me everything either. I feel like there's more, I just don't know what it is."

"What governments know?" Dominick asked, still wondering how this could possibly be going on behind the backs of all the people on Earth and no one knowing or seeing anything. After all, it has been thousands of years that they have been coming back and forth and seemed to do everything secretly and behind the scenes not wanting to reveal themselves.

"They said that the major governments know the ones with power. Most U.S. presidents when they enter office are told. The same with the head of Parliament, European Union Leaders, The U.N., that's all I remember. I was pretty shocked by that time."

"Most presidents, so they don't tell all of them?"

"They said there have been a couple that they felt wouldn't have been able to handle knowing."

"I don't understand. These people are pacifists; they don't have weapons or even know how to fight with anyone. Why would our government even care or want to cooperate with them?"

"That's what I mean about not knowing everything. You heard what Ginny said on the Traveler, how they disabled the nuclear weapons to keep us from blowing ourselves up. They have advanced technology and that might be enough to cause the governments to cooperate with them. I really don't know . . . but it's a lot to deal with hearing it all in a single day!"

"I'll ask Thomas about it tomorrow."

"What are you doing with him tomorrow?"

"Just hanging out, like today. We went to the lake and had a picnic, it was a lot of fun, and we had a good time."

"I suppose Willow was there."

"She was. Her father is bringing her, and her mother, back with him when we go home."

Drew looked at Dominick, "He is, is he." Drew wasn't surprised by that in the least.

"Yep, I can't wait for Patrick to meet her. We can go on double dates with him and his new girlfriend. I think her name is Jenny. Do you have anything planned for tomorrow?"

Drew knew better than to argue with Dominick over this, and he really had no bad feelings against Willow, she seemed like a nice girl. He just didn't like the way the relationship was being pushed by Thomas and Wilton. He couldn't understand why Wilton wouldn't be more concerned about his only child wanting to be in a relationship with Dominick who came from such a different background.

"I'm going with Tegan tomorrow to see the ships that they want to use to transport people to the new planet. They still haven't told me much about where it is or anything for that matter, only that it's forty-one light years away from Earth, that's something like fifty million miles. I can't even imagine that, this whole thing seems so unreal."

"Yeah, I know what you mean."

+ + + + + + + + +

The next morning Dominick woke to the sound of his father getting a shower. When Drew came out of the bathroom shaved and dressed, he looked more like himself. Dominick rolled over and dozed back off.

Drew continued to get ready for the day ahead of him, when he noticed the time he went to wake Dominick.

"Dominick, it's getting late." Drew said as he gently shook his son's shoulder.

"What time is it?"

"Almost nine."

"Okay, I better get in the shower, Thomas will be here soon."

Drew heard a knock at the door after Dominick got into the shower. He opened the door to find Thomas standing there alone. "Hi, come on in, he's not ready yet, he just got into the shower."

"I'm early anyway."

"What are you up to today?" Drew asked.

"My mother wants to meet Dominick so I thought we would swing by my parent's house. Then Bethany and I were going to take Willow and Dominick to the theater to see one of the current plays that their putting on."

"That sounds like a full day."

Thomas nodded, "Are you spending the day with my father and brother?"

"Yes as a matter of fact, they're taking me to see the ships that are going to be used to transport people from Earth to the new planet."

Thomas nodded showing he understood but didn't say anything else about the subject.

Drew surmised that since Thomas wasn't surprised in the least by what they were discussing that he had to know as much as Tegan. After considering his options, Drew decided to ask Thomas a few questions. "Your dad told me about the plan to evacuate Earth but not much about the new planet. How different is the planet that you've found for us compared to Earth?"

"It's more similar to Earth than it is to our planet, but it has two moons. It is also larger, almost three times the size of Earth, and it has more land mass. There is an ocean and it's salty like yours, but the biggest difference is that the only life there is vegetation."

"How can that be, doesn't there have to be some type of animals for plants to have carbon dioxide?"

"On Earth that is the case but on this planet, there are plants that breathe oxygen and put off carbon dioxide, along with plants like the ones you're used to."

Drew took in what Thomas was saying. How much information he was being exposed to in the course of a few days was mindboggling. "It's been bothering me that the planet is so far away from here and Earth, isn't there somewhere closer than that?"

"No, there's not a planet that would work out any closer than that. We wouldn't be able to put you on a planet that was already inhabited, that wouldn't be very fair to the populations that were already there."

"Inhabited! By who?" Drew asked, shocked at the implications.

"It's true that there are other planets that are closer, but they have intelligent beings occupying them. They may not be as advanced as either one of our societies but the planets belonged to them first. It just wouldn't be right and it wouldn't work anyway. Think about it, what would your people do if they had to share a planet with anything other than vegetation?"

Drew shook his head, "I get your point. So you must do alot of exploring then if you know about all these other worlds."

"We have a Project for researching the galaxy, yes."

"Just the galaxy?"

"So far, it's extremely large. It's a separate Project from the one my family and I work with but I do know that there are many planets with life out there."

"Are there any that are more advanced than yours?" Drew asked fearing the answer.

"Not in our galaxy, I think if there was we would have ran into them by now."

Dominick finished with his shower and heard Thomas and his dad talking, he hurried getting dressed. "Hi, sorry to keep you waiting."

"You're not. We were having a rather stimulating conversation." Thomas said.

"Oh really," Dominick glanced at his dad, "about what?"

"The galaxy, did you know they have another Project that is dedicated to exploring other planets?" Drew asked.

"No, the subject never came up."

Sensing a little tension Thomas laughed. "We have many Projects for all sorts of things like exploring stars, the black hole at the center of the galaxy, and oceans."

"Oceans?" Dominick was excited since this was his favorite subject.

"Yes, most planets have them, so we want to understand their significance."

"I suppose that makes sense." Drew said looking at Dominick, who shrugged.

"You'll have to take me to the Ocean Project one day so I can see what you have found!" Dominick said excitedly.

Thomas stood, "I'm sure we can arrange that. Are we ready to go?"

"Yeah, do I need anything special?"

"No not today."

As Thomas and Dominick walked toward the door Thomas turned back to Drew, "Take care Drew; I'll have him back after dinner."

"Alright, I'm meeting your father in about a half hour and won't be back till then myself." Drew explained.

Dominick smiled, "Have a good time."

Drew walked toward them and closed the door once they left. He then took a seat in the chair in the living space. He really wished he could call his wife and talk to her about Dominick and Willow. The only peace he had was that at least they weren't left alone too long. Thomas was doing a good job as chaperone. Hearing a knock stirred Drew from his thoughts. He picked up his wallet wondering why he even bothered to carry it; it was more of a habit than a necessity here. He then walked toward the door expecting Tegan.

Opening the door he came face to face with a tall blonde man, "Oh, I was expecting Tegan or Timothy Torem. Do you have the right address?"

"I believe I do, my name is Kinnock Kaunda, and I am the representative of the Administrative Service for this particular zone."

Drew felt his blood run cold, "The Administrative Service, I haven't heard of you. Do you want to come in?"

"Thank you." Kinnock walked into the apartment and waited for Drew to shut the door. "I thought it was important to meet you and introduce myself."

Drew held out his hand, "It's nice to meet you." The men shook.

"Do you mind if I sit, I walked from my office?"

"Of course not, be my guest."

As Kinnock turned to sit Drew felt his heart beating in his chest, he was wondering if this would be when he would finally see the true nature of these people. After all, if they were human like him and everyone else, how could they be as perfect as they presented themselves? Drew sat down on the chair across from Kinnock and watched as he removed his hat and held it in his hands. He certainly looked official in his pressed tan pants and jacket that had a braided blue belt at his waist; it reminded Drew of a military uniform. Drew waited for Kinnock to speak first since he was uncomfortable not knowing the reason for his visit.

Kinnock looked at Drew, meeting his eyes. "I wanted to relate to you how important your visit is to us, we have waited a long time for this day. Tegan's family and my family go back to a man named Kaunda who left Aerthen with his family for this planet. My family is descended from his daughter Nishka who kept her father's name, Kaunda, as our surname. Tegan's ancestors took the name of Kaunda's son Torem as theirs. Kaunda's brother was Domern, who I am sure you now realize, was your ancestor."

"Yes, Thomas showed us the record of genealogy he brought with him." Drew was starting to relax. This visit didn't appear to be one of an official nature.

"I felt that it was important to come in person to meet you, my father sends his regards. He is the Chief Administrator in our Central Council and was planning to come in person. However, an urgent matter has kept him from traveling from our Council Headquarters. I hope this does not offend you." Kinnock had a worried look on his face.

"Don't be concerned, I'm not offended. I wouldn't want him to neglect his service to your people."

Kinnock's expression relaxed, "That is a relief. We work hard to find ways to keep peace with your world. Ever since the Riven it has not been the same between us."

"Thomas mentioned the Riven when I first met him, what exactly happened?"

"It was a dark time in our history. We finally were able to return to Aerthen to reunite with the members of our society and their families who stayed behind. Back then, it took us twelve years to travel one way, and when we arrived, they did not want anything to do with us. The leaders and adults who knew us had passed away and the new generation of leaders felt we had abandoned them. The worst part was that they attacked us and tried to kill us. They would have succeeded in killing us all if it was not for a group of men led by a man named James. He and three other men of other households did not believe the lies that the rest believed and they came to our defense. The group escaped with the help of these men, however, two of our ancestors were severely injured, and one passed away on the way back to Aerthen II."

"What ever happened to the families that protected you? Did the rest of the people turn against them?" Drew wondered not hearing about them before this.

"They have descendants that are still our friends, they watch out for us when we visit your world. We would never have been able to help your ancestors in the ways that we have if it was not for those four families. When we evacuate your populations to the new planet we intend to set them up as the leaders of your people."

It took a few seconds for what Kinnock just said to register, "What did you just say?" He asked bewildered.

"When your populations are moved to your new home, we want to see the members of the four families become the new leaders of your people on that world. We do not trust anyone else to lead you into a new direction and away from the way your people and governments conduct themselves."

"I'm sorry!" Drew answered standing up from his seat. "Do you really think the leaders of the world will just let some unknown members of those families usurp their authority? They'll use whatever weapons they have at their disposal to keep their power, you know our history!" Drew was beginning to feel that everyone on this planet was naïve if this is what they truly believed could happen so easily. No technological advantage would be worth the governments giving up their power peacefully. It didn't matter where they were relocated.

"There is so much that you do not understand and I am sorry for that Drew. We have always wanted to be open with your people, but even our existence became a secret for fear of your ancestors attacking us again. Everything we have done has been conducted in secret ever since the Riven, out of fear for our safety."

"What don't I understand?" Drew wondered, he could tell by the way that Kinnock spoke that whatever it was that he didn't understand was something huge.

"There is no harm in telling you, it will not be long until we reveal ourselves to your world now."

"Is that so you can relocate us to the other planet?" Drew asked a little sarcastically.

"That is correct."

"What's the big secret then, I mean other than the fact that you exist and have been intervening in our history since the Riven?" He almost shouted.

Drew's nerves were on edge, this was the final straw. He had started to become edgy when he first learned about Thomas. Then this issue with Willow and the great catastrophe he had just learned about that was coming, along with the relocation and now some other even greater secret just was too much. Drew shook his head realizing he was raising his voice. He looked at Kinnock who seemed startled by his reaction. "Listen, I'm sorry, this has just been alot to learn about these last few months, and especially what I've seen and heard since I arrived here . . . I didn't mean to yell."

"I understand. Do you want to hear what I was going to say?" Kinnock wondered.

"Yes, better to hear it from you than when everyone else learns about it on Earth."

Kinnock chuckled slightly, "I suppose you feel as our ancestors did here when the homeship returned and they learned about the Riven, it was shocking to them."

"I guess the tides have turned." Drew said, thinking about the irony in the situation.

"I was going to let you in on the best kept secret in your history." Kinnock stated, smiling at Drew.

"Yes, okay, so there's a secret other than your existence, and it's bigger. I can't wait to hear this! You know you really need to learn how to make alcohol, especially if you bring any more of us here and tell us this stuff."

"I am sure there is something we can offer you in its place. I will talk to the science department."

"Please do, it would make this a great deal easier." Drew took a deep breath, "Okay, let's get this over with, tell me what I don't know."

"The four families already rule your world, they are called the Council."

Drew looked at Kinnock dumbfounded, he didn't believe him. "What . . . how? You said yourself that the governments are corrupt, if the families are in control why are the governments allowed to conduct themselves that way?"

"They do not interfere in the lives of your individual countries and the way they deal with one other. They mainly look after us and make sure that our plans succeed."

"So how are they the rulers then?" Drew was beginning to feel exasperated.

"When they do contact any leader on your world, their demands are never turned down, the world leaders know that they have to listen to them."

"Why on Earth would they feel that they have to listen to a group of people who have no military power? That makes no sense."

"Because Drew, they are aware of our existence, and know that the four families are our representatives."

Drew felt irritated at what he was beginning to perceive as a conversation that was going in circles. "Alright, so what would you do? You aren't warriors, you don't have an army or even weapons for that matter. Do you?"

"No we do not; we have never fallen as you have. We do not need weapons or a military. What we have is the ability to keep your world safe and your people alive, and they know that."

"How do you keep us alive?" Drew asked, not sure if he really wanted to go down this path or not.

"Has Thomas shared any of our interventions you mentioned earlier?"

"He talked about manipulating the argument of whether AC or DC was the better electricity current, and we were also told about your failure with the atomic bomb."

"Yes, that was unfortunate, so we had to take another direction. Let me ask you Drew, did you really believe that a mold spore just happened to land on a petri dish in 1928, allowing Dr. Fleming to discover penicillin? Or that the idea that Cleisthenes had of a democratic government in ancient Greece was his own?"

"I don't know anything about Greece, but the mold thing always bothered me as a scientist."

"As well it should have, the mold was placed by one of the four family members who worked closely with Dr. Fleming. As for Cleisthenes, one of our original Project members was his influence. By 500 B.C. in your timeline, we had discovered how to form a bridge and travel to your world in less than a day, rather than it taking twelve years. The Aerthen Project came into existence and we started to send groups of our own people to all corners of your world to assist you. We have been there ever since. The four families have grown in numbers over their generations and they are apart of every government and institution that has any importance in your world."

"Does everyone here know about all this?" Drew wondered.

"Most of it they do, yes. Only those involved in the Project, and the Administrative Service, since we are the government, know everything about your world. Although our description and function is not the same as what your definition of a government might be. It is true that everyone here knows you exist, and has heard of you since they have been old enough to rationalize what they hear. However, most do not know the extent to which you have fallen; if they did, they would be petrified of you. We report to our citizens how things are going with your world and the environment, they also know of our plans to move your population to another planet because, unfortunately, we cannot change the course of your planet's furtherance. The planet you live on is still young and continuing to stabilize. Our people also know how, over the years, we have diverted meteors heading your way on a number of occasions to save you. But they do not know how we have kept you from destroying yourselves."

"So that's another reason why our leaders know they need you."

"It is."

"Is there anything else that I should know, any other big secrets, or plans that you have?"

Chuckling once again Kinnock added, "I think it is enough for now." He smiled, "That is all of the major matters, anything I have not mentioned pales in comparison to these!"

"Thank goodness, I don't think I could handle anything else!"

"If you are ready, Tegan is waiting for us at Project Headquarters. I told him I would bring you there when we were done."

33

During the drive to Project Headquarters, Drew was thinking over the conversation that he and Kinnock just had. He was curious about a couple of the remarks Kinnock had made but didn't expand on. "Can I ask you something?"

"Of course, go ahead."

"At the apartment you mentioned that my definition of government was different from yours. What did you mean by that?"

"Our function is different. On your world, the government rules, makes laws, and enforces their authority. Here we are merely coordinators between Projects and the different zones."

"What do you coordinate?"

"Mostly information to make sure our endeavors run smoothly when the Projects have overlapping interests. We also organize conferences between the zones and we host the yearly elections."

"What are the zones that you keep mentioning and what kind of elections."

"You are curious!" Kinnock exclaimed.

"I'm sorry, I just find your way of life fascinating, and want to know more about it."

"There is nothing wrong with that, I find it refreshing. The zones can be compared to your states. We apportion our land mass so that we have a way to organize our lives. For example, our government headquarters is in zone one and this is zone three. If I needed to send a package to my superior, I would mark the package with his name, structure numeral, and the name of the lane much as you would. Instead of putting a state I would write that he is located in zone one."

"I see that's almost exactly the same way our postal service works."

"The elections we have are not much different than the kind you have in your country. However, we have them yearly. Each zone has a representative that communicates what is happening in their zone to the government headquarters, and each Project has a representative. We elect them yearly, some have been representatives for many years, and others change more frequently. I represent our zone and Tegan represents the Aerthen Project."

"Interesting." Drew wondered who made the laws here if the government didn't. "Who makes laws and decisions when problems arise?"

"We do not have laws; there is no need for them. Doing what is right in the mind of our creator is a natural part of our thoughts and behavior. When we disagree on a subject we bring together other members of the Project or zone and discuss our ideas until we all agree."

"What if you can't come to an agreement?"

"Then we do nothing. If we cannot agree on the way to proceed with an idea then we believe that there is a reason we cannot agree so we do nothing."

"Doesn't that cause hurt feelings and bitterness between you?"

"No, why would it?"

"I don't know it's just how things are where I come from. People want their way that's why we have laws and courts to keep order and make decisions when we disagree."

"Oh yes, because of your fallen nature." Kinnock answered in an understanding tone of voice.

"Why do you keep referring to us as fallen? What does that mean?"

"You know the answer to that already."

"I do?"

"You use to be the same as we are, but after the flood and catastrophe you chose to disobey the creator. That is what we refer to as being fallen."

"Do you mean sin?"

"That might be your word for it. I am not familiar with many of your words, Tegan may know if that is a synonym since he is more familiar with your world."

"I'll have to ask him." Drew thought it better to leave the subject alone. A religious discussion wasn't something he was really interested in having at this point in time. He had too much to think about as it was without adding religion to the mix.

+ + + + + + + + + +

Dominick and Thomas had a relaxing visit with Thomas's mother. She was a thin woman who had a limp when she walked and carried her left arm in a sling. Thomas helped her make them breakfast after she insisted she wasn't going to allow them to leave with empty stomachs. Dominick knew that she had some kind of a health issue from an accident but wasn't sure exactly what it was and didn't want to ask.

When they left his parent's house and drove toward the center of the zone, Dominick thought that Thomas seemed to be more relaxed than usual. "That was a nice visit with your mother, she seems very nice."

"I rarely get to see her anymore, she looked good today."

Dominick smiled not really knowing what to say.

"Bethany and Willow should be at the theater by the time we get there."

"What are we going to see?"

"Bethany says it's the newest play that's been sweeping the zones, everyone's talking about it. It's a comedy about two brothers and a friend who decide to live in the wilderness zone and the situations they run into."

"What's the wilderness zone?"

"It's the forested area that lies to the south of here, about four thousand miles away near the midline of our world. Nobody actually lives there because it gets very warm. But there is a large variety of animal life that inhabits the area. Actually over half of the species there we brought with us from Aerthen, so you'll see some familiar faces!" Thomas said laughing.

"Are the animals as friendly as the ones around here?" Dominick hoped they were he really enjoyed his encounters with the wild animals on Aerthen II.

"Yes they are. They don't get to see humans very often so when anyone goes there they pay quite a good deal of attention to them. I suppose the play will find humor with that scenario."

"I can't wait; I haven't seen a play in a long time." Dominick continued to look out the window of the rambler, the name the people here used for cars, and admired the stone buildings. It was amazing how they shaped and molded the stone with such intricate designs making each building a little different.

"There's the theater." Thomas announced a few minutes later pointing ahead to another stone structure; this one had a round roof.

They parked the rambler and walked to the theater entrance. After they entered the lobby, Dominick noticed Bethany and Willow sitting far to the left in an area with plants and a fountain. Bethany noticed them at the same time and stood motioning to Willow.

When Willow saw Dominick, she immediately smiled and started to walk toward him. It made him warm inside to see her reaction to him. She looked even more beautiful wearing a pink dress covered in small flowers; the pastel colors made her hair seem even blonder.

"I missed you!" Willow said when she was close enough for Dominick to hear her. She then reached up to kiss him.

Dominick reached out and pulled her close to him as they gently kissed and then hugged. "I missed you too." He whispered into her ear.

They parted, but continued to hold hands as they followed Thomas and Bethany inside the theater. The two couples sat as close to the front as they could, finding seats in the fifth row. Dominick put his arm around Willow as she cuddled up as close to him as possible despite having a chair arm between them.

Thomas watched them carefully out of the corner of his eye. He knew that it would not be in their best interest to be alone together for any length of time. He wondered, and also worried a little, about how it was going to be possible to chaperone the two of them once they returned to Aerthen.

After the play, they decided to visit another of their favorite restaurants. While they waited for their orders, they laughed about the different scenes in the play that they each enjoyed the most. Dominick's favorite was when the monkeys came swooping out of the trees and led the young men back to their cave. The way the monkeys pulled at their ears and clothes and kept offering them food made him laugh until his side hurt. He had tears in his eyes watching as a baby monkey climbed onto the top of the head of one of the men, curled up, and then fell asleep. The man didn't want to move and disturb his new friend so he sat straight up only moving his eyes back and forth.

After dinner Thomas drove Willow home first, Dominick walked her to her door and then went inside to say hello to Professor Walters. They shared the high points of their evening's entertainment with Willow's parents who then excused themselves and went into the kitchen.

Dominick found it very hard to say goodnight and leave Willow, but he knew that Thomas and Bethany were waiting outside. "I'll see you tomorrow, I'm sure Thomas has some new adventure planned for us!"

Willow giggled, "I'm sure he does. I have something for you." Willow quickly walked out of the room and returned a few minutes later with what looked like a cell phone. "I picked this up so that we could call each other."

Dominick was excited, "How does it work?"

"You just push the button on the side, when it lights up say 'Call Willow' and it will automatically connect to my communicator. I programmed it this morning."

"This is great! Will they work when we get back on Earth?"

"I do not know. I will have to ask my father. He calls my mother from Aerthen on a communicator similar to this, but I am not sure if these will work there."

Feeling that he was taking too long to say goodnight, Dominick looked at Willow, "I don't want to leave, but Thomas will be wondering where I am."

"I know I hope that we can spend more time alone soon." Willow said. She felt loneliness creep in after they kissed goodnight and watched as Dominick started toward the door.

"Goodnight." Dominick called to Professor Walters and Mrs. Walters who had stepped into the kitchen to give him and Willow a few minutes alone.

"Goodnight Dominick, say hello to your father for us." Professor Walters said, walking out of the kitchen and back into the living area.

Lorna Walters followed behind her husband smiling, "See you soon."

Walking out the door of Willow's home was hard for Dominick, he missed her already, and when he was away from her, she was the only thing he really thought about.

When Dominick returned to the rambler, the mood was heavy. Thomas was on his phone and Bethany had her hand on his shoulder, when she looked at Dominick, he could see the stress in her eyes. "What's wrong?" He asked softly not to interfere with Thomas's call.

"Something happened on Aerthen, Thomas will tell us in a minute."

Thomas listened more than he spoke, after what seemed like hours he finally hung up from his conversation. He looked back and forth at Bethany and Dominick. "Lawrence Larose and Diane Dineen called a few hours ago and said that the Sargasso seaweed growth in the Atlantic Ocean has exploded, it is growing and spreading exponentially. It's making it hard for smaller boats to travel and if it gets much thicker the larger ships will also have a hard time sailing through it!"

"What does that mean?" Dominick wondered.

"I don't know. We have an emergency meeting tomorrow at Project Headquarters, I'll find out more then."

"Do you think we'll have to return sooner?" Bethany asked.

"I'm not sure." Thomas replied. They drove in silence back to the apartment where Dominick and his dad were staying.

"I'll be in touch and let you know what's going on." Thomas said, looking over his shoulder at Dominick.

Dominick wasn't sure why they seemed so concerned. He knew about phenomena's like the red tide where algae grew out of control. One of the reasons why he had become interested in marine biology was because of the red tide. To him this event with the seaweed was probably nothing different. "Alright, see ya later."

Drew hadn't returned yet from his day with Tegan, it was almost seven o'clock according to the clock on the kitchen wall. Dominick wondered if his dad would know more about what was happening when he returned to the apartment for the night.

+ + + + + + + + + +

Dominick was tired of waiting for his father to get back; it was now almost eight, so he decided to lay down. He hadn't slept well since they arrived, he had been too excited about meeting Willow to be able to think or do anything, even sleep. Once he laid down, the lack of a goodnight's rest caught up with him and he dozed off quickly.

"Dominick, Dominick. Wake up." Drew called to his son. He hated waking him but under the circumstances, he couldn't wait until morning.

"Dad?" Dominick turned to look at his father. "What's going on?"

"Something big, there's an emergency meeting tomorrow for all the members of the Aerthen Project. Tegan says that the Earth may have sped up its change starting with the oceans."

"Thomas got a phone call tonight about the same thing. He said there's something going on with the seaweed starting to block shipping lanes." Dominick sat up, yawning. "I don't understand why they're so concerned about seaweed."

"It's not normal seaweed, it mutated somehow. I think that's why they are so concerned."

"I suppose they'll tell us about it after the meeting. Do you think everyone back home is alright?" Dominick asked. Concerned for his mother, sister, and friends.

"I'm sure they are." Drew reassured him.

"What about our vacation, will it be cut short?" The thought of leaving began to bother him; he was worried Willow might not go back with them now.

"I don't know we'll have to wait and see. Will you be able to get back to sleep, I shouldn't have woken you, but I needed to be sure you knew about this."

"I'm okay. I can sleep in tomorrow anyway. With the meeting our plans had to be shelved for now."

Drew smiled, then patted Dominick on the shoulder. "Try to get back to sleep, okay."

"I will."

Drew stood and then walked out of Dominick's bedroom. He turned before shutting the door and glanced over at Dominick who had once again laid down and was under the covers.

When he heard the door shut, Dominick waited a few minutes and then took out the phone Willow gave him. He pushed the symbols she had shown him, then said, "Call Willow", and waited.

"Hi Dominick, I'm so glad you called. I was thinking about you."

"I was thinking about you too. I won't be going with Thomas tomorrow so I won't be able to see you."

"We can still see each other. Do you want to come over to my home? My parents will be at the meeting too."

"The one Thomas and Bethany have to go to about my planet?"

"Yes."

"I would love to come over to your house . . . but how would I get there?"

"I can come over and get you, it's not that far. The shuttle runs down the main thoroughfare two lanes away from your apartment building."

"Alright, what time do you want me to meet you?"

"I will come over right after my parents leave, so about nine o'clock."

"I'll be downstairs at nine. I can't wait to see you again."

Giggling Willow answered, "I wish we didn't have to wait till the morning to be together."

"Me too."

"Goodnight, I love you." She said disconnecting her end.

Dominick laid in bed holding onto the phone. He didn't think he would get much sleep now. He also hoped that his father wouldn't give him a hard time in the morning when he wanted to leave.

Drew stayed up late thinking about everything he had heard and seen since they arrived on Aerthen II. He was also worried about what was going on back on Earth. He didn't understand why they were reacting so seriously about the seaweed, what could it possibly do that would be so harmful? Blocking a few shipping lanes wasn't that big of a deal since they could change their courses, it was probably a fluke anyway and everything would go back to normal sooner rather than later. He looked up at the clock in his room, it was two in the morning, he rolled over and closed his eyes finally feeling tired.

34

When Dominick woke up the next morning, he showered, ate breakfast, and waited for his father to get up. At eight-fifty he decided he would write a note saying that he went with Willow and would be back later, he then left the apartment and went to meet her.

He stood outside waiting, a few minutes later he heard Willow call to him, "Dominick, Dominick, I am over here!"

He turned to the right and smiled, he then ran the half block to meet her. When they met up, they hugged and quickly kissed on the lips.

"What are we going to do today?" Dominick asked.

"Let us go back to my house. We can talk about what it will be like when we go to Aerthen, and you can tell me what kinds of clothes I will need. My father told me that it is cold there."

"It gets a lot colder there in the winter, and it will be the dead of winter when we return. Do you have warm clothes and a coat?"

"Dominick, I do not even know what a coat is!" She laughed and grabbed his hand pulling him down the street.

They walked for over an hour and Willow pointed out the stores where she and her mother would shop. "Do you want something to eat before we go to my house? I would like something."

Even though he ate, he still felt hungry, "Sure do you have money?"

"Money? What it that?" Willow asked.

Dominick hadn't paid much attention when they ate out and just assumed that Thomas or Tegan had paid the bill. "You know, what you use to pay someone when you get something from their store or restaurant."

"We never do anything like that, I do not understand? Do you do that on your world?"

"Yeah, we work to make money and then use it to buy what we need and to pay for things we want to do. Don't your parents get paid for working as professors?"

"No. We do what we like and help society by doing it. I want to be a caretaker and comfort sick people. When I finish at the university, I want to help at the infirmary. I am learning about remedies right now and how they work."

Dominick thought about what she said, it seemed odd, he remembered Thomas saying something about not liking

299

how people on Earth relied on money so much. "So what you're saying is that you don't get paid for working you just decide what you want to do, learn how, and then do it for free?"

"You are not making sense. I want to be a medic and help people. My parents wanted to teach to help, that is why we do it. The man at the theater likes to put on plays and coach the actors to entertain and make people laugh. Farmers like to grow crops and are happy when we enjoy what they produce. I only know how it works here."

"It sounds like it might be better here, if you don't have money back home then you can't buy food and there are people starving."

"Starving? No one gives them food?"

"No, not always. Let's change the subject, how much farther is it to your home?"

"Only two lanes away."

"Do you still want something to eat?" Dominick felt a change in her mood.

"Not really."

Dominick stopped, "Willow, don't be sad, please. I didn't mean to upset you."

"I just do not understand the way it is on Aerthen. I have to remember that you are fallen and not think about what I cannot change. My father says that all we can do is help when it is possible and not get emotionally involved with what we see and hear there."

"I think that's what most of us do who live there. I know I
can't help the people with no money or homes, so I just
don't dwell on it. Are you sure you don't want to stop and
eat?"

"Maybe I should eat something, then we can just relax
when we get to my home. There is a sarnie shop on the
next lane. Do you want to go there?"

Dominick pulled Willow close to him before they
continued on their way, "Sure, let's go." They walked
while Dominick kept his arm around her. He felt he needed
to show support and comfort her since she was clearly
upset.

After eating at the sarnie shop, which Dominick thought
resembled a delicatessen back home, they headed to
Willow's home. Dominick noticed that she was her usual
self again, light and bubbly. He wanted to avoid talking
about the conditions back home so that he didn't upset her
again.

Willow sat on the couch in her living space and Dominick
sat next to her. "Would you like anything to drink?" She
asked.

"No, I'm fine. What do you do for fun? Do you have any
hobbies?"

"I like to paint, but I have not done it in a long while. The
university takes up most of my time these days. What
about you, Dominick, do you have a hobby?"

"No, I really don't. But I like to play basketball with my
friends. I can't wait for you to meet my best friend,

Patrick. He has a new girlfriend and we can all hang out together when we get back."

"I think that will be alot of fun." Willow said snuggling up to Dominick who put his arm around her; he then turned to his side facing her.

Willow put her head back so that Dominick would kiss her. They snuggled and kissed on the sofa, Willow's body movements were exhilarating to Dominick and he wanted more of her than just a kiss. She seemed as though she wanted the same as she pushed her hips toward him now that he was lying practically on top of her. He was about to lose control, he started to move his hand up her shirt and touch her when suddenly, Thomas's words jumped into his mind, "She will never understand . . ."

Dominick pulled away, "Willow, we have to stop, I'm sorry, I . . . I need to stop."

"Alright." Willow said sitting up. "Is anything wrong?"

Dominick looked at her; he didn't know what to say. "It's not that I don't want to . . . I'm just worried."

"What are you worried about?"

"I'm worried that you could be hurt if our relationship doesn't work out."

"Why would it not work out, I thought we loved each other!"

"I do love you . . . and I know you love me because . . . I can feel it. But I wouldn't be able to support you, I'm still in school, there is a lot going on and I don't know . . . I just don't know."

"What is alot? What do you not know?" Willow asked.

"Well . . . the differences in the way relationships work here, for one."

"What happens with relationships on your world?" Willow had never thought about there being a difference.

"What do you mean?" Dominick wanted to be sure what she meant before answering. He didn't want to make the wrong assumption and make things worse.

"Here when we want to spend our lives with someone we join together physically in order to establish our commitment to one another."

"That's how Thomas explained it to me too . . . at home . . . we don't have to be together for life to do that."

"You do not!" Willow was surprised.

"No, men and women do it all the time and then move on with other relationships if they don't get married and stay together."

"Married? Is that how you join?"

"Yes it is, we join by getting married, it's a ceremony that our families and friends watch while we pledge our love to each other."

"So . . . have you joined with other girls then, without being married?" Willow asked beginning to feel queasy at the thought of him being with another girl. She really hoped Dominick would say no.

"Willow do we really have to talk about this?"

Willow started to cry, "I have to know."

"Alright then." Dominick took a deep breath. "Just one time, with a girl I knew in high school. We went out for two years then she went to college down south so we just stop seeing each other. I haven't talked to her for over four months."

Willow felt awkward. "So she is your partner then?" She started to get up off the couch, not wanting Dominick to see her cry.

Dominick grabbed her hand and held on. "No she isn't. It's not like that there, I told you. We didn't get married, that's the only thing that counts. Thomas told me how your relationships work here and I don't want to hurt you."

"Hurt me?"

"Yes, I really care about you and I would love to spend the rest of my life with you. But I'm confused."

"What are you confused about? Either you want to be partners with me or you do not!"

"Willow, please understand, if we join together now I would want to take care of you, and to do that I need a job and money on Earth . . . Aerthen."

"When will you be able to do that?"

"I just started college. It would be about four years from now on Earth. Is it normal to decide to be together at our age here? It's really not on Earth . . . or Aerthen, whatever you want to call it. We don't usually marry until we're older, after we graduate college and can afford to live on our own."

Willow stared at Dominick.

Dominick felt like it was hours, he didn't know what to say or do, he was terrified he would lose her.

"I see." She finally said. "We choose a partner whenever one comes into our life. Sometimes when we are young and sometimes when we are older. There is no set time."

"Willow don't take this wrong, okay." Dominick feared she wouldn't understand what he was going through with their relationship.

"Take what wrong?" She looked into his eyes and could see his pain.

"I'm just afraid that if something happens and we can't stay together that you'll be hurt. What happens if you join with someone and then you don't stay together here?"

Willow looked at Dominick with a confused look, "That never happens."

"In our case it could. I'm from another world, on my world I couldn't support you right now. Thomas says I can't stay here where it would be much easier for us to be together. I'm afraid Willow, do you understand? I don't want you to get hurt because of me."

"I only want to be with you . . . we can wait until you think the time is right. Does that help?"

Still holding onto Willow's wrist, he pulled her back onto the couch where she landed on his lap. "That would make everything better." He whispered into her ear pulling her close.

Willow wrapped her arms around his neck, "I have no intention of being separated from you, no matter where you go that is where I will go too."

Dominick laughed to himself thinking what she said sounded so cliché. But he knew she was sincere. "I will never go anywhere without you either. I love you so much."

They sat together on the couch holding one another until they fell asleep in each other's arms. When the door opened neither of them heard Wilton and Lorna return.

"Look Wilton, how sweet." Lorna commented seeing the two asleep on the couch.

Wilton smiled, "Remember when we were young and in love? Nothing else mattered to us. I suspect it is the same for them."

"You are right about that. Look at them they do not have a care in the world."

Wilton reached for Lorna; she turned and walked the two steps to her partner. They gently kissed each other on the lips and hugged.

"Will you be alright when we go to Aerthen?" Wilton asked, worried for her.

"I will as long as you stay close to me."

"Do you think Willow will have any problems? She has never been told what really happens there!"

"She only sees Dominick, Wilton. There is nothing more important to her; I think she will be fine."

"Should we tell them or wait and tell Willow of our change in plans?" Wilton asked.

"We should let Drew tell Dominick, he would feel violated if we usurped his authority as a parent."

"You are always right my dear. Now what are we going to have for our meal? I am hungry after that meeting."

"Shh." Lorna whispered. "I think Willow is starting to wake up. We should go and start our meal so that it is ready when they wake."

+ + + + + + + + + +

Dominick felt Willow move and he woke up. He looked out the window and noticed that it was getting dark. He glanced at his watch it was almost eight o'clock. It felt good sitting with Willow so he relaxed. Then he started to hear voices in the kitchen, Professor Walters, Mrs. Walters, and … his dad? He listened closer to be sure. There was no doubt about it his father was in the kitchen. He couldn't really hear what they were saying their voices were muffled and purposely low, he imagined it was so they wouldn't wake them.

"Willow." Dominick gently rocked her shoulder. "Willow, can you hear me?"

Willow yawned and stretched, she looked up at him smiling, "How long did we sleep?"

"I'm not sure, It's getting late. I think my dad is here talking to your parents in the kitchen."

Willow sat up and looked questioningly at Dominick while listening to the voices. "That is odd, why would he come here and then not wake us up?"

"I don't know maybe we should go find out."

The two stood and walked toward the kitchen. Dominick stopped and starred, surprised to see not only was his father there but also Thomas and Tegan.

"What's going on?" He asked sensing that this was not a casual visit.

"Well look who finally woke up!" Thomas said with a smile. "We've been running out of subjects to discuss waiting."

"You could have woke us up, why didn't you?" Dominick asked.

"That would not have been polite, you both seemed very comfortable." Tegan stated.

"Why is everyone here?" Willow asked discerning the heavy emotional mood in the room.

After what seemed like an eternity, Thomas finally spoke up. "We were just discussing the results of our meeting today with Drew."

Dominick looked at his father and realized that he was looking a little pale and was unusually quiet. "Dad what's going on?"

"Why don't you and Willow come and take a seat, this involves both of you too." Drew said.

Glancing back and forth at one another, Dominick picked up Willow's hand and felt her tremble. He held onto her and walked over to the table where Wilton had pulled over two chairs from the corner for them to sit in.

When they were seated, Thomas started the conversation. "I'll catch you both up before we continue, okay."

Dominick and Willow nodded their heads yes. Then Dominick spoke up, also sensing that whatever was going on had to be significant. "How bad is it?"

"That depends on how you look at it." Drew answered.

Dominick looked at his father, "Do you think it's bad?"

"Not for you and I, no I don't." Drew answered.

Dominick felt relieved, "Okay then, what's happening?" He asked looking at Thomas.

"As you know we had an emergency meeting today at Project Headquarters. The reason for that was the new data that we have acquired from Aerthen . . . Earth. It seems that the planet has started a cycle that we didn't see coming."

"You mean like when you didn't see the polar shift coming when you left a long time ago?" Dominick asked.

"Similar to that, yes." Tegan interjected.

"The ocean's plant life has started to transform into what we can only surmise to be a covering or shield that is overlaying the seas. It has become almost impossible for small to medium sized vessels to travel through the area. We believe that in another few months even the largest ocean liners will not be able to sail through the growing seaweed." Thomas explained.

"Can't they just go around it?" Dominick asked.

"The problem is that it will cover the Atlantic Ocean in about three months and we have found some of the weed in the Pacific and Indian Oceans as well." Thomas said. "The currents are starting to spread the weed and we fear it will soon be in every ocean and possibly start to travel up rivers."

"It will cause the shipping industry to come to a halt which will do a great deal of damage to trade and the economy." Drew added.

"Damage?" Dominick questioned.

"Ships carry cargo from country to country, importing and exporting almost everything from food to cars and oil. Without the ability to send products across the oceans it will have a large impact on the global economy and the availability people have to essential manufactured goods." Drew explained.

"Can't they send the stuff on airplanes?" Dominick wondered.

"Some of it I suppose, but that's not the only problem. Tegan was about to tell us the rest when you and Willow came in." Drew answered.

Willow continued to hold Dominick's hand under the table. Dominick could tell she was scared by what all this could mean for them. He put his arm around her and pulled her toward him to try and comfort her as Tegan stated to explain further.

"From what we can deduce, the seaweed is not only growing exponentially but has also changed its molecular structure making it almost impossible to cut through, which is why the ships cannot travel by pushing it aside. It is becoming almost a solid mass on the ocean surface. We have not been able to stop the transformation with any type of compounds in our labs."

"What have you tried?" Drew asked familiar with lab procedures.

"We have tried to return the plant molecular structure to its original state, when that didn't work we tried to put a code in it to stop it from multiplying. That also was unsuccessful. The good news is that it is not effecting the marine life. Whales and other oxygen breathing mammals have been able to surface without any difficulties that we can see." Tegan hesitated, "The most disturbing result of the weed is that it is disturbing ocean currents."

"The currents run so deep, how is it doing that? Wouldn't it just float with them?" Drew interposed.

"At first that is exactly what it did. Which is how we believe it is travelling to the other oceans. However, the original areas in which the seaweed variation arose, the Sargasso Sea, have seen the seaweed not only float but start to accumulate into the depths as well. This has caused the Gulf Stream current to slow slightly and we fear it will continue to reduce the current's speed."

Dominick realized the implications of this from his studies in oceanography. "That's not good; the whole world's climate would be effected if that happens. There could be another ice age!"

"Yes there could." Wilton added. "That is what caused us to accelerate the plan to evacuate the planet. Kareem Kaunda, who is the Head of the Administrative Service, called a meeting with all the Project Heads to move the plan up."

"Is Kareem Kinnock's father?" Drew asked remembering his conversation with Kinnock.

"He is." Tegan answered. "He was going to contact Suren Samgi on Aerthen to have the Council put their part of the plan into effect as soon as possible."

Drew recalled hearing about the Council from his previous conversation with Kinnock; they were the supposed actual leaders on Earth, and he found that the most disturbing out of everything he had heard or learned here.

Dominick remembered hearing the name Suren before. Then he remembered it was on the shuttle after the missile was fired at them when Thomas and Sully were talking and Sully called Suren on the phone.

"When will all this take place?" Drew asked.

"The exact time frame has not been established. Much of that depends on what the Council is able to arrange with the world leaders on Aerthen. They usually meet every two years secretly in the United States on the western coast. This will be the first time that there has been an unscheduled meeting. It may take a few weeks to be able to gather them together." Tegan explained.

"Who will be there?" Dominick asked.

"The heads of the key governments and organizations of your world. They will have to make an excuse as to why they are leaving their responsibilities and schedules unexpectedly. The UN will also send members to represent the countries that do not have representation at the meeting."

Drew remained silent, he had not been able to get beyond the shock of all the revelations he already was trying to digest emotionally and intellectually, now all this had come to light. He wondered how he would ever be able to return home and go back to his 9 to 5 job and daily routine. He was beginning to realize that his life had changed dramatically and would never be the same!

Dominick looked from Tegan to Thomas, "Will we be leaving sooner?"

"That depends. Right now we don't have any plans to cut our trip short." Thomas said.

Dominick squeezed Willows hand. "Okay." Was all he said, his only concern was his relationship with Willow and not wanting their time on her world to end quite yet.

35

The next morning Thomas took Dominick to pick Willow up for a day together with him and Bethany.

When Dominick knocked on her door, Willow must have been standing right behind it because she pulled the door open as soon as he knocked, and quickly hugged Dominick around his waist. "My father says that we are still going to be able to go back to Aerthen with you." She said excitedly.

"Good, I was getting worried with all the changes in their plans that are going on." He answered hugging her back and smelling the perfumed smell of her hair.

"Me too. I asked my father if you could stay here with me if he would not let me go there, but he said that our peoples could never live together on our world."

Her statement alarmed Dominick. "What does that mean exactly? You come to our world all the time and stay there!"

"I know we do, I was upset after he told me that because I was afraid that we would not be able to be with each other. My mother noticed how upset I was and she told me that if people from Aerthen lived here they would bring conflict with them."

"Conflict?" Dominick blurted out pulling back from her. "I thought they cared about the people on my world!"

"We do. But when my mother and father said I could still go back with you, I forgot about the rest of what they told me. I should have asked them. I am sorry." Willow said looking down, feeling as though she disappointed Dominick.

Noticing her change in affect, Dominick wanted to reassure her. "Willow don't worry about it, the only thing that matters is that we can be together somewhere. It doesn't really matter where does it?"

Willow looked up into Dominick's eyes, he seemed so strong to her, "You mean that . . . I can tell."

"More than you'll ever know." He thought at that moment that she was the sweetest girl he had ever known. "I love you Willow, I think I would die if I had to live without you."

"I love you too!" Willow reached upward standing on her toes to kiss Dominick.

Dominick likewise reached down to meet her. After a tender kiss, they hugged tightly.

"What's taking you two so long?"

Hearing Bethany's voice behind him, Dominick loosened his hug on Willow and turned his head. "Sorry, we'll be right there."

Willow giggled, "I forgot they were in the rambler waiting."

"Yeah . . . me too." Dominick said laughing. He picked up her hand, and led her down the walkway to Thomas's rambler where he and Bethany were waiting.

Dominick opened the back door of the rambler for Willow to climb in first. Once she was seated, he climbed in after her and shut the door. He thought that he should apologize to Thomas for taking so long since he knew they were on a schedule to get to the history galleria. He leaned forward, closer to the seat in front of him and toward Thomas. "Thomas, I'm sorry that it took me so long to get Willow."

"No apology necessary, we were just wondering what was taking so long and wanted to be sure that you two were okay."

"Yeah we're okay but . . ."

Thomas sensed Dominick's hesitation and wondered what was bothering him. "What's up?"

Unsure if he wanted to talk about it, Dominick shrugged, "Nothing. It's okay."

"If there is something bothering you it's better to talk about it, don't you think?"

"Nay, I'm fine."

Willow looked over at Dominick, "Maybe we should talk about it." She tried to whisper. "It is bothering me too Dominick."

Bethany overheard some of what Willow said. "What's bothering you Willow is something wrong, did something happen?"

Willow squeezed Dominick's hand. "Nothing happened. I told Dominick something my father said. We both were a little upset by it."

"What did he say?" Thomas asked.

"I was worried that I would be separated from Dominick. My father told me that I could be with Dominick as long as I went to Aerthen, but that no one from Aerthen could live here. My mother said that it was because they would bring conflict to us."

Dominick watched Thomas and Bethany as Willow explained. They were looking at each other but not toward him and Willow.

"Is that true?" Dominick asked feeling betrayed.

"It isn't because we don't want you here. We would like nothing more than to be able to be one people again. I don't have to tell you what would happen if our populations mixed, you know what your people would do to us, don't you?"

Dominick felt his anger start to diminish. "Then why are you so happy that I'm with Willow, that we're together? I would think you wouldn't want us to be, especially not her parents."

"You have to be able to look at situations in more than one dimension. You and Willow together isn't the same as our populations being together in larger numbers. That's when trouble would start."

"I'm one person, why can't one person from my world live here then?"

"Why are you so insistent about this?" Bethany asked.

"I would rather Willow not come to Earth! I really don't have to explain why do I?"

"Dominick it is okay, calm down." Willow said holding onto Dominick's arm. "I will be alright on Aerthen with you. I know I will!"

Dominick put his hand over his forehead and took a deep breath trying to calm down. He was afraid he was scaring Willow.

Thomas pulled the rambler over and parked along the side of the road. "The reason we can't let just one of you come here is because it wouldn't be fair. How could we let you live here and say no to everyone else?"

Dominick thought about what he was saying. "Who would find out?"

Aerthen

"Someday everyone on your world will know about us, it isn't something that we can keep secret forever, especially with our upcoming plans." Thomas explained.

"Okay, maybe you're right. But I don't like it."

"At least we will be together." Willow said. "That is all I want!"

"That's what is important right now for you two. The rest will take of itself. I promise." Thomas said.

"You can't promise that!" Dominick said sarcastically.

"Ah, but I can! It's how the universe is set up, the way it all works!"

"Are you kidding me? You sound like some kind of guru or something!"

Thomas laughed, "Nope, it's true. Everything works together for the good when your desire is motivated with a pure heart."

Dominick still wasn't sure if Thomas was teasing him, placating them, or what, when both Thomas and Bethany's phones rang taking their attention in a different direction.

Thomas answered first, "Hello." . . . "Alright we'll be right there. I have to drop Dominick and Willow off first."

Bethany also answered her phone after looking at who was calling, "What's up Lawrence?" . . . "Alright, yes, I'll be in touch." She hung up and looked over at Thomas who was still listening to whoever was talking to him.

Thomas glanced at Bethany and then into the back seat while he listened. "That shouldn't be a problem; I think he will be able to handle it." . . . "I'll talk to him myself when we get back to Aerthen." . . . "Okay Timothy, see you soon."

"What's going on?" Dominick asked.

"It seems that we have to leave for Aerthen in two days. The Council has decided on how they want to reveal our plans to Aerthen leaders and handle the evacuation of the people, and I have to be there for the meeting."

"I'll have to be there too. Lawrence and Diane are in the Atlantic working on the seaweed mutations and won't be available to discuss the situation themselves." Bethany said.

"We both have to meet with my brother and the rest of the team in an hour." Thomas glanced back, "Where do you two want to go?"

"Can we go to the apartment? Is that okay with you Willow?"

Willow nodded.

"That's probably for the best. Your father will be there won't he?"

"He should be."

"Good, we can explain to him what's going on then. Sorry we're going to miss the galleria, you really would have enjoyed it." Bethany said disappointedly.

"Hopefully we can go some other time." Dominick said.

"I'm sure we will." Thomas acknowledged.

They drove in silence concentrating on the information they just received. Dominick and Willow cuddled in the back seat.

Willow was nervous knowing that they would be leaving sooner for Aerthen than expected. "I have to get in touch with my school and friends to let them know I will be away."

"Okay." Dominick answered. "Will it be a problem with your schooling if you're gone too long?"

"No, I can pick up where I left off whenever I get back. My friend Celera is expecting me to go on a camping trip with her in a couple weeks. I will have to let her know I will be away."

"I'm sorry, are you disappointed?"

"Not really, I will be with you." Willow snuggled up to him. "You are my life now."

Dominick never felt so happy. He knew that he had found the person with whom he could spend the rest of his life. Willow was so different from the other girls he had dated back on Earth, he felt she needed him, and he wanted to take care of her. He held her smelling the scent of her hair as they pulled up in front of the apartment.

Willow scooted to the door and climbed out of the rambler following Dominick. She was getting nervous about the sudden change in plans and wanted to remain close to him.

The two couples walked together silently until they entered the living space of the apartment. Drew was sitting at the table writing notes on a pad he had brought with him when the door opened. He looked at Thomas and knew something had changed. "What's going on now?" he asked.

"We are going to be heading back to Aerthen in two days, there have been further developments, and the Council is ready to make their move." Thomas explained.

"Is there anything you need before we head out?" Bethany asked.

"No, Dominick and I will be ready when it comes time to go. Just let us know when you are coming to pick us up."

"We probably won't see you until then unfortunately. There are just too many details we need to iron out in the next couple of days before we go." Thomas explained.

"That's okay." Dominick tried to reassure Thomas. "Willow has some loose ends to tie up too. I suppose we will be busy with those."

"I'll watch out for them until then." Drew said winking at Thomas.

Thomas smiled realizing Drew shared his concern for Dominick and Willow. Then he and Bethany headed out to attend to business.

Once the door was closed, Drew turned to Dominick, "Tegan called a few minutes ago, we have to leave in the morning, not a couple of days from now! I didn't want to say anything to Thomas since we are guests here, he'll find out at the meeting."

Willow gasped, "I am going to have to make a few calls, do you mind? It shouldn't take me too long."

"Of course not!" Dominick said, smiling and then laughing.

"Why are you laughing, what is funny?" Willow asked, a little confused by his reaction.

Dominick hugged her and said, "You just used your first contraction, you are going to fit in fine back on Aerthen!"

AUTHOR INFORMATION

twitter.com/cathleenryan333

cathleenryan333@yahoo.com

facebook.com/cathleenryan333

cathleenryan333.wix.com/cathleen-ryan

AERTHEN CHARACTERS AND PLACES

Aden= Place where world populations gathered after the flood.

Administrative Service= Central government on Aerthen II.

Aerthen= Planet. People are vegetarians where eating meat is unheard of.

Aerthen Party= Type of religion that believes nature is alive and in harmony with everything.

Aerthen

Aerthen Project= Monitoring of Earth.

Ashford, England= Headquarters of the four families on Earth.

Bethany Bier= Thomas's girlfriend. Political advisor to a senator from NY in Washington.

Bridget Bier= Co-pilot of current home ship, Bethany's cousin.

Bottleneck= A severe decrease in human population size which reduces the variation in the gene pool. The smaller genetic diversity that remains passes on their genes to future offspring. This causes a lower genetic variety. This also reduces the strength of the population and their ability to survive.

Celera= Willow's best friend on Aerthen II.

Central Council= The leaders of the four families. Meet and live in Ashford, England.

Cylinders= Suspended animation beds.

Diane Dineen= Oceanographer.

Domern= Brother of Kaunda who stays behind on Aerthen along with thousands of others. Member of the Aerthen Party/religious sect.

Dane Domern= Dominick's great-grand father who knew Thomas's great-grandfather.

Dominick Domern= Marine biology student, also interested in archeology.

Dominions= Individual countries, a total of thirty.

Donna Domern= Dominick's sister who is in college taking courses for elementary teaching.

Douglas Domern= Dominick's grandfather.

Drew Domern= Dominick's father who is a forensic scientist who specializes in blood and body fluids.

Early training academy= Public school system.

Flying eye rovers= Drones.

Ginny= Co-pilot aboard the Traveler.

George= Co-worker of Drew Domern at the forensic lab who specializes in documents.

Haplogroups= Pertain to deep ancestral origins dating back thousands of years.

High speed= Light speed.

Homeship= Space ship.

Hover Position= 932,000 miles from Earth, called Lagrange Points, are locations in space where objects placed there tend to stay without any assistance. It is possible for an object to exist at the point it is placed for an unlimited amount of time; there are five Lagrange Points.

Jenny= Patrick's girlfriend.

Jim Jr.= Follows Thomas along with Wayne.

Jim Sr.= Jim Jr.'s father, head Council member for the four families.

John= Part of student government at the college, also worked at the front desk of the dorm where Dominick lived.

Aerthen

Kareem Kaunda= Head of Aerthen II administrative service.

Kinnock Kaunda= Member of the administrative service on Aerthen II.

Kaunda= Husband of Milka, and father of Torem and Nishka. Captain in the lawmaker service/police force and one of several captains who are in charge of security for the Southern Dominion.

Lana Larose-Tarbuk= Trent Tarbuk's spouse.

Lanes= Streets.

Lawrence Larose= Works with Diane Dineen also an oceanographer.

Little Aerthen= Moon.

Lorna Latrell Walters= Wilton Walters wife.

Luremia= First civilization.

Mandy= Dominick's high school girlfriend who moved to Georgia for college.

Major Tarbuk= Kaunda's immediate superior, over the captains.

Max and Donald= Friends of Dominick and Patrick.

Metropolis= City.

Midline= Equator.

Milka= Wife of Kaunda, mother of Torem and Nishka.

Native born= Born on Earth.

Nishka= Daughter of Kaunda and Milka. Twelve years old.

Orbiter= Satellite.

Patrick= Dominick Domern's high school friend and college roommate.

Professor Bier= Lead scientist.

Professor Wilton Walters= Dominick's archeology professor. Is sixty-two but athletic.

Protector= Law enforcement.

Provost= President.

Provost Golan= Current president of Aerthen II.

Puffs= Clouds.

Rambler= Car.

Rebekah Domern= Dominick's mother.

Resources= Elements/forces of nature such as wind, water, soil.

Riven= The split between the population that stayed behind and the ones who left for Aerthen II.

Ron Jr.= Part of team assigned to Thomas.

Ron Sr.= Ron Jr.'s father, Council member.

Samgi= Lead pilot.

Senator from NY= State senator that Bethany works for.

Shadow Government= (SG) Ron is in charge of the local group along with Luke. Jim and Wayne are on the road.

Aerthen

Jim Sr. is head of the shadow government located in England.

Starscopes= Telescopes.

Sully Samgi= Pilot of current day home ship and shuttle.

Suren Samgi= Member of Council in England.

Talbot Torem= Thomas's great-grand father who befriended Dane Domern.

Technology Command= Space program.

Tegan Torem= Father of Thomas and Timothy and the head of the Aerthen Program.

Thomas Torem= Dominick's cousin who came to find him.

Timothy Torem= Dominick's cousin, Thomas's older brother and one of the Program directors who oversees the Aerthen Project.

Torem= Son of Kaunda and Milka. Ten years old.

Tony Tarbuk= Volcanologist

Trent Tarbuk= Thomas Torem's contact on Aerthen II.

Vapor= Condensation of water.

Vince Visor= Climatologist who was the most senior of the group sent to Earth.

Watchers= Four families who have passed down the history of Aerthen and the families who left and have returned to assist the people who stayed behind. Their mission is to watch them and assist them if ever needed.

Water ship= Large boats.

Wayne= Security guard at lab.

Wayne= Follows Thomas along with Jim.

Willow Walters= Daughter of Prof. Walters and Lorna Walters.

Wilhelm Wagner= Wayne's father and Council member.

Wilma and Warren Wagner= Wayne's older sister and brother.

Made in the USA
Middletown, DE
28 July 2015